***Good women do not go around pretending to be married when they aren't."***

"I think you're getting more riled up about this than necessary."

"I'm not speaking to you," she said again.

The whole thing was so absurd and she was so furious, he couldn't stop the smile.

"This is not funny, Eli."

"No it isn't, sweetheart.

"And don't call me *sweetheart*."

He hid his humor behind a cool tone. "My sincerest apology."

"I don't want an apology, I just want to be who I was when I got out of bed this morning. Jewel Crowley, spinster—not Jewel Crowley, supposedly married to the Colored Casanova of Cass County."

## *Other* Avon Romances

THE GOVERNESS WEARS SCARLET *by Sari Robins*
THE KISS *by Sophia Nash*
THE NIGHT BEFORE THE WEDDING *by Debra Mullins*
RETURN OF THE ROGUE *by Donna Fletcher*
SEDUCED BY SIN *by Kimberly Logan*
TEMPTATION OF THE WARRIOR *by Margo Maguire*
THREE NIGHTS OF SIN *by Anne Mallory*

## *Coming Soon*

AT THE BRIDE HUNT BALL *by Olivia Parker*
HIS DARK AND DANGEROUS WAYS *by Edith Layton*

## *And Don't Miss These Exciting* ROMANTIC TREASURES *from Avon Books*

HOW TO PROPOSE TO A PRINCE *by Kathryn Caskie*
NEVER TRUST A SCOUNDREL *by Gayle Callen*
A NOTORIOUS PROPOSITION *by Adele Ashworth*

# Beverly Jenkins

# Jewel

AVON
An Imprint of HarperCollins*Publishers*

This is a work of fiction. Names, characters, places, and incidents are products of the author's imagination or are used fictitiously and are not to be construed as real. Any resemblance to actual events, locales, organizations, or persons, living or dead, is entirely coincidental.

AVON BOOKS
*An Imprint of* HarperCollins*Publishers*
10 East 53rd Street
New York, New York 10022-5299


ISBN: 978-0-06-116135-3
**www.avonromance.com**



First Avon Books paperback printing: May 2008



Printed in the U.S.A.

10 9 8 7 6 5 4 3 2 1

*To my mother-in-law,*
*Joy L. Kelley,*
*my own Abigail*

# JEWEL

# Prologue

*May 3, 1881*
*Boston*

Cecile was furious. The doddering old reprobate she'd stooped to marry two weeks ago in order to get at his supposed fortune was in reality as poor as he was ancient. His name was Lucius Briles, and lying beneath him on their wedding night, while he grunted and pushed and ran his crone-like hands over her naked flesh, had forced bile into her throat, but she'd sent her mind elsewhere until he was done, confident riches would be her reward. However, her talk with his barrister yesterday revealed that his wealth was a façade. The fine Boston mansion, the carriages, the china and sparkling silverware all belonged to the bank, which planned to begin foreclosure proceedings in a few days. Everything from horses to candlesticks would be sold, leaving the newlyweds with no alternative but to reside with his dog-faced daughter, Bethany, a woman who'd disliked Cecile on sight and had done everything in her power to keep the nuptials from taking place. Cecile now wished she'd not dismissed Bethany so out of hand. Lucius Briles was not the man she'd thought him to be, and because of that, she would have to vanish as she always did after a successful fleecing, only this time there'd been no fleece, just a nasty old man who wanted to put his hands up her skirt.

Her anger knew no bounds as she paced the confines of her well-appointed bedroom. How was she supposed to survive without money for new gowns, hairdressers and the like? She'd made a good living these past six years marrying wealthy men and then absconding with their riches. Briles was just the latest in a long line of the many, but the first to not have a pot to piss in or a window to toss it out of. She faulted herself for not spending more time studying him before making her play for his affections. The local newspaper had portrayed him as a pillar of Boston's representative society, a man of such wealth and stature the great Fred Douglass himself had once dined at the Brileses' table. She'd taken the information as gospel not knowing Briles was in hock up to his ear trumpet and smelly wooden teeth.

She'd been in Boston six weeks now and had journeyed to the city in order to escape the Pinkertons sicced on her by her last husband, a San Francisco businessman named Frank Sorrell. She'd stayed married to Sorrell just long enough to worm her way into his bed, heart, and bank accounts before disappearing. Frank had been quick, though; the Pinkerton he'd hired caught up with her at the train station a few days later and she'd had to bed the detective in order to wiggle free. When he awakened the next morning to find her gone, along with his wallet, she was certain he'd not been happy, but she'd wanted payments for her services and felt it only right.

Upon arriving in Boston, her plan had been to find another mark, relieve him of his funds, and take a steamer to Canada hoping the Pinkertons would give up the chase and go after other prey, but at the moment she didn't have enough money to get her any where.

So now, she looked around the bedroom in search of items she could pawn. It didn't matter that everything in the house belonged to the bank, she had a more pressing need. To that end, she opened the trunk she'd dragged out of the attic and began to fill it with whatever she could find: heavy ornate candlesticks, the silverware from her morning meal, she even took down the framed portraits of Lucius and his first wife hanging in the hallway because the frames looked valuable. The cache wasn't nearly enough, but she'd search the rest of the house in a few moments. Now she had to finish her packing, so she began removing her gowns from her wardrobe.

"Leaving?" The smug voice belonged to the dog-faced daughter, Bethany.

Cecile didn't turn around. "I'm going to visit a cousin in New York." She continued removing her gowns from the armoire. "And well-brought-up women do not enter a room without announcing themselves first."

"What would you know about the habits of well-raised women?"

"Enough to know that you are not."

"Neither are you, according to the wire I received today from a Pinkerton."

Cecile paused but only for a moment, then began placing her face paints into a small carpetbag. "Have you been fabricating tales, Bethany? I know you've never cared for me, but Pinkertons? That's a bit over the top even for you."

"According to the wire, fabrications aren't needed. Pinkertons have been trying to run you to ground for years. Apparently you make your living preying on men like my father."

"I've no idea what you're babbling about."

"No? Then maybe when the man arrives he can voice it in a language you do understand."

"What man?"

"The Pinkerton. He'll be coming here later and is very interested in speaking with you."

Cecile's mind was racing beneath her cool, distant exterior. "About what?"

"The other men you've embezzled."

"You're babbling again, Bethany."

"I think not. When you first began showing an interest in my father I sensed something wasn't right. An acquaintance suggested I share my fears with Pinkertons' Boston office and I did. They made some inquiries on my behalf, and lo and behold a woman fitting your description turned up in their arrest sheets."

"There are thousands of women fitting my description all over the country."

"But none make their living by marrying multiple husbands and stealing from them."

Cecile didn't care for the superior haughtiness flashing in Bethany's basset brown eyes any more than she liked hearing that she might be heading for arrest. On the pretext of placing her nightclothes in the trunk, Cecile walked over to it and wrapped her hand around one of the heavy candlesticks hidden beneath her gowns. Employing a trick as old as Methuselah, she trilled, "Well, hello, Lucius."

When Bethany turned to the door expecting to see her father, Cecile brought the candlestick down on the back of her head with such force she fell to the floor. Cecile struck her again to make sure she was dead. Staring down at the pool of blood spreading slowly beneath Bethany's head, Cecile felt the glow of satisfaction. "Had you been smart, my dear stepdaughter, you would have kept your mouth shut and left me unawares of the Pinkerton's interest. Instead, you had to gloat and tell all. Now look at you. Those nasty little puppies you call children are going to be motherless, all because you couldn't stand not throwing up what you knew in my face. Stupid."

It came to Cecile that she had been stupid as well. Murder was a very serious offense. Had she been thinking, she would have struck Bethany only hard enough to render her senseless, tied and gagged her and stuffed her in a closet somewhere. Instead, she'd killed her. Now she was really going to have to go to ground, and in a place no one, not even the Pinkertons, would think to look. While she thought about where that might be, she quickly changed into the widow's weeds she always traveled in.

Everyone treated widows with deference. Men opened doors, gave her their seats. A few had even purchased train tickets for her when she claimed to have lost her own due to the stresses brought on by grief. It was the ruse she'd have to employ now because she had no time to pawn anything and it was imperative that she get on a train and leave Boston immediately. Not knowing when the Pinkerton planned to arrive, or if he were already secreted outside watching the house, made her exit a risky one, but she had no choice.

Adjusting her veil, she straightened her rustling silk skirt and picked up her black handbag. All of her glorious gowns and other personal items would have to be left behind. She'd have to travel light, but was confident in her abilities to play on the kindness of strangers in order to take care of her immediate needs. Looking down at Bethany's dead dog-face one last time, she stepped over the body and left the room. Walking quickly down the hallway to the stairs that led to the front door, she'd decided where she'd go. She'd spend a month or so making sure she wasn't being tailed, then she'd head back to the place where all her marriages began. Grayson Grove. She wondered if Nate and Eli Grayson would be glad to see her? Smiling at her own cleverness, she closed the door and set out for the train station.

# Chapter 1

*Grayson Grove*
*Cass County, Michigan*
*May 3, 1881*

Surrounded by the Eden-like green of the countryside, Eli Grayson drove his horse-drawn wagon down the bumpy road toward town. Towering trees wearing the first fresh leaves of spring lined his passage and drew the eye up to a cloudless blue sky. Birdsongs filled his ears while the warmth of the early May breeze made the harsh raw winds of winter just a memory.

Eventually the road led out of the trees and into the sunlight and the landscape gave way to meadows filled with blooming wildflowers spread out like God's opened paint box. Taking in the beautiful vista, Eli knew of no other place he'd rather be than Grayson Grove. It was established in the 1830s by his grandparents who'd come from Carolina to what was then the Michigan Territory. Armed with their freedom papers and money enough to purchase land, courtesy of their dead master's will, they and the thirty other freed slaves who'd accompanied them founded the settlement Eli's grandmother Dorcas christened Grayson Grove.

Over the years the number of Grove residents had increased, making the settlement now a township, one of three all-Black townships in Cass County.

Back then, the only business in the clearing that became the town's center had been the Grayson General Store. Now, as Eli made his way down Main Street, in addition to the long-established Vern's Barbershop, Bates Undertaking, and the Grayson livery stood the doc's office operated by Eli's cousin-in-law, Dr. Viveca Lancaster Grayson. Other new enterprises serving the Grove were the seamstress shop run by Adelaide Kane, and the Grayson Lending Library founded a few years back by lifelong family friend Maddie Loomis. Nestled next to the library was the boarded-up storefront that once housed the town's newspaper, the *Gazette*. As founder and editor, Eli had worked tirelessly for nearly a decade to publish a paper the area could be proud of, but as the bigger nationally syndicated papers began to encroach on his territory, he had little money to invest in new presses or salaries to hire additional help in order to compete. He'd taken out bank loans and borrowed money from friends and family, all in an effort to keep the paper afloat, but last year he'd faced reality. Not only were his bank notes overdue, he couldn't repay his friends. Granted they knew he'd eventually make good on the debts, but he didn't know when, or how.

So, he sat on the wagon seat staring at what had once been his life's blood. It was his plan to reopen the newspaper, but like the repayment of his debts he had no idea how or when. Sighing with frustration, he took one last look at his boarded-up dreams then continued down the street to the general store.

For such an early hour, there were quite a few buggies and wagons tied up near the businesses he passed. Some of the people on the walks waved to him and called out, "Morning, Eli."

He waved back, sending them his patented grin. All were friends and neighbors, and each face represented a memory of growing up—like Mr. Welch, whose apples he used to steal, and Mrs. Potts, who used to rap him across the knuckles with a wooden ruler whenever he pulled some prank in school or forgot his homework. In spite of the uncertainties Eli faced with the *Gazette*, he loved the Grove and after having traveled all over the nation, it was still the only place he cared to be.

Miss Edna Lee had been running the general store since Eli was in short pants, and no one was kinder. Although she was in her sixties now and slowing down a bit, the New Orleans–born octoroon had aged beautifully and was, like all the other women in the Grove, smart as a whip. "Morning, Eli," she called out cheerily as the tin bell above the door announced his arrival. Her long silver hair was braided into two long plaits and secured low on her neck, another Miss Edna fixture.

"Morning, Miss Edna."

A chorus of greetings from the customers inside buying tools, farm implements, and other necessities also marked his entrance. He got a nod from the store's regulars, who were drinking coffee and watching the morning's checker game.

"When's Nate and the doc due back?" Aaron Patterson asked as he kinged his opponent, his twin brother Abraham, now scowling from his seat on the other side of the black-and-red board perched on top of an old cracker barrel.

Nate Grayson was Eli's cousin. He was also the Grove's mayor and sheriff. The doc was his wife, Viveca. "Not for another month," Eli answered, taking his coffee mug down from where it hung on the pegboard near Edna's front counter. Most of the adults in the Grove had a mug hanging in the store. Nate and Viveca were in California visiting her parents. With them on the trip were their fourteen- and fifteen-year-old daughters, Magic and Satin, and their twin sons, four-year-old Jacob and Joseph.

Eli poured the dark brew Miss Edna always kept hot no matter the season into his cup and added, "The way Viveca's mama loves her grandchildren, it may be years before she lets them come home again."

Everyone nodded in agreement. They'd met Mr. and Mrs. Lancaster when they'd visited the Grove five years ago. Francesca Lancaster had as much an irrepressible spirit as her fearless doctor daughter.

The Grove general store also served as the post office. Miss Edna handed him a few envelopes. "These came in last evening."

"Thanks." With his coffee mug in hand and the mail tucked into the pocket of his worn blue cotton shirt, Eli called out his goodbyes, waved, and walked down to the mayor's office. He'd been asked to look after the Grove's business matters while Nate was away.

Inside the office, he sat at the desk, and while sipping at the best coffee in the state, scanned the mail. Most of the envelopes addressed to Nate held items like land deeds and notices from the state's capitol on upcoming or recently passed laws. Nothing in the correspondences appeared to need immediate attention, so he added them to the pile on the desk. There were also a couple of letters for Viveca. One, from her missionary sister Jess in Liberia, he tucked into the top desk drawer for safekeeping. At the bottom of the stack was a letter addressed to Eli. He didn't recognize the New York return address, but opened it and quickly read the hand-penned page inside. The more he read, the wider his eyes became. Excited, he read it again to make sure of the wording, then he tossed the letter in the air and shouted for joy.

The letter was from G. W. Hicks, owner of the largest Black newspaper syndicate in the country. Hicks was interested in adding the *Gazette* to his holdings, and he was coming to the Grove to speak with Eli about the idea! Eli wanted to dance on the desk, do handsprings, do cartwheels. Hicks had a sterling reputation. With his backing the *Gazette* could go far. Picking up the letter he read it again and this time looked for the date Hicks planned to arrive. Eli checked the calendar on the desk and his eyes widened again. Mail delivery was always slow in the Grove and in this instance it had been remarkably so. Hicks was due to arrive tomorrow on the ten o' clock train from Detroit! Draining the rest of his coffee, Eli hastily left his cousin's office and locked up. Filled with heart-pounding excitement, he all but ran down the walk to the *Gazette*'s office to get it ready for Hicks's visit.

It was dark inside and after a year of being boarded up the dust in the air could be seen against the slat of sunlight coming in through the opened door at Eli's back. Back when he'd closed the place the costly glass windows that had fronted the establishment were taken down and stored, and plywood nailed up over the openings. Looking around now, he wished he could put the panes back in, but there wasn't time. The plywood probably wouldn't make a good first impression, but if he took it down and it rained, the ancient press might be ruined and that would be even worse. His only option was to sweep the floors, get rid of the dust, and hope that if he brought enough lanterns along tomorrow Hicks could see the layout inside.

Vernon Stevenson, owner of the barbershop and godfather to Nate's daughter, Magic, wandered in. "What're you doing, Eli?"

He explained and a grin split the barber's face as he hooted, "Hot damn! That's good news. Be nice to have the *Gazette* going again. You planning on cleaning the place up?"

Eli nodded while wondering if mice had gotten in over the winter.

"Be glad to lend a hand if you need one. No customers at that moment. I'll grab some brooms."

By later that morning the news that Eli was expecting an important visitor who might help him reopen the *Gazette* spread across the Grove. It also brought volunteers to help with the cleaning, among them his mother, Abigail, and her husband, the irascible old lumber beast Adam Crowley.

"Is it true, Eli?" his mother asked excitedly as she moved into the doorway aided by her carved ebony cane. "G. W. Hicks wants to buy the *Gazette*?"

Eli greeted his mother with a smile. "Not sure about the buying, but he might be interested in adding us to his syndicate."

Pleased, Adam nodded. "Be a good thing."

"Yes it would be." They stepped outside so he could talk to them and not be in the way of the sweeping.

Abigail searched her son's face. "Adam and I truly hope this will be the offer we've all been praying for."

"Even if you are a Democrat," her husband tossed out with a grin, arms crossed over his massive chest.

The topic of Eli's political affiliation was a never-ending, yet friendly, debate between the two men. "Everybody's going to be a Democrat before long, Adam," Eli pointed out confidently. "You'll see."

"Not while I'm living."

Eli counted himself amongst the small but rising number of Black men registered to vote as Democrats. With the majority of the race still in the pockets of what the national press called the Lily White Republicans, Eli and other like-minded individuals were showing their disillusionment with the party of Lincoln and its increasing refusal to back issues most important to its Black constituency by aligning themselves with the much-hated Democrats. Of course, he had nothing but contempt for the southern members of the party who'd rather commit murder than allow Black men to vote, but the Republicans were taking Black votes for granted. Something had to be done to shake them up, and Eli and the other Black Democrats hoped this would be a way to bring that about. "Adam, if all men of good conscience would just consider . . ."

Abigail held up a hand. She'd heard this argument a hundred times before. Looking pointedly between the two men she loved best, she stated, "You two can pick up this eternal argument at another time. G. W. Hicks is the topic for now. When will he arrive?"

Eli grinned at Adam. Although Abigail would never admit it, she was as irascible as her husband. "Tomorrow's train."

"How long do you think he'll stay?" Adam asked.

Eli shrugged. "But I've talked to the Quilt Ladies. They'll be putting him up while he's here."

The Quilt ladies were the self-appointed moral society of the Grove and the owners of the best boardinghouse and dining room in the area.

"He'll enjoy that," Abigail added. "Caroline and her ladies can be harpies sometimes, but they run a fine house."

A short while later, the work was done. Eli thought everything looked fine and hoped Hicks would agree.

After having dinner with Abigail and Adam, Eli went home to his small cabin and dug out the *Gazette*'s ledgers, along with some of the old copies of the paper he'd saved and his subscription lists. He was sure Hicks would want to review the financial aspects of the operation, so he planned to have them available.

At the height of the *Gazette*'s popularity, there'd been subscribers as far west as Chicago and as far north as Muskegon. The Detroit area had its own Black papers, very popular papers, but the *Gazette* had a few subscriptions on that side of the state as well. Then, after his funds ran out, he had nothing. No subscribers, no newspaper. Hicks was supposed to be a man of vision. Eli hoped it was true because reopening the *Gazette* would put purpose back into his life.

It hadn't always been that way, though. In fact it had taken him quite some time to figure out what to do with his life because, as a young man, chasing women had been his one and only passion. On many occasions his mother had accused him of being too handsome and too arrogant for his own good, and she'd been correct. Every scrap of trouble he'd ever gotten himself into had been because of his affinity for the softer sex. Back then he'd juggled women like a performer in a circus act with mistresses in Kalamazoo, Niles, Muskegon and one particularly talented brown-skinned beauty across the lake in Chicago. Filled with hubris he'd even committed the cardinal sin of sleeping with Nate's first wife, Cecile, while Nate was away fighting Lincoln's war. All their lives they'd been close as brothers, but after Nate learned the adulterous truth, Cecile was sent packing, divorce papers in hand, and Eli? Nate refused to speak to him, or acknowledge his presence. As far as Nate was concerned Eli no longer existed.

Eli dropped his head into his hands at the painful memory. The guilt and shame had been so much he'd turned to the bottle, becoming pariah to both family and friends. Although the liquor had him convinced that being an outcast hadn't mattered, it had.

Then, five years ago, Dr. Viveca Lancaster blew into the Grove like a western cyclone. After the dust died, she and Nate had fallen in love, and Eli and Nate began taking small steps toward reconciliation. Eli doubted Nate would ever fully forgive him, nor would Eli ever forgive himself, but the cousins were closer now than they'd been in a long while and were pleased with the healing of the rift everyone in the Grove thought permanent.

With that episode no longer coloring every aspect of his life, he was doing his best to stay on the straight and narrow. Being the publisher and editor of the *Gazette* had been instrumental in helping him achieve that. Now having caught the attention of G. W. Hicks the future looked bright.

The train from Detroit was late, which only added to Eli's nervousness. When it finally arrived in a hail of smoke, whistles, and brimstone, he had to inhale deeply to regain a semblance of calm. Dressed in his best brown suit and with his Sunday hat in hand he searched the faces of the passengers exiting from the train for the man he'd come to greet. A woman with two small children stepped down onto the platform first, followed by a bearded elderly man and an equally old woman. When no one else appeared, he wondered if maybe Hicks had missed the train somehow, and his feelings began to deflate. Then down stepped a portly dark-skinned man sporting graying mut-tonchops, and dressed in a fine black vested suit and snow white shirt, and Eli began to relax, even as the nervousness took wing again. G. W. Hicks. Had to be him. The newspaper magnate looked a bit rumpled as would be expected after the long journey from New York, but he had an air of au-thority about him that seemed to radiate.

Eli walked over and inquired politely, "Mr. Hicks?"

The man gave him a quick up and down. "Yes. And you are?"

Eli stuck out his hand. "Eli Grayson. Welcome to Michigan, sir."

"Pleased to meet you, Grayson," he offered with a firm grip. "Hoped my letter would arrive ahead of me. Post can be slow."

"Yes, it can. I received your letter yesterday. Do you have a trunk?"

"I do."

"Then let's find the porter so we can be on our way."

On the ride back to the Grove, Hicks seemed content to enjoy the view. He didn't volunteer any conversation so Eli remained silent, too, but he could see his visitor taking in the trees and the rolling land with what appeared to be apprecia-tive eyes.

Hicks finally asked, "You born here?"

"Yes, sir. My grandparents settled here back in the thirties."

"Really?"

"Yes. Came here from Carolina."

"All that way?"

Eli nodded.

"I was born in Philadelphia. There's a good-sized rural area still within the city's boundaries but nothing as grand as this. Land here takes a man's breath away."

The assessment pleased Eli. "That it does."

"What are the winters like?"

"Harsh and long, but when spring finally comes, we're reminded why my grandparents chose this place."

"Beautiful country."

Eli sensed he'd passed the first hurdle. It was as if the land knew it needed to make a good impression and was showing itself off with style. The sun was shining and the sky was blue. It had rained last night for a short time and as a result the countryside was lush and emerald green for as far as one could see.

"Beautiful country," Hicks voiced again before lapsing back into silence.

Eli wanted to discuss the reason for the visit but decided it best to wait and let Hicks initiate the conversation.

They made it to town an hour later, and as they slowly drove down Main Street Eli pointed out the businesses.

Hicks glanced around. "No idea you lived in such a small town. Your editorials have such scope I assumed you were from larger environs."

Inside, Eli grinned in response to the praise. Outwardly, he showed only polite calm. "I wasn't aware you knew anything about my writing until your letter arrived, sir."

"Know a lot about it. Know you're a Democrat, too."

Eli stilled, and forced his voice to remain casual. "That going to be a problem?"

"If it was son, I wouldn't have come," he stated bluntly. "I like a man willing to climb out on a limb. Even when I think he's wrong."

Eli knew that Hicks and Adam Crowley would hit it off right away should the two ever meet. "My stepfather holds the same opinion."

"Sounds like a smart man."

Eli drove on. He could see folks on the walks eyeing his passage. Everyone knew Eli would be bringing the newspaper man to town that day. A few people even called out welcomes to Hicks, and that seemed to surprise him as well.

Eli explained, "There are no secrets in a place as small as this. Everybody knows who you are and why you're here."

"And why do they think I'm here?'

"To put the *Gazette* back into business."

Hicks didn't comment but asked instead. "How many people here can read?"

"Everybody. Male and female. It's the law."

"The law?"

Eli met his startled eyes. "Yes, sir. If you're born here you have to attend school."

"Females, as well?"

"Particularly females. My grandmother Dorcas had that written into the Grove's original charter."

"How interesting."

"Men from other places who marry Grove women don't always appreciate having a wife who can think circles around them. We on the other hand don't mind. Accustomed to it, I guess."

Hicks sat back. "Incredible."

Eli smiled inwardly. Incredible indeed.

They rolled past the doc's office with the big sign out front Nate had erected a few years back.

"Town has a doctor?"

"Yes, sir. My cousin-in-law, Viveca.

"Viveca? The doctor's a female?"

"Yes. She's originally from California. Got her training at the Woman's Medical College of Pennsylvania."

"Prestigious institution."

"We're grateful to have her. Not many townships have their own doc.

"Or a lending library." Hicks nodded at the building as they rode by. "Who'd have thought such a small place could be so progressive? I'm very impressed, Grayson."

"Thank you, sir." Eli's voice was even-toned but inside he was cheering.

As they drove by the storefront that had housed the *Gazette*, Eli pointed it out, and Hicks replied, "Looking forward to seeing the inside."

"Whenever you're ready, sir."

* * *

Because of all the prizes and ribbons their beautiful hand-stitched quilts had won at county fairs over the years, Caroline Ross, Poppy Pernell, and Brenna Sanders were known as The Quilt Ladies. The elderly ivory-skinned ladies with their antebellum hoop skirts and elaborately coiffed gray ringlets considered themselves morally superior to their neighbors due to the miscegenation in their bloodlines. As a result, when they weren't winning prizes they were overseeing the morals of the Grove whether the residents wanted them in their business or not.

Usually they acted like queens among the rabble, but when Eli introduced them to Hicks, they fluttered around him like butterflies.

Caroline Ross, wearing a faded green gown with hooped skirts, stepped forward and gushed, "Welcome to the Grove, Mr. Hicks. I'm Caroline Ross. We are honored to have such a distinguished guest in our midst."

Hicks looked surprised by both her and her attire and he eyed Eli for a moment, but Eli kept his face void of reaction as Hicks replied, "Thank you, Miss Ross."

She then introduced the others: Poppy, who owned the house, and the violet-eyed Brenna.

"I hope you won't be put off by the Grove's country ways," Brenna stated "We've been doing our best to bring a modicum of culture here."

"On the contrary, I'm finding the Grove to be most progressive."

"Really?" From her voice one would have thought he'd voiced a preference for women with twin heads.

Hicks explained, "You have a doctor and a lending library. Not many places can boast that."

"Our doctor has Spanish blood. She's really quite the lady, " Poppy said with a smile. Of the three Quilt Ladies, Poppy got along with the rest of the Grove the best.

"Just don't play billiards with her," cracked a new voice. Out of the back walked Maddie Loomis dressed in her usual brown buckskins. In spite of her unconventional attire, she was one of the most beautiful women in the county: tall, lean, with jet black eyes, and the sleek fluid movements of a cougar.

Hicks blinked.

Eli made the introductions. "Mr. G. W. Hicks, Maddie Loomis. She runs the lending library."

Maddie stuck out her hand. "Pleased to meet you."

The gesture seemed to throw him, too, then he shook. "Pleased to make your acquaintance as well."

She turned to Caroline. "I think the dogs got all the rats in your cellar. If you see anymore just let me know."

"Thanks, Maddie."

"You're welcome. Mr. Hicks, nice meeting you, Eli. See you later."

"Bye, Maddie."

Hicks watched her departure, then seeming to realize he was still staring at the door through which she'd exited, he shook himself back to the matter at hand.

Caroline asked, "Would you like to see your room now."

"Yes. Please."

Eli sensed Maddie had made an impression but wasn't sure whether it had been good or bad.

They were taken to a spacious bedroom on the second floor. Putting down his leather travel bag, Hicks looked around. "This will do nicely, Miss Ross."

"We hoped it would. Would you like something to eat? We'll be serving luncheon in about thirty minutes."

"I'd like that. In the meantime, Grayson, why don't you show me your operation."

"I'd be honored."

At the *Gazette* office Eli stuck the key in the lock. "I took down the glass, so I'm not sure how much you'll be able to see."

Once the door was opened, he lit a lantern to supplement the swath of sunlight streaming in behind them.

Hicks stared around the dimly lit space, then settled his gaze on the printing press. "Pretty old press."

"I believe *ancient* is more the word, sir."

"Only the one?"

Eli nodded.

Hicks took another slow look around, then said, "I've seen enough."

On the ride back to the boardinghouse, Hicks kept his thoughts to himself. Eli didn't say anything either, but he was worried because of the visit's brevity. When they reached their destination, Hicks stepped down from the wagon. "I'm going to go in and get something to eat, then rest up for a bit. I'd like to have supper with you this evening if we can. What time do they serve?"

"Four. Doors close at six."

"Then let's plan on five. Do they happen to have a private room?"

"Yes. Ask Mrs. Ross. She'll arrange it."

"I'm impressed by you and your town, Grayson. Since I don't own any newspapers in this area, we ought to be able to work something out."

An elated Eli wanted to jump up and down. "Thank you, sir."

"Bring your books and your wife. Like to meet her, too."

"My wife?"

Hicks nodded. "Only hire married men. Been my experience that bachelors are unreliable and undependable. A man with a wife and family will give you an honest-day's work."

Eli froze.

"She can come, can't she?"

"Uh. Yes. Yes, she can."

"Good. Looking forward to our discussion."

"So am I, sir."

Hicks walked to the door and Eli turned the wagon around. Stunned and speechless he drove away. He supposed he should have told the man the truth, but he'd been so taken aback by the ramifications of the caveat, he'd said the first thing that popped into his head. Now it was too late. If he went back and confessed, Hicks would not only find another newspaper to fund, he'd think Eli was a liar. Outdone, he asked himself, "Where in hell am I going to find a wife?"

# Chapter 2

It was wash day, and a weary Jewel Crowley was glad she was almost done. Doing laundry for her five brothers was work enough, but when sheets, pillow slips, shirts and the rest were tossed in, it was a wonder she got it all done before the sun went down. At twenty-four years of age, she was by society's measure a spinster. She had no husband and no prospects for one, but she had plenty of wash, she thought wryly, adding six more pairs of denims to the nearly full clotheslines strung between the trees in the field next to the house. She blamed her lack of suitors on the Grove's remote location—no one of any interest ever came to the Grove—and on the fact that Adam Crowley was her father, and Noah, Abraham, Jeremiah, Ezekiel, and Paul were her brothers. No potential suitor in his right mind would come calling knowing he'd have to face down six burly lumber beasts guarding her like archangels girded for war, so her life was rooted with them instead. Not that she minded. She had a good life, good family and friends, but when she went Home to the Lord, she wanted to have something on her headstone besides She Took Care of Her Brothers.

Jewel was intelligent enough to know she could have a full life without a husband. She had only to look at Viveca, who'd been a doctor before marrying Nathaniel Grayson, or Abigail, who instead of spending her widowed years pining for a mate, had focused her energies on ways to uplift the race and women as well. Even Jewel's good friend Maddie, whose unconventional past had made her a pariah to many in the Grove, had settled into a good life with her books and her hunting dogs. Jewel herself was noted for her committee work and her way with roses, a talent that gave her income and some measure of independence, but she didn't want to be still doing wash while the world passed her by and when she was old and gray.

She'd just started hanging up the last tub of wet clothes when she saw Eli Grayson's buggy pull to a stop in front of the house. She'd heard about the fancy New York publisher who was coming to town to talk about the *Gazette*. She hoped the meeting between the two would go well. Everyone else in town missed reading Eli's newspaper, even if he was a Democrat.

"Afternoon, Jewel," he said walking up, giving her that smile. Jewel had known Eli her entire life. He was wearing his lady-killer smile. She was immediately suspicious.

"Eli," she replied as she hung up socks. "What brings you by?"

"Just thought I'd stop over and see how you were."

"Oh really? Can't remember you ever doing that before."

"Is there a law against me inquiring after your health?"

"Eli, I'm busy here and I have supper to get ready. What are you fishing for?"

"You doubt my motive?"

"Is my pa a Republican?"

He covered his heart with a hand. "You wound me, fair maiden."

She shook her head at his silliness. "What do you want?"

"Have this problem and I need a favor."

"What type of problem and what type of favor?"

"G. W. Hicks is in town to talk about maybe adding the *Gazette* to his stable."

"I heard. How's it faring?"

"Well, he has this small stipulation."

"And it is?"

"I need a wife."

She snorted a laugh before she could stop herself.

"You find that funny?"

"You need a wife like a goat needs an embroidery hoop." She hung up another pair of socks. There were so many she wondered if they were somehow breeding when nobody was looking.

"I'm serious, Jewel."

"And I'm not?"

Eli knew this would be difficult; Jewel Crowley could be as irascible as her pa. "This may be my last chance to make something out of the *Gazette*. His papers are read all over the country. I can't let this opportunity pass."

"You're not making sense. What does Hicks buying the *Gazette* have to do with you needing a wife?"

"Hicks believes bachelors are undependable and unreliable."

She stopped. "Should I speak to that or remain silent?"

"The latter, please." His smoke black eyes twinkled with amusement. She also had one of the wittiest tongues in the Grove. "Hicks won't consider the *Gazette* unless I have a wife."

She fished more socks out of the tub and added them to the line. "So, who are you marrying? Do you need me to make a cake? Is that what this is about?"

"No, Jewel. I figure, if I can get someone to pretend to be my wife for the short time Hicks is here, no one will be the wiser."

She shrugged and, after hanging up the last two socks, picked up the empty tub and rested it on her hip. "Sounds half-baked to me, but if you believe you can pull it off, I'll keep your secret if I run into Hicks while he's here." She walked away.

Eli raised his eyes to the heavens for strength, then hurried to catch up with her.

"Hicks wants to meet her at dinner this evening."

"Okay. So who're you going to ask?"

"You."

She stopped, stared and began to laugh. "Me? Did you fall out of bed on your head this morning? I'm going to fix dinner."

He touched her gently on the arm. "Do I look as if I'm laughing?"

Jewel searched his face again, the handsomest male face in the county. "You have women in Kalamazoo, Chicago, and all points in between. Use one of them."

"None of them can be here by five this evening."

"Then find someone else. What about Lenore?" Lenore's father, James, ran the Grove mill. She was silly and vain, but she was unmarried.

"Lenore Wilson couldn't keep a secret if she was dead."

"What about Celeste Keppler over in Niles?"

"She's a lumber beast, Jewel. The rest of the time she doesn't even wear shoes."

"So shallow, Eli."

His lips thinned. "This is not funny."

"No, it's not, but I'm out of suggestions." She was once again in motion and striding through the cropped grass toward the house.

"Jewel—"

"Go away, Eli. I don't have time for your foolishness."

"Jewel, if you'd just listen."

"I've heard all I need to hear. No."

"Please, Jewel—"

"Pestering me to death is not going to change my mind."

He gently grabbed her hand to keep her near. "You're the only choice I have."

Jewel ignored the warmth from his touch sliding up her arm, or at least tried to. "Then you are in a serious fix," she pointed out disengaging her hand.

"That's why I'm here. I truly, truly need your help."

"And so will my reputation when word gets out that I pretended to be your wife."

"Your reputation will be fine. We're just going to have dinner with him. It isn't like we're going to stand up and make a grand announcement that we're married. Afterwards, we'll tell him you went to visit a sick aunt in Muskegon, or some other place. He'll only be here a couple days. He'll never have to see you again, or you him. Please, Jewel. Think about what the *Gazette* means to the Grove."

"Think about what size skinning knife my pa's going to use on your hide if he finds out."

"He won't."

"Why not ask Maddie?"

"Hicks has already met her. Please, Jewel, I'm begging. I'll do anything you ask in exchange. I'll grovel, crawl on my belly like a snake. I'll eat worms, dirt. You name it, I'll do it."

The fervent plea sounded so boyish, she couldn't keep her smile from showing.

"That smile gives me hope."

"Save the charm for your mistresses."

Eyes filled with humor, he went silent for a moment then asked again, softly, "Please, Jewel."

She sighed. "If I say yes, I know I'm going to regret it. I can feel it as sure as I can feel the sun on my face."

"You won't, I promise. One hour. That's all. Nothing's going to happen. We'll be dining in the Quilt Ladies' private room. No one will even know what we're discussing."

"Can't you just tell him the truth?"

"If I do, he'll bankroll a newspaper somewhere else because he'll think I'm a liar."

"Which in this case you are."

"Jewel, please. Please."

She sighed again and ran her hands over her face. "Okay. One dinner. One hour. One. That's all."

"Thank you!" Grabbing her around the waist, he swung her around and the pleasure in his dark face made him even more handsome. "Thank you!"

Laughing, she protested, "Put me down, you loon!"

"I could kiss you."

"Don't."

He set her down.

The power of him was so overwhelming, she had to turn away or become a puddle at his feet. Grabbing hold of herself, she kept her tone cool. "We'll be eating at the boardinghouse?"

"Yes. I'll come back and pick you up around four so we can arrive together."

She looked down at the denims she was wearing. "I suppose I should put on a dress."

"Would you, please."

She shot him a look. "I'll see you later."

"I owe you, Jewel."

"Yes, you do," and she went into the house.

It was a little past two in the afternoon, so Jewel had time to start the roast chickens and peel some potatoes for dinner. Her brothers, all of whom cut lumber and built houses for her father's company were working over near Niles. Most times they were back by midafternoon. She had no idea how she was going to get gussied up and leave the house without them becoming suspicious. The only time she paid attention to her looks was for church on Sundays, but they'd known Eli all of their lives, too, and would probably go along with his ruse. However, there was no way her father would sanction such a harebrained scheme. Grove fathers guarded their daughters' reputations the way dragons guarded gold, and Adam Crowley was no exception. Eli's reputation as a ladies' man was legendary. Her pa would be the first to admit Eli had become much more focused in life over the past few years, but that wouldn't matter. Eli was a Lothario and Jewel was a virgin, and as far as her father was concerned never the twain shall meet.

Supper was just about done cooking when her brothers came home. They tromped in loud and boisterous and greeted her with smiles. Meg, their mother, had died during Jewel's eleventh year, and after her death, Jewel took over the running of the house. While her father and brothers felled lumber she handled everything from the wash to the cooking to the gardening, but refused to let her brothers help even when they insisted because she'd promised her mother on her death bed that she would take care of the Crowley men, and because Jewel could do the chores so much faster than they. But by the time she turned eighteen, she was so overwhelmed and overworked it had taken a visit from Dr. Lancaster to convince her to let the five big strong men help out. These days, Jewel continued to be the main housekeeper, but thanks to their assistance she was no longer tired all day every day, and in the evenings they took care of the dishes and righted the kitchen; a blessing.

While her brothers ate, she hurried to her room to wash up and get dressed. Thanks to the shopping trips to Detroit and Chicago initiated by Dr. Lancaster and Abigail, Jewel owned a fairly decent amount of ladies' attire—not that the Grove offered myriad opportunities to wear any of her purchases, outside of church or the occasional town dance, but this evening she was pretending to be the wife of Eli Grayson, and she thought her blue skirt and jacket would be an appropriate choice. Looking into the wooden framed mirror on her vanity table, she paused as she tied back her thick ebony hair with a matching blue ribbon, then shook her head at the ridiculous plan. Nothing good was going to come of this, but it was hard to tell him no. Most of the young women in the Grove had at one time or another been sweet on both Eli and his handsome older cousin Nate, and Jewel was no exception. However unlike the others who'd grown up and turned their hearts toward more realistic suitors, Jewel's heart had settled on Eli and dug in, and she had no explanation why. She found her attraction to him silly and embarrassing. He never saw her as anyone other than the Crowleys' little sister, and because she knew there was no way on God's green earth she could compete with the fancy and sophisticated ladies he lavished his affections upon, she'd never let him know her feelings. Nor would she ever. The last thing she needed was his pity or, heaven forbid, his laughter. Now that his widowed mother, Abigail, was married to her widower father, he was family, not blood, but another brother none-the-less, and that was the only relationship she needed or expected.

Refusing to think anymore on the subject, she put the finishing touches to her attire, gave her reflection one last critical glance, and left her room.

Her brothers had finished dinner by then, and were outdoors relaxing under the big oaks behind the house. She needed to tell them her plans for the evening, but before she went out to join them she looked around to make sure her father hadn't stopped by to visit while she'd been dressing. If he were about he'd surely ask where she was headed, and since she'd never lied to her father and doubted she ever would, she'd have to confess the truth and then all perdition would break loose.

But as she peered out of the window in the parlor, she didn't see him.

Outside, Paul, the eldest, took one look at her in her blue finery, and confusion creased his brow. "Is there church tonight?"

She pulled on her matching crocheted gloves. "No." She then explained Eli's proposal. For a moment there was silence.

Jeremiah, who most favored their mother and was second in the sibling line, asked, "And you agreed to this?"

She shrugged. "Eli is family now. I'm simply helping him out."

Noah cracked, "That's what Pa's going to put on his headstone."

The brothers laughed. Zeke, who was shorter but wider than his brothers, said, "I think it's a good plan."

Abraham shook his head. "You're the one who thought setting up an ice shanty on the lake in *April* was a good plan."

More laughs. Zeke hung his head in embarrassment. He'd been fourteen at the time and so full of himself he refused to listen when his older brothers tried to explain the dangers of ice fishing in April. When the thinning ice under his shanty broke away and drifted into open water, taking him and the shanty on a perilous fifteen-mile ride down river, he realized the soundness of their advice. Only after the floe ground into a larger, more stable stretch of ice was he able to leave it and get back to shore.

Paul brought the conversation back to the matter at hand. "Personally, I hope Eli's plan works.

Her brothers nodded.

Jewel added, "And I hope Pa doesn't find out."

Everyone agreed with that, too.

Eli drove up a few moments later, and after setting the brake on his buggy, walked over to where the Crowleys were gathered. Once greetings were exchanged, he turned to Jewel. "Ready?"

"As I'll ever be."

"Then let's get going. We don't want to be late." He offered his arm. She studied it for a moment, then rolled her eyes and stalked off to the buggy. Eli turned to her brothers. "And we wonder why she doesn't have a beau."

They all laughed and Eli hurried to catch up.

When he joined her in the buggy, he looked her way. "You know, if this plan is to succeed, you're going to have to act as if you like me."

"I like you fine."

"Then can you take that sour look off your face? You're supposed to be my wife."

Exasperated, she sat back against the seat. "We're going to be late." Sighing with an exasperation of his own, he signaled the horse with the reins.

As he drove past the enormous willow tree that stood on the edge of the Crowley property and out to the road, he glanced her way again, taking in her blue outfit. "You look nice."

"Thanks," she responded before asking, "Suppose Hicks wants to know how long we've been married?"

Eli shrugged. "How about we say a couple of years?"

"Do we have children?"

"No."

"Good. Pretending to be married is lie enough."

He was beginning to think that shoeless lumber beast Celeste Keppler might have been a better choice. He did note how different Jewel looked when she took the time to fix herself up, though. Because of the unconventional influence of Dr. Viveca Lancaster Grayson, many of the women in the Grove had taken to wearing denim trousers when they did chores, and since everyone knew Jewel worked from sun up to sun down he'd be willing to bet she slept in her denims as well. The only time she seemed to be without them was on Sundays. In reality, she was a beauty. She had clear brown skin, thick rippling dark hair, and a pair of intelligent black eyes that could shine with laughter one moment and cut you like an ax blade the next. She could be incredibly generous—case in point, her agreeing to help him with Hicks—but she also had a wrath that could flay the hide off a grizzly bear. As a result, all of the Crowley men went out of their way to keep her happy, one because they loved her to no end, and two because she was a terror when angry. "Remember the time your brothers and I tore down the clotheslines playing lacrosse."

"I do, and you all never did it again."

He chuckled. "Birdshot can be a powerful deterrent."

On the day in question she'd asked that they not play lacrosse in the field until the laundry she had hanging on the lines dried and was taken down, but being older they'd dismissed both her and her request.

"We couldn't believe you were shooting at us." One moment they'd been running pell-mell up and down the field passing the ball back and forth with their webbed sticks, and the next, birdshot filled the air sending them cursing, ducking, and scrambling for cover.

"I couldn't believe you all tore down two lines of wash and went on playing as if it was meaningless. I was furious."

"We could tell." Once the shooting stopped, she made them pick up every piece of wash, restring the lines, and rehang the laundry, but she didn't rewash anything. "Paul said you didn't wash clothes again for a month."

"I did for Pa and me, but not for them. Made them suffer the July heat with dirty linens on their beds and unwashed clothes on their backs. The wash and I received a lot more respect after that." She looked his way. "Whatever made you think about that?"

"Just musing on your many facets."

"My facets," she echoed skeptically.

"Yes. You have a generous side and a side that shoots."

"I see. Then I'll make sure I keep the latter hidden while we're with Hicks. No sense in dazzling him with my scintillating personality."

He grinned. "You know, you're going to make some man a fine wife one day."

"And you say that, because?"

"You've a great wit. You run an efficient household and you're not bad to look at."

Amused she turned to the passing landscape. "That's quite the compliment coming from you."

"I'm serious."

"I'm sure you are, but considering your way with the ladies, any woman with half a brain would never take you seriously."

"You wound me again."

"And you undoubtedly flirt in your sleep."

The famous Grayson smile split his dark features. "You think I'm flirting with you?"

"With me? No."

Her cynical-sounding reply gave him pause, and for the first time in his life Eli evaluated her the way he would had he indeed been flirting. He'd already alluded to her beauty, but why hadn't he noticed the alluring ripeness of her mouth before, and when had her body become so curvaceous? He put those distracting thoughts aside. If Adam Crowley got even a hint that he might be assessing Jewel the way a man would a woman, the old lumber beast would come looking for him armed and loaded for bear.

When they reached the Quilt Ladies' establishment, the large number of vehicles parked outside attested to the many diners inside. "You think all these folks are here to get a gander at Hicks?" Jewel asked.

"We small-towners take our amusements where we can."

He came around to her side of the buggy and offered up a hand. She paused, eyed him, then remembering her role let him assist her down without making a fuss. She was glad she'd worn gloves, though, because they shielded her hand against the unsettling warmth of his touch. She took a moment to smooth her skirt. When she felt capable of facing him again, she looked him in the eyes. "You're certain you want to go through with this?"

"I am."

"Then I'll do my best not to foul the plan."

"See? Your generous side."

His vivid eyes were one of his most powerful weapons, she found herself thinking. Shaking herself back to reality, she covered her lapse by saying dismissively, "Let's just go in. The sooner we're done the sooner I can return home."

Amused by all that she was, Eli walked her to the door and decided that if she ever did find a beau, he'd have to be a very special man indeed.

Upon entering the Quilt Ladies' small but tastefully decorated establishment, they saw that all eight tables in the main room were occupied and that every eye was turned their way. Jewel tried not to squirm under the casual scrutiny and nodded greetings. Kicking herself for agreeing to this, she prayed the evening would go quickly.

Caroline Ross, wearing a mint green gown with tiny yellow bows on the hooped skirt swayed over and greeted them warmly, "Eli, hello again. Mr. Hicks is waiting for you in the back room. Jewel, I'm afraid finding you a seat may take some time."

Eli cleared his throat. "She's with me."

"Really?"

Jewel explained hastily, "He thought I might like to meet Mr. Hicks. I, uh, have some ideas for the *Gazette*. A ladies' column." She summoned up what she hoped passed for a genuine smile.

"Ah," Caroline voiced but studied Jewel long enough to give her a repeat case of the squirms. "This way."

She led them through the room. The packed-in diners viewed their passing with unabashed interest. A few even whispered, "Good luck, Eli."

When she showed them into the small private room, Hicks was seated at the lone white-clothed table. He'd changed to a brown suit and at their approach rose to his feet.

Eli turned to Caroline, "Thank you."

It was easy to see she wanted to hover, but Eli didn't want her eavesdropping when he introduced Jewel as his wife. "Miss Ross, can you bring us something cold to drink. We're parched from the drive."

"Oh. Of course. Excuse me. I'll send someone right in." She exited and closed the door softly behind her.

By then Hicks was looking between Eli and Jewel with an expectancy that couldn't be ignored, so Eli plunged in. "G. W. Hicks, this is my wife, Jewel Grayson."

His smile was kind. "Pleased to meet you, Mrs. Grayson."

"Thank you. I'm pleased as well. The Grove is very honored to host such an esteemed visitor."

Hicks gestured to the chairs. "Please. Join me."

After they were settled, Hicks gave Jewel a polite glance and said to Eli, "Grayson, you didn't tell me your wife was so lovely."

Jewel kept her face composed.

Eli eyed her fondly. "She's lovely, intelligent, and witty as well. Marrying her was the best thing I've ever done."

Jewel almost rolled her eyes but remembered her role, and said with a feigned shyness, "Thank you, Eli. That was very sweet."

He reached over and covered her hand with his. Instinct made her want to pull back, but the subtle pressure of his hand kept hers immobile.

Hicks seemed to be pleased by the show of affection. "How long have you been married?"

"A couple of years," they both answered.

"Children?"

"No." Again in unison.

"I'm sure that will come with time."

Jewel smiled falsely.

The waiter entered with a pitcher of iced tea, sparing her any further talk of babies. He poured some of the amber liquid into their glass tumblers, and once done, said, "I'll be back with your meals."

He departed and closed the door. Hicks again had his attention on Jewel. "Are you a Grove native, Mrs. Grayson?"

"Yes, sir."

"What do you think of your husband's newspaper?"

"I enjoyed it. I took issue with his editorials at times, but that's to be expected, him being a Democrat and all."

Hicks grinned. "If women had the vote, which party would you prefer?"

"That's between me and the ballot box. No?"

That sat him back.

Eli inwardly cringed.

Jewel took a small sip of tea.

Hicks observed her for a silent moment more, then looked impressed. "Grayson, you said the women here were unique. You were not wrong." He raised his glass in salute. "To you, Mrs. Grayson, and intelligent women everywhere."

Jewel raised hers in response and hoped the food would arrive soon.

For the next hour, they ate their meals of roast duck and vegetables and discussed the political issues of the day. The state of Tennessee had recently enacted a new Jim Crow law that was being roundly denounced by Black newspapers from Boston to Los Angeles. The statute, which endorsed the segregation of railroad coaches, had employed the new term *separate but equal*.

Eli cracked bitterly, "Separate, yes. Equal, no."

Hicks agreed. "There's nothing equal about riding in a cattle car. The race is heading down a slippery slope with this legislation because Tennessee has given other states the phrase they need to further distance us from our rights."

Jewel silently agreed as well. The country seemed less and less interested in applying the freedoms promised in the Constitution to its darker citizens. Reconstruction had been dead for years and the Redemptionists in the South were murdering Black men and women separately and equally.

"And that is why the race's newspapers are so vital," Eli said, leaning forward to make his point. "No one else is going to bang our drum. The *Chicago Tribune* said we Blacks are going to disappear from national politics, and they may be correct, but as long as there is one Black editor left standing we will not go silently."

"Hear, hear," Hicks voiced, pleased. "Which is exactly one of the reasons why I'm choosing you and your paper, Grayson. You won't go silently."

He eyed the two of them and then rose to his feet. "Will you come with me, please?"

She and Eli shared a look but followed him out to the main dining room.

He called out in a loud voice, "Ladies and gentlemen of the Grove, may I have your attention."

Feeling uneasy under the scrutiny of the diners, Jewel wondered what he was going to say.

When it was quiet, he continued, "I'd like to welcome into my newspaper family the newly appointed editor of the *Gazette,* Eli Grayson. Let's give him and his lovely wife, Jewel, a hand."

Every mouth in the place dropped, and in the silence, Jewel wished she knew how to faint because that was what she wanted to do.

As if they'd needed a moment to recover from the startling announcement, the diners began to applaud enthusiastically while staring at each other in surprise and shock.

Eli knew this wasn't good. Seeing the storm gathering in Jewel's face, he bowed to the cheering crowd, and said out of the side of his mouth, "Smile darling."

So she did, but she whispered furiously, "Is this what you meant when you said nothing was going to happen?" Short of telling the truth and opening up an even larger can of worms, there was no way out, at least for the moment. The news of their marriage would spread so quickly that by the time the moon rose, people all over the county would be asking each other, "Did you hear about

Eli Grayson and Jewel Crowley?" She wanted to shoot somebody. Preferably Eli.

Eli knew that he and Jewel needed to leave the diner before one of their neighbors came over to offer congratulations and began asking questions neither of them was prepared to answer. His hastily conceived plan had gotten away from him as quickly as a toboggan on a hill of fresh snow, so once the applause died and they were again seated in the private room, he said, "Mr. Hicks, I am honored by your faith in me, and you won't be sorry you tapped me. However, Jewel hasn't been feeling well, and I promised her I'd get her home early so she could lie down."

"Oh, of course, why didn't you say something before?"

Eli asked, "Can you and I meet sometime tomorrow?"

"Certainly. How about here around nine?"

"Perfect." He turned to Jewel. "Are you ready, sweetheart?"

She kicked him beneath the table. Enjoying his muffled groan of pain, she responded quietly, "Yes, dear. Mr. Hicks, it was a pleasure meeting you."

"I hope you feel better. I'm looking forward to dining with you and your husband again, soon."

Jewel nodded politely and let Eli lead her from the dining room, all the while trying to ignore the diners looking after them with wide-eyed wonder.

# Chapter 3

Outside, they walked over to the buggy. Jewel had steam pouring out of her ears. When he politely offered a hand to assist her up, she promptly slapped it away and got in under her own power.

"Did you have to kick me so hard?"

"I told you this was a harebrained plan."

"That you agreed to."

"I'm not speaking to you."

With her arms clamped over her chest she looked like a female version of her father. He held on to his grin. "Jewel—"

She snarled, "If you don't get this buggy moving, I swear I'll drive off and leave you right here."

Knowing this was not the best place to have this argument, he climbed up onto the seat and drove the buggy out of town. He waited until they reached the countryside before saying, "I didn't know he was going to stand up and say what he did. When he leaves town, we'll tell folks it was a mistake."

"Yes, my mistake for saying yes. Good women do not go around pretending to be married when they aren't."

"I think you're getting more riled up about this than necessary."

"I'm not speaking to you," she said again.

The whole thing was so absurd and she was so furious, he couldn't stop the smile.

"This is not funny, Eli."

"No it isn't, sweetheart."

"And don't call me *sweetheart*."

He hid his humor behind a cool tone. "My sincerest apology."

"I don't want an apology, I just want to be who I was when I got out of bed this morning. Jewel Crowley, spinster—not Jewel Crowley, supposedly married to the Colored Casanova of Cass County."

He laughed. He couldn't help himself. "Is that what folks call me?"

She didn't respond.

"You could do worse, you know. In fact, I'd pick me over being a spinster any day of the week."

A less self-assured man would have cringed under the glare she gave him, but he simply turned his attention back to his driving. He supposed the only way to make this right was to do what he should have done from the beginning, which was to tell Hicks the truth and let the consequences fall where they may. Reopening the *Gazette* had been a dream he desperately wanted to see realized, but not at her expense. "I'll tell Hicks the truth in the morning."

"That would be best," she replied tightly. Too late by far, but best.

"If he doesn't want the *Gazette* in his syndicate, I'll come up with another way to catch the brass ring."

Jewel knew losing Hicks's support would deflate all of Eli's plans, but she didn't offer any sympathies because it was going to take a month of Sundays to convince folks that she and Eli hadn't secretly run off to become man and wife, if they could be convinced at all. In reality, convincing shouldn't be necessary. Anybody with half a brain would know the two of them weren't married, but as he stated earlier, small-town folks took their amusement where they could find it. The speculation and spectacle surrounding this debacle would be like finding gold.

"This will all be ironed out. I promise."

She didn't respond.

He looked her way. "Still not talking to me?'

"No."

His chuckle softly rippled the silence. "Okay. Let's leave that for a moment and go back to another subject. You'd really prefer spinsterhood over marriage to me?"

"Yes, because I like my life the way it is. I have my family, my committee work, and my roses. I don't wish to be married to someone who has to look up *monogamy* in Mr. Webster's dictionary."

"Ouch, Jewel. I'd be monogamous with the right woman. Just haven't met her yet."

She rolled her eyes.

"Such disbelief."

"Such balderdash."

"Such truth."

He met her eyes and the power in them seemed to reach out and stroke her. Unnerved, she looked away.

"Jewel?" he called softly.

She turned.

"I am sorry."

"I know, Eli. Just take me home."

When he brought the buggy to a halt in front of the Crowley home, she didn't wait for him to help her down. As soon as he stopped, she hopped down and ran up the walk to the door. Regretting the mess he'd gotten her into, he waited to make sure she went inside before driving away.

Paul was in the parlor reading when Jewel came in. He took one look at her face and asked, "Did it go that badly?"

She pulled off her gloves and related the story.

His eyes widened. "Hicks told everyone you two were married?"

"Yes."

"What did Eli say?"

"Nothing, and neither did I. We were so astonished, there wasn't much we could say."

"Is he going to tell Hicks the truth?"

"In the morning."

"Let's hope that will be the end of it. Poor Eli. There goes his hope for the *Gazette*."

"Poor Eli? What about me? They applauded, Paul. Everyone in town is going to believe I'm his wife."

"Could be worse."

She glared.

He grinned. "Fixing this may be like trying to shove a bear into a mouse hole, but let things settle a bit. They may not go as badly as you believe."

"Pa's going to throw a fit."

"There is that. He's not going to like you being gossiped about."

She pressed her hands to her head. "Nor that I brought it on myself. I think I'll just kill myself now and save him the trouble."

He smiled. Of all her brothers she loved Paul the best. Growing up, he'd stood up for her, and when the other four tortured her he'd come to her rescue. He was a good ten years older than she, but always had time to listen. Like now. "I'm going to change out of these clothes. Where's everyone else?"

"Turkey hunting. Should be back before dark." He looked at the misery in his baby sister's face and said, "Don't worry Jewel. I'm betting everyone will understand and it'll just blow over."

Tight-lipped, she hoped he was right, and left him to his reading.

Later, wearing her denims and brogans, Jewel went out to the barn to sort through the rose plants she'd been trying to get to all day. Roses were her passion. In another month the Grove's roses would begin blooming everywhere, and she was responsible for planting and caring for most of them. Her reputation with the thorny beauties was so well known around the county that wealthy White homes and churches also employed her services. Harrison's Yellows were her favorites. They were showy, usually the first roses to bloom and were long lasting. They were also easily divided by a hatchet, which made them not as costly as other varieties to replace.

Jewel was in the process of making sure all the roots of the bare canes she planned to put in for Maddie Loomis in the morning were still nice and damp in the buckets she had them resting in when Abigail walked in leaning on her cane. "Evening, Jewel."

"How are you?" Jewel loved her stepmother. Many of Abigail's friends called her Gail. She'd been one of the many Grove women who'd helped raise Jewel after the death of her mother, and when Abigail finally relented and married Jewel's father a few years back, no one had been happier.

"I was on my way home from the Historical Society meeting, thought I'd stop and see how you were doing."

"I'm fine. Tired, though. Washday today." Jewel was trying to work up the nerve to talk to her about the boardinghouse incident but wasn't having much success. "How's Pa?"

"Doing well. He wanted to stay and play checkers at the general store, so I left him there. Miss

Edna said if you have any rose canes you're not planting, she'd like a few."

"Okay. After I'm done at Maddie's tomorrow I'll go by the store."

"Jewel? Are you sure you're well? You look—"

"Hello," a familiar voice trilled. "Jewel, are you in the barn?"

Abigail and Jewel shared a look. Caroline Ross?

Sure enough, she and her hooped gown swayed into the barn. For the life of her, Jewel could never figure out how Caroline and the others drove with all that fabric billowing about. More importantly, Jewel knew Caroline had heard Hicks's declaration at dinner and prayed the woman didn't mention it now. "What brings you by?"

Caroline grinned. "Who says there are no secrets in the Grove? When Hicks made that announcement you could have knocked me over with a feather. How long have you two sly ones been married?"

Jewel's worst fears had come true. She dragged her hands across her face.

Abigail looked on in confusion. "Married?"

Before Abigail could continue, Jewel said, "It's all a mistake, Miss Ross. A very silly mistake."

She smiled. "Oh, I see. It's still supposed to be a secret. Cat's already out of the bag, though, don't you think? You and Eli. That is something."

Abigail stared openmouthed.

Caroline added, "And Jewel, you just glowed. We all noticed it."

"Glowed?" Jewel echoed.

Caroline nodded, "You know? *Glowed.* As in a babe is on the way. Is it true what everyone is saying?"

Jewel's eyes widened like plates. She'd left the boardinghouse less than two hours ago, and already rumor had her carrying Eli's child! She somehow managed to say, "As I said, Miss Ross, Hicks made a mistake. Everyone knows Eli and I aren't married."

Abigail began to cough so violently, Jewel went hastily to her side. "Do you need water?"

"No. A seat." She sat down on a large crate and began to fan herself with her handkerchief.

Jewel knew it was time to send Caroline Ross packing. "Miss Ross, I'm going to get Gail some water. Thank you for visiting. I'd be real appreciative if you'd tell folks that I'm neither married nor carrying."

Caroline winked. "The babe's supposed to be a secret, too, isn't it? I won't say a word. I promise." She headed toward the barn entrance, then stopped and look back at Jewel. "Congratulations," she offered with a conspiratorial whisper.

When she was gone, an appalled Jewel turned to a stunned Abigail who asked, "What in heavens was that about? You and Eli married?"

Jewel sighed and told her the story, and when she was finished, Abigail gasped, "Oh my word!"

"And now, apparently folks believe I'm carrying, too."

For a long moment all Abigail could do was stare in astonishment and disbelief. "Eli has to straighten this out right away. If Hicks leaves town because of the truth, so be it. Good lord, what was he thinking?"

"About the *Gazette*."

"Whose first headline will be: *Gazette* Editor Eli Grayson Hung by Adam Crowley."

"I know. Maybe Pa won't hear the rumors."

"Only if he's deaf. I'm betting Caroline Ross is at this moment spreading the word to anyone who will listen." Abigail leaned back against the barn wall, thinking. "If I can get to your father before he hears the gossip and explain things, maybe he can be convinced to wait and see if this will all pass over before he levels his bear gun on my son."

Jewel knew how much her father loved Abigail and that at times would listen to her when he refused to listen to anyone else. She had a way with him second only to Jewel, but he could be stubborn and bullheaded to a fault when it came to his daughter's well-being. "Maybe he'll fool us all and deal with this in a level-headed manner."

"Optimism is a virtue, dear, but remember that time you were ill, when Viveca first came to be the doctor here, and Adam had your brother shanghai her in the middle of the night to come tend to you?"

Jewel did. Nate Grayson had been very upset

by her father's actions, but her pa hadn't cared. Jewel's health had been his only concern.

Abigail roused herself. "I'll go home and see if he's there. Let's hope we can get this all put to rest. As far as society is concerned, all we women have is our reputation and we can't have yours trampled by something as foolish as this."

"Thanks, Gail."

"You're welcome. Now you go on back to your roses and I'll see to your father. Wish me luck."

"You know I do."

When Abigail was gone, Jewel finished up the roses and walked back to the house thinking this had to be one of the worst days of her life.

Taking advantage of the day's fading light, Eli was seated on the porch of his cabin organizing the items he planned to present to Hicks in the morning. "If the man doesn't leave town after I tell him the truth," he mused aloud sarcastically.

His conversation with himself faded as he watched Adam Crowley ride up. Wondering what he might want and hoping nothing had happened to his mother, Eli stood and watched his stepfather dismount and march up to meet him.

"Evening, Adam. Something wrong with Mother?"

"No," he answered tersely. "I need to talk to you."

Eli studied the granite-set face. "Out here or inside?"

"Inside."

Eli led the way, and when the screen door closed behind them, Adam didn't mince words. "What is this about you and Jewel being married?"

Eli froze, then wondered if the old lumberjack would let him live long enough to provide an explanation. "It was a ruse."

Adam crossed his arms over his barrel-like chest and waited.

Eli told him the story, leaving nothing out and making sure to place the blame squarely on himself. "Jewel was simply trying to help me."

"And now?"

"Hopefully, after I tell Hicks the truth in the morning, things will quiet down. How'd you find out?"

"Miss Edna's store. Everyone in town's talking. I even received a few congratulations on the upcoming birth of my grandchild."

Eli stared.

Adam's eyes gleamed grimly. "Thought that would get your attention. Not only are you and my Jewel supposedly married, but apparently she's carrying your child!"

The last part of the sentence was shouted so loudly, Eli swore the roof rattled.

Eli was angry at the gossips, at the damage done to Jewel's reputation, and at himself. She'd tried to warn him but he'd been so focused on his own needs, he hadn't listened.

"Son, I understand why you thought the ruse was necessary, the *Gazette* means the world to us all, but couldn't you have gotten someone else? Why my Jewel?"

"I'll marry her." Those were three words Eli never thought he'd hear himself say to anyone's father.

"What?"

"I said, I'll marry her," he repeated, looking Adam square in the eyes.

"The hell you will."

"I sell newspapers, Adam. People like scandal. No matter what we say about the ruse, some people are still going to believe the worst, and they're going to talk about her from here to Chicago. I won't allow it. She was just trying to do me a good turn."

"You honestly believe I'm going to let you marry my only daughter?"

"Do you know of any other way to stop the gossiping, short of her moving away? The people in the Grove who are our friends will take our denials as truth, but what about the others. What about the people who hire her to grow their roses. Some have been willing to overlook her color, but salacious rumors about whether she's married or not, or carrying or not, could cost her her business." Eli pulled in a deep breath, adding, "This mess is entirely my fault."

"Yes, it is, but at least you're being honorable about it." Adam studied him for a long time. "Suppose I say yes to your marrying her. What kind of husband are you meaning to be?"

"I'll not shame her and I'll be faithful to her. That's really what you're asking, isn't it?"

"Damn right. This is my Jewel we're discussing."

"I'm not going to pretend that I love her, but I will care for her, and provide for her to the best of my abilities until death parts us."

"She's going to put up a whale of a fight."

"I know."

"Probably get out that bird gun of hers and shoot us both."

They shared a look, and for the first time since Adam's arrival, Eli allowed himself a small smile. "That is a given, too."

Both men agreed that the sooner the vows took place the better everything would be, so while Eli went to get dressed, Adam rode off to fetch the reverend. Eli planned to meet them at the Crowley home in an hour. He imagined Jewel would explode when presented with his proposal, and expected no less.

"Hell of a way to start a marriage," he mumbled as he did up his tie in the mirror. *Marriage.* He paused a moment to contemplate the word. It was going to affect his life like nothing had since his ill-fated affair with Nate's wife, Cecile. After the disastrous results, he swore he'd never rain havoc down on the life of anyone he cared about ever again, and because he'd known Jewel all her life she qualified as one of those people.

No, he didn't love her; he doubted he ever would, not in the way Nate loved Viveca, or the way Adam loved Abigail. There would be no grand passion in this, but he would treat her with kindness and respect. He'd told her she'd make some man a fine wife one day, he just didn't know that man would be him.

That evening at the Crowley home, Jewel's brothers were engaged in an arm-wrestling competition, one of the thousands they'd had since childhood, and their boisterous cheers filled the air. As always Jewel played judge. None of the brothers trusted the others not to favor one contestant over the other, so over the years, she became responsible for making sure the grips were fair, that no one had his elbow over the line on the smooth surface of the huge tree stump used for the matches, or started too soon.

Paul, being the oldest and the strongest, hadn't lost to any of his brothers ever. His opponent this time around was Ezekiel, who was beginning to rival Paul in strength and determination.

Jewel's serious face showed the import of her task as she checked their grips, elbows, and stances. Their eyes were focused on each other, their hands locked. Once she was assured everything was as it should be, she signaled with her handkerchief and the battle began.

Not that it lasted very long. The grinning Paul looked into his sibling's straining face then slammed Zeke's hand down flat for the win. Paul's supporters yelled in triumph while Zeke's offered up resigned smiles and their money.

Jewel was just putting her winnings into the pocket of her denims when she saw Abigail drive up.

"What she's doing out this late?" Paul asked as they all watched her step down. "Hope nothing has happened."

Jewel could see by the stern set of Abigail's mouth and the force of her cane against the ground as she crossed the field that something had. She hoped she hadn't come to say Caroline Ross had been spreading more rumors.

"Evening everyone," Abigail said, then turned to Jewel. "There's something we need to discuss. Let's go to the house."

Jewel noted that her face gave nothing away. Paul and the others wore questioning looks but kept their curiosity unspoken.

Once inside, Abigail took a seat in the parlor and set her cane near. "Would you close the door, please, Jewel."

Although Abigail's face was still unreadable, Jewel got the sense that something was very wrong. "Pa's not dead or anything?"

Abigail offered a wisp of a smile. "No, dear, your father's fine."

"Then what's happened?" she asked, closing the door.

Like her husband, Abigail didn't mince words. "Eli has proposed marriage."

"To whom?"

"To you."

Jewel was certain she'd misheard her. "Why?"

"Because its all over town that you're carrying his child."

"Everyone knows Caroline Ross is a busybody, no one's going to believe her."

"Unfortunately, that isn't true. Edna said you and Eli are being talked about just about everywhere. Your father is very concerned." Abigail added, "As am I."

"You spoke with him, then?"

"I did and he's fit to be tied. Challenged Jim Miller to a fight a short while ago because of his disparaging remarks about the child being conceived out of wedlock. When he said you should be banned from the church, Vernon had to step in before they came to blows."

Jewel sighed her frustration. This was disastrous.

"So, Eli will be here shortly, and your father's on his way to get Reverend Anderson."

"What?" she shouted.

When Abigail nodded, eyes sympathetic, Jewel stated tightly, "I'm honored that Eli wants to be honorable, but I don't want to marry him any more than he wants to marry me."

"I know. It's your reputation, dear. Maybe in another hundred years such things won't matter, but they matter very much in this world today. And my son is a good man."

A frustrated Jewel put her hands over her face and peered at Abigail through spread fingers. "This is not what I want to do."

Abigail nodded. "I' know, and I've spent the last hour trying to figure a way around it but nothing else comes to mind."

"And I'm supposed to be his wife, *forever?"*

Abigail's face told all.

"There has to be a way out that doesn't include this."

Gail met the stricken eyes of her stepdaughter, and noted how much she favored her late mother. "If you can offer a solution, it would be welcomed, but in the meantime, you should go and get dressed. The men will be here soon." With caring in her voice, she asked, "Do you need assistance?"

Jewel shook her head. "No. Thank you, though." And with her back tense and her face stony, she exited the parlor.

In her room, Jewel wanted to break something, shoot something, climb on the roof and wail like a child. She knew it was a terribly unchristian of her to think this, but was Eli drinking again? In her mind, he had to be, to come up with something this farfetched and think it would work—but then again, he'd thought fooling Hicks would work. She sighed at the injustice of it all. In spite of her silly adolescent feelings for him she had no desire to be his wife. She knew he had a penchant for the ladies, so would he be faithful to her and his vows? He'd boasted of his ability to be true with the right woman—one he hadn't met yet, he'd been quick to admit—so where did that leave her? Realistically, it left her at the mercy of a society that refused to consider the idea of a woman being intelligent enough to make her own decisions, decisions that shouldn't be driven by the aftereffects of gossip and innuendo.

She opened her wardrobe and cynically eyed her choices. Her attention settled first on the stylish black walking costume she wore to funerals, but thought that would be a very childish way to protest. Almost as childish as considering running away from home, which had crossed her mind. But she wasn't twelve years of age; she was twenty-four, fully grown, and a Crowley. She needed to act accordingly, even if she found the idea of the approaching wedding appalling.

As she sorted through her dresses, a part of her continued to search for a way out of the noose. Then the answer came to her. It was going to cause the top of her father's head to fly off when he heard it, but truthfully, she didn't much care. It was a way out and she'd take it.

Filled with relief, she decided on the same blue outfit she'd worn earlier. The gown would always be associated with that evening's disastrous dinner and there was no sense in attaching fresh bad memories to another set of clothing.

She'd just finished brushing and retying her hair when a soft knock on the door made her turn. Walking over, she opened it to find her father on the other side.

He looked grim. "May I come in?"

She wanted to deny him but he was her father. "Certainly." She stepped back to let him enter.

"Are you ready?"

"No," she offered bluntly.

"Jewel, I'm sorry, but Eli's doing this for you."

"So I'm told."

Father and daughter eyed each other for a moment, then Adam said, "I know you're angry but I won't have your name dragged in the dirt."

"I understand that, but understand this—I'm going to be angry for some time, Pa."

"He's promised to be faithful."

Not wanting to discuss her own fears on the subject, she turned from him and said coolly, "It doesn't matter. This won't be a love match, so he's free to venture where he will as long as he's discreet." She pulled on her gloves.

He stared.

"I'm being realistic, Papa. I know men have their needs, and besides, I plan to have him divorce me in a few years anyway."

His eyes widened farther. "Divorce? What are you talking about?"

"It's my way out of this mess. I read about divorce in a pamphlet I saw at the Intelligence Society meeting last month." At the time she'd no idea how valuable the article would be to her personally. "Divorce is a lot more widespread and accepted these days, especially out west."

"We're not out west," he growled ominously.

"No, we're not, but we're not in the eighteenth century, when women had no voice in their futures, either."

Adam grabbed tufts of his graying hair. "I knew Abigail starting that Society would be the death of me. Do you think I want you to marry this way?"

"Apparently you do, Pa, because you didn't say no to him."

"But the gossip!" he snarled.

"I know about the gossip," she shot back. "And I know how it can ruin a woman's name which is why I'm agreeing to this foolishness, but I don't have to like it and I don't have to stay married until death."

He looked ready to explode.

She held on to her own temper. "Now, unless you want to argue more, I think we should go get this done."

Adam looked at his youngest. She'd always been feisty, had to be in order to survive in the all-male Crowley household, but leave it to her to find a novel way out of her predicament. He didn't care for her solution. Divorce carried it's own stigma, but he could only shake his head in awed amusement. He had no idea if she'd really go through with the divorce and trade one stigma for another, but she was a Crowley if nothing else and she was not going to go meekly like a lamb led to slaughter. "Eli has no idea what he's in for, does he?"

She allowed herself a small smile. "I'm sure he doesn't."

"I'll pray for him."

"That might be good. Pray for me, too, because I'll probably rue this day for the rest of my life."

Tight-lipped at her pronouncement, Adam held out his arm and Jewel let herself be escorted to the parlor.

# Chapter 4

"I now pronounce you man and wife."

Reverend Anderson's words fell between the now married couple. Eli had never seen a more frozen-faced bride in all his days; Jewel just wanted it all to be over so she could return to the solitude of her room.

"Under normal circumstances, this is where I invite the groom to kiss his new bride."

Jewel shot him such a hot scowl that he added hastily, "But in this situation, I believe we'll simply applaud."

In attendance were her surprised brothers and Adam and Abigail. All applauded politely. When the clapping faded, the reverend looked at the newlyweds and offered sagely, "Sometimes God sees possibilities where we see none. I ask that you give this union a chance. May you both be blessed."

Because there'd been no time to plan for the event there was no celebratory wedding dinner prepared or even punch. After giving his daughter a solemn kiss on her brow, Adam excused himself to take the reverend home, leaving everyone else to stand around in the awkward silence.

Gail finally said, "I'm sure the two of you have things to discuss, so we'll leave you to it."

Her brothers mumbled their agreements. Everyone filed out, the parlor door was closed softly, and Mr. and Mrs. Eli Grayson were alone.

After a long silence, Jewel's chin rose and she trained her eyes on his. "Now what?"

"Not sure. I suppose we should see about getting your things moved to my cabin."

"Why?"

"Because married people usually reside under the same roof."

"This is not a usual marriage, so I plan to stay here."

"I'm not moving in with your brothers."

"I'm not suggesting you do. You've given me your name and I'm thankful, but that's all. I'm going to return to my life and you to yours. In a year or two you can divorce me."

"Divorce?" he asked, sounding like her father.

"Yes, divorce. It's not as if this is a love match, so feel free to dally where you like as long as you are discreet."

Eli cocked his head at her. "You want me to be unfaithful?"

"I'm being realistic, Eli. A man has needs."

"Needs usually enjoyed with his wife."

The tone of his voice set off alarm bells in her head. She searched his face and saw patient amusement. "Surely you don't want to share a marriage bed—with me?"

"Why not with you?"

"Because we both know I'm not one of those pampered, soft-skinned women you prefer."

"And what makes you think you know what kind of woman I prefer. Has it occurred to you that I might find the task of picking a rose covered with thorns a challenge?"

Jewel blinked. In his eyes and stance she read trouble of a kind she wasn't certain she knew how to fight.

He told her softly, "And, no, this isn't a love match, but it could be fun if you'd let it."

"I don't want fun. I just want to be who I was, and what I was before you showed up this afternoon."

"A spinster."

"An unmarried young woman."

"Same thing." On the ride over to the Crowley house that evening, Eli had decided not to fight the choice he'd made to marry her. Jewel was beautiful, intelligent, and strong spirited; all qualities he'd have wanted in a true wife, so why not make a go of it. Granted, he usually steered clear of innocents; he preferred his women as experienced as he, but at this moment, the idea of drawing passionate sighs from Jewel's lips instead of vinegar had him already envisioning the pleasure he wanted to give to his virgin bride. "So you don't want a wedding night."

"No."

"We'll save it, then."

The light of amusement in his eyes did not help her mood. "You're not taking this seriously enough for me."

"I'm not taking this seriously at all, to be truthful. We are man and wife, and I'd like to make the best of it."

"Meaning you'd like to bed me."

"You're a beautiful woman, Jewel. No getting around that, but there's more to marriage. Look at Viveca and Nate. Look at our parents."

"They love each other. We don't."

He had to admit, she had him there. "A point for your side."

She rolled her eyes. He was way too handsome for his own good and she was certain there were women who'd take him under any conditions. She was not one of them.

Eli scanned the tight set of her chin. Admittedly, divorce was a way out—and trust her to come up with such an outrageous solution. His decision to try and make the marriage at least tolerable was apparently all for naught. "The reverend has agreed not to divulge the true date of the wedding. That way we can tell our nosy neighbors we were married some time ago, but wanted to keep the news from your father."

"That's as good a lie as any, I suppose. Anything else?"

"Yes. We're married. You're going to have to act as if you care for me when we're out together."

"I can do that."

He knew how angry she must be; no one liked being forced into a situation not of their choosing. Truthfully, he wasn't happy either, but he'd done the honorable thing whether she appreciated it or not. "I'm going to meet with Hicks in the morning and then I'll come back here so we can iron this out."

Jewel knew she'd have to surrender sooner or later, but she preferred the latter. "Fine," she said, not bothering to hide her displeasure. "Anything else?"

He shook his head.

"Then I'll say good night." Without further word she walked to the closed parlor door and opened it.

"Good night, wife."

The tone of his voice made her stop. Turning back, she found herself snared by the directness of his gaze. Her realization that women probably succumbed to him at the drop of a hat finally made her break the contact and continue her exit, but on legs far less steady than she cared to admit.

Eli watched her go. Life certainly wasn't going to be dull or easy from now on, but he had something his prickly new bride lacked—patience. He'd simply have to wait her out.

Before leaving to return home, Eli wanted to talk with her brothers and to his mother, in that order. He found the brothers upstairs in the big book-lined study that had been Adam Crowley's during Eli's youth. At his entrance all conversation stopped and every eye turned his way. Not sure where he stood with them now, he plunged ahead. "I just came to tell you all the same thing I told your father. I plan to care for Jewel and provide for her to the best of my abilities as long as we are married." He then added, "Which according to her may not be for very long."

Seeing the confusion on their faces, he explained. "She wants a divorce as soon as things settle down."

"What?" her brothers bellowed in unison.

"My feelings exactly. And she doesn't plan to live with me either it seems. She's in her room now even as we speak."

Paul chuckled and shook his head. "Here you are offering to do the honorable thing and I'm betting you feel like you stepped into a bear trap."

"She is something."

Zeke said, "But she has to live with you. She's your wife."

"Explained that. She didn't buy it."

The brothers shared amused looks.

"So what are you going to do?" Abe asked.

Eli shrugged. "Can't simply throw her over my shoulder and drag her off."

"No you can't," Noah pointed out.

"Not and live to talk about it come the morning," Jeremiah added.

Paul said, "Abigail says you're going to tell folks

that you and Jewel have been secretly married. How's anybody going to believe it if she continues to live here?"

Eli shrugged again.

"Maybe she'll come to her senses in the morning," Zeke offered.

Eli thought turtles would fly first, but he kept that to himself. "I'm meeting with Hicks in the morning, then I'll come back and see if she and I can agree on anything."

"Good luck," Jeremiah said.

Paul added, "You're an honorable man, Eli."

The others nodded their agreement.

The five men in the room were the closest Eli had to brothers and he responded with a heartfelt "Thanks."

He found his mother sitting outside on the porch bench. She looked up and said, "I'm very proud of you."

He took a seat on the railing. "Jewel sure isn't. She's refusing to live with me."

Abigail smiled in the darkness. "She comes from stubborn stock."

"And she wants me to divorce her once things have quieted down."

"Now why didn't I think of that?"

Amusement filled him. "Of course you'd think that a good idea."

"No, I think it's brilliant idea. Divorce has its stigma but I know a few divorced women in Kalamazoo and Muskegon who are living life on their own terms, and doing well. Frankly, by century's end, I believe divorce is going to become more and more acceptable." She added solemnly, "Had that option been available during my first marriage, I'd probably not need this cane."

Eli knew of the abuse she'd suffered at the hands of his father. He'd married her not for love but as a way to get at her fortune. Since her fall down a flight of stairs during one of the man's rages, the cane had become a necessity. The thoughts brought Eli a rage of his own, so he set them aside and concentrated on the matter at hand. "Any suggestions?"

She shrugged. "You're the Lothario."

"She doesn't want a wedding night."

"Of course not, Eli. Would you if you were in her shoes?"

He thought it over. "Probably not, but I've convinced myself to try and make this marriage work."

"Really?"

"If I were in the market for a wife, she'd fit the mold."

"Interesting. I was under the impression you were doing this under duress."

"I am. No man wants to be forced into marrying, but I am at an age where thoughts of settling down with one woman don't give me hives anymore."

"And you'd be true to her?"

"Yes, Mother," he said firmly.

"Arranged marriages have been known to blossom." She eyed him in the darkness. "Give her time. Maybe use some of that legendary charm I keep hearing so much about."

Embarrassment caused his head to drop. "If I tried that she'd probably blast me with her bird gun. I'll opt for appealing to her logic for now."

"Whatever you think is best." She placed her hand affectionately over his. "You've done a good thing here this evening, Eli. The reward will come."

"Let's hope you're right." He sighed wistfully. "We can hardly act married if she's living here."

"She may have a change of heart come morning."

Again, he didn't think so, but rather than beat a dead horse he stood then leaned down to give her a soft kiss on her cheek. "I'll see you tomorrow."

"Good night, son."

That next morning, Jewel woke up in a foul mood. Because she'd tossed and turned all night she'd hadn't gotten a lick of sleep. As she set breakfast on the table for her brothers, they took one look at her sternly set face and didn't say a word outside of "Good morning." No one wanted the storm to break over them. In light of that, they ate as quickly as their stomachs would allow, then hightailed it out of the house for the drive to work.

Alone in the house, Jewel finished up the dishes then sat at the table to sip her coffee and to mull over her fate. Eli kept sliding into her thoughts and she kept pushing him away. She didn't want to think of him any more than she wanted to think about them being man and wife. Having to face the questions and the inevitable congratulations sure to come from the Grove's residents was something else she wanted to avoid, even as the parts of herself that had been sweet on Eli were quietly elated by yesterday's turn of events. But the practical, no-nonsense Jewel was appalled by that side of herself, and was determined to keep those silly feelings from growing and taking charge. She needed to be stoic and emotionless if she were to survive until the divorce. Otherwise all she had to look forward to was a broken heart, and she refused to be that woman.

With that in mind, she put her empty cup in the sink and went out to the barn to get the roses she planned to plant for Maddie.

Eli awakened with Jewel on his mind, and although he knew he had no business doing so, he thought about what it might be like to awaken with her warm against his side. He'd bet he was the only married man in creation ever to spend his wedding night alone. Grim but resigned he got out of bed to get ready for his day.

On his way into town, he set aside thoughts of his recalcitrant wife and focused his attention on the meeting with Hicks. At least he would no longer be lying about having a wife, he thought sarcastically. Redirecting his mind away from his marriage again, his first hope was that Hicks would purchase new printing presses for the *Gazette*. The one presently in the office, an Albion handpress, was an 1862 model that he kept running with rigged parts and prayer. With a proper press, he could produce a proper paper formatted more in line with the times, thus making it more attractive to the advertisers that kept a paper afloat. Maybe by year's end, if the new *Gazette* proved to be a success, he might even turn enough of a profit to repay some of his creditors. Obviously he was putting the cart in front of the horse but as his mother was fond of saying, If you don't have dreams, they won't come true.

Hicks was waiting for him on the Quilt Ladies' porch. "Is there somewhere else we can meet, Grayson? Mrs. Ross is making a pest of herself. Keeps going on about her late husband as if she wants me to take the poor man's place."

"Let's use the mayor's office."

As they walked back down Main Street, Hicks asked, "How's your wife this morning? Feeling better I hope."

"Much better," Eli lied. "Thanks for asking."

They passed a few people on the walk and acknowledged them with nods.

"She's quite a beauty, and intelligent as well. You're a lucky man, Grayson."

"Luckiest man in the world, sir." Hoping to steer the conversation away from Jewel, he asked, "How many papers are in your syndicate, Mr. Hicks?"

"Call me G.W., since we're going to be working together."

"Thank you. Please call me Eli."

He nodded then answered the question. "I own eleven papers. Most are back east, but two are in California and one is in Canada. Don't get out to see the California operations much, but they're pulling their weight financially."

"So the *Gazette* will be number twelve."

"Correct. Looking at acquiring some others in Illinois and Ohio as well, but I want to get you up and running first."

Pleased by that, Eli stuck the key into the door of the mayor's office and let them in. Once the men were seated the true discussion began. They talked printing presses, business advertisements, and whether there'd be enough pages in the *Gazette* to carry the political drawings of Black cartoonist Henry J. Lewis, whose work began appearing in *Harper's Weekly* in 1879. As talk moved to geographical locations, Eli brought out a map so that G.W. could see the state's layout. He then pointed out how far the Grove was from Detroit and how close it was to Chicago.

"I never realized Chicago sat on the other side of your Lake Michigan."

"We're close neighbors. In its prime, the *Gazette* had subscribers there, too. Many folks in this area do daywork in Chicago and travel home on the weekends. Having the *Gazette* mailed to them keeps them abreast of news they might have missed."

Hicks looked impressed, then asked bluntly, "How deep in debt are you?"

Eli quoted the figure.

"That much?"

"Yes, sir."

"We'll see if we can whittle that down a bit once everything is in place."

Although Eli had no idea how Hicks planned to handle that, he was grateful for the support.

"Do you know of any property for sale here?" G.W. asked.

"There are some plots in town and out. May I ask why?"

"I like this Grove of yours. Might like to build here."

"Really?" He wasn't sure if that was a good thing or not. It would certainly not be good for his marriage. Jewel would have to be the smiling wife a lot more than she'd care to be. "We're way off the beaten path here, sir."

"I like that aspect, though, and the Grove's progressiveness. In fact, I'm finding a lot to my liking, Mrs. Ross excluded."

"She can be a trial." He wasn't sure where this was all going. "So you want to move here?"

"I might. Who do I see about the properties?"

"Adam Crowley has a few plots out by his place. Miss Edna over at the store has some land for sale as well."

"Where can I find Crowley?"

"Right now, he and his sons are over in Niles. Adam owns a house-building business. Used to be a lumber beast."

Hicks looked confused.

"Back east they're called lumberjacks."

"Ah."

"He's my father-in-law."

Hicks surprise was plain.

"And because he and my widowed mother married a few years back, he's also my stepfather."

Hicks's lips lifted in a smile. "So your wife is his daughter, which also makes her your stepsister?"

"Something like that."

"Nothing like small towns."

Eli agreed.

"When can I meet Crowley?"

"This evening after he's done working soon enough?"

"Perfect. In the meantime, is there a telegraph office in town?"

"No, but the one over in Calvin Center is close. That's a township just a few miles away."

"Can I pay someone to take me?"

"I'll drive you. Won't take more than a hour there and back."

"I'll get my papers."

"I have to see if there's any mail, so how about we meet at the store?"

Their agreement made, the men parted ways.

Eli walked up the street to the store, all the while wondering if Hicks would really settle in the Grove, and how that might affect him and Jewel. Deciding he had enough to worry about at the moment, he let it lie.

Reaching the store, he stepped inside, and as all eyes turned his way, he knew what he had to do. Taking a deep breath he announced, "Yes, Jewel and I are married. Have been for a while."

Applause erupted, smiles appeared on many faces. Losers of bets paid up while smug-looking winners collected.

"So when's the celebration?" Vernon asked.

"What celebration?"

"The one you're having to announce the marriage. You and Jewel are two of our own. You have to have something so folks can come by and offer congratulations."

Eli supposed it was a good idea; not one he particularly liked, nor would Jewel, but the saving grace of it was that once it was over, the Grove could go back to being a sleepy little township, and folks could focus their attention elsewhere. "I'll talk to Jewel and let you know. I want to finish up this business with Hicks, first."

They all nodded understandingly and returned to what they'd been doing.

Miss Edna handed him the mail and said for

his ears only, "You did an honorable thing offering her your name. She'll come around."

Eli shuffled through the small stack of envelopes. "But will it happen before the turn of the century?" He gave her a kiss on the cheek. "Thanks for the mail."

She smiled and watched him slip out the door.

"So, do you think I was right to agree to this marriage business?"

Maddie looked Jewel's way. They were digging holes in Maddie's front yard to hold the new rose bushes. "Take it from an old whore, when folks hiss at you in church, or cross the street when they see you approach, it hurts your heart, even though you tell yourself it doesn't." Maddie was a Grove native and had grown up with Eli and his cousin Nate. Years ago, she'd owned the Emporium, the town's only whorehouse, and had suffered all manner of meanness from the good people in the area.

"So your answer is yes?"

"Much as I hate to see you railroaded this way, that is my answer. It could be worse, you know, at least Eli is smart, clean, and easy on the eyes."

Thinking about how she and Eli parted last night, she offered emotionlessly, "We didn't have a wedding night."

Maddie stopped digging. "He probably knows you're an innocent and wants to give you time to adjust."

"No, it was me. I didn't want it."

"And your reason? If I may be so nosy to ask?"

"Because it's Eli," she said as if the answer was clearly obvious. "I don't want to be compared to all the other women he's had."

"Who said you would be?"

"But I don't know anything, Maddie." Her embarrassment was plain. "Not about that."

"You don't have to. He knows enough for half the state and that's to your advantage."

"Why?"

"Because the last thing you need on a wedding night is two people who don't know what the hell they're doing. With the right man, relations can be earth shattering."

"I don't want earth shattering."

"Yes, you do."

"I do?"

Maddie grinned. "Trust me. You do."

Jewel couldn't hold back a smile. "Lord."

"It will be okay. If and when the times comes just let him lead until you learn the ins and outs. There's probably a reason the women call him the Colored Casanova of Cass County." Maddie caught a glimpse of Jewel's face. "Am I embarrassing you?"

"Yes."

"Not trying to. Just giving you facts. Having a man who knows how to make a woman's body sing puts you head and shoulders above a good portion of the women in the world, so count your blessings."

"But I don't want to be married to him."

"I understand that, but you are married to him, so until the divorce you can either keep eating sour lemons or take them and make lemonade."

Jewel forced the shovel into the dirt. "I hate it when you're wise, Maddie Loomis."

Smiling, Maddie nodded. "I know."

# Chapter 5

Once all the holes were dug, Maddie headed off to open the library for the day while Jewel stayed behind to put in the roses. Adding manure to the holes from the pile in the yard courtesy of one of the local dairy farmers, she mixed it in with the clean topsoil, mounded it into a cone and set a plant atop each. She then filled in the sides of the hole with more dirt, making sure to keep the crown at the base of the plant exposed, then firmed up the soil. By the time she got all ten plants in, it was early afternoon and she was a muddy, manure-smelling mess. Taking a moment to admire her handiwork, she visually inspected the spacing and decided that when the plants bloomed, they would be a beautiful accent to Maddie's front porch.

She was gathering up the shovels and hand tools to return them to Maddie's barn when Eli rode up on his horse. He was still not anyone she wanted to see, but remembering Maddie's advice about lemonade, she bested her irritation as he walked up and forced herself to be pleasant, or as pleasant as she could manage. "Eli."

"Jewel," he said in response to her greeting. "How are you?"

"Fine. You?"

"I'm fine, too."

He was wearing a nice brown suit and he certainly looked fine even to her cynical eyes. "Got Maddie's roses in."

"I see. They look pretty scrawny."

She didn't take offense because he was right. The dark brown plants looked like twigs. "They do, but they'll be fat and green before long."

"I'm sure Maddie will be pleased."

They were making small talk and they both knew it.

He asked, "Will you have dinner with me?"

That caught her off guard, that, and his tone. "I, um, promised Miss Edna I'd see about putting in roses for her when I was done here."

"It's pretty late in the day. I'm sure she won't mind waiting until tomorrow."

Jewel found herself looking everywhere but into his eyes. "I suppose you're right." Only then did she look directly at him and into the eyes that had been affecting her equilibrium since he'd waltzed with her at her fourteenth birthday party. "I need to clean up, first."

He surveyed her muddy denims, shirt, and brogans. "I can wait."

The timbre of his voice made it sound as if he were referring to something else entirely and she got the shakes. She cleared her throat. "Meet me at the house in about an hour."

He nodded, held her gaze just long enough to make her remember Maddie's talk about earth shattering, then she grabbed up the tools, placed them in the wheelbarrow, and pushed it toward the barn. When she hazarded a look back over her shoulder, he was still standing there watching. She turned around quickly, her lips tight.

Only a few houses in the Grove had plumbing indoors, and because the Crowleys were in the home-building business theirs was one. It had been installed two years ago and Jewel thought the shower the greatest invention since the washing machine. With her hair tied up in a bandanna to keep it dry, she stood beneath the heated water and let it wash away the soil and stink. Even a woman as no-nonsense as she had a fondness for scented soap, so when she finished washing and wrapped herself in a big drying sheet, she was clean and smelled of roses.

The brazier heating her curling iron was ready when she returned to her room, so she combed out her bangs, curled them, then braided the rest of her hair into a long plait that she circled and pinned low on her neck. Choosing a simple black skirt and white blouse, she dressed, then stuck her black-stockinged feet into a pair of leather slippers. Her accessories were simple. Around her neck was the gold heart-shaped locket her father had given her for Christmas a few years back, and in her ears the silver filigree hoops she'd purchased in Chicago last summer. All in all, she thought she looked presentable. Eli was probably accustomed to a woman with more dash, but that couldn't be helped.

Her brothers didn't balk about having to oversee their own dinner when she told them earlier of her plans with Eli, so when she came downstairs dressed and ready to go, they were in the kitchen putting the last touches to their meal of rabbit and vegetables. Jeremiah had cooking skills second only to Jewel's, so he was in charge. "Smells good," she told him.

"You look nice," he said, setting the pan with the done rabbits on the stove top. The rest of her brothers agreed.

Smiling her thanks, she said, "I need to ask a favor."

"And it is?" Paul asked

"Will you all build me a house?"

They stared.

"As soon as possible."

"Why a house?" Abe asked.

"Because since I can't get out of this marriage right away, I'm going to take Maddie's advice and make lemonade out the lemons I've been dealt, which means Eli and I need someplace to stay. Together. And his cabin is too small."

"Told you she'd come to her senses," Zeke reminded everyone with pride in his voice.

The look she shot him would have made another man wish he'd kept his mouth shut, but because he was her brother he simply grinned.

The smiling Noah asked, "How many bedrooms?"

"Just two."

He shrugged. "Okay. We can always add more if you need more rooms later."

"I don't think that'll be necessary. After the divorce and Eli moves on, I want to have a place to call my own."

The brothers shared a look.

"What?" she asked.

They all shook their heads. "Nothing," Jeremiah replied on everyone's behalf. "Have you talked to Pa about this?"

"No, not yet."

"Well do, and we'll get started soon as he says the word. You want it on your land?"

"Yes." Each of the siblings had a designated thirty-acre plot given to them at birth. The only restriction on its use was that it couldn't be sold outside of the family. Adam Crowley was convinced that in the future land would be at a premium and he was determined that theirs remain under Crowley control.

The chime of the door pull sounded in the kitchen. "That must be Eli," she said, hoping her sudden case of nerves didn't show.

It did.

"Have a good time," Paul offered up.

Jewel had no idea what kind of time she was going to have, but replied, "Thanks," and went to answer the door.

Eli thought she looked lovely. Even though

her attire was plain, it made her appear soft and feminine. The man in him found this version of her a marked improvement over the manure-wearing woman she'd been earlier in the day. She smelled better, too, he noted as he drove the buggy away from the Crowley house, but he kept the compliments unspoken for now. "Where would you like to eat?"

"Anywhere but the Quilt Ladies'." Having to deal with Caroline Ross was not Jewel's idea of a good time.

"Hoping you'd say that."

"Why? Do you have another place in mind?"

"Yep, but it's a surprise."

"And you're not going to tell me," she stated.

"Then it wouldn't be a surprise." Glancing over he took in the crossness in her face and posture. "When was the last time you did something just for the sheer fun of it?"

The question was met with silence.

"Can't answer that, can you?"

Jewel sent him a leveling look, which he of course ignored.

"You need more fun in your life, Jewel Grayson."

"Really?" Her tone was somewhere between sarcasm and irritation. Hearing herself addressed by her new name didn't improve her mood.

"Yes, you do. So in celebration of our first day of married life, we're going to have some fun."

Jewel wondered why the fates had placed him of all people in her life, but because she had no answer, she sat back and waited to see what this fun would turn out to be.

They were traveling through one of the Grove's most beautiful meadows. On each side of the two-track road they were bumping along, oxeye daisies bloomed, alongside red clover and the fading petals of white trillium. In response to the breezy day, the vast expanse of wildflowers rippled like the multicolored waves of an exotic sea. "This has to be the loveliest place on earth in the spring," Jewel said in a voice laden with reverence.

Eli noted the genuine feeling in her tone. "Then let's find a place to stop."

"What for?"

"Our picnic."

Her jaw dropped.

He liked making her speechless, he realized, and wondered how many other ways it could be accomplished. Pleased with himself, he drove a few more feet, then pulled off the road and stopped. "How's this?"

She was still staring his way.

"What?" he asked easily.

"A picnic?"

He shrugged, "Why not? I have food and everything." Setting the brake, he stepped down then came around to her side. "Care to join me?"

She studied him and decided once again that he was far too handsome for his own good. From the cut of his jaw to the playful, smoke gray eyes, a mere woman didn't stand a chance. So she surrendered, took his hand, and let him assist her down.

The touch was brief, but long enough for her fingers to feel singed, even after the contact ended. Needing to take her mind off of him and collect herself, she scanned the beautiful setting for a moment before slowly turning his way. "Maddie said I should make lemonade out the lemons in my life."

Eli wasn't sure what she was referencing, so he said simply, "Smart woman, that Maddie. So what are you going to do with the advice?"

"Have Pa and the boys build me a house."

"Really?" he asked studying her. "Why?"

"So when the divorce is over I can have a place of my own."

"Ah. When are you having them build this house of yours?" Arms crossed over his chest, he waited.

Jewel sensed that maybe now hadn't been the right time to have this conversation. "As soon as possible."

"You can't have your divorce right away, Jewel."

"I know, but I'd like to move into the place as soon as it's finished."

"And I'll be, where?"

"In the house, too."

"I see."

She held his probing gaze then had to look away.

"So we're going to live as man and wife?" he asked.

"On the outside, yes."

"And on the inside?"

Unable to decipher his mood, she nervously turned her attention back to the flowers spread out around them. "I'll have one room and you'll have the other."

"Ah," he uttered again.

"It's the best I can do. For now," she added softly, although she hadn't meant to, at least not out loud.

Eli's eyebrow rose and he wondered if she knew how interesting he found her last two words. "If you want us to have separate rooms, for now, that's what we'll have. I've never forced a woman in my life so have no worries on that count."

The quiet emphasis he'd placed on *for now*, made her wish she'd chosen her words more cautiously, especially when the memory of Maddie's talk about earth shattering and all that it entailed suddenly rose unbidden. Not wanting to visit that for any amount of coin, she hastily sent the memory back to wherever it had come from.

Eli knew she was a virgin, but he wondered if she'd ever been kissed. He couldn't remember her being courted by anyone, but with Adam and her brothers guarding her so ferociously, he supposed potential suitors hadn't the nerve to come calling. Having charmed his share of women in the past, he wondered how she'd react were he to pay attention to her in the way a man does with a woman he's interested in. Would her kisses be as volatile and lightning charged as she? He knew he should be directing his thoughts elsewhere, but he was finding that the more he was around her, the more intriguing she seemed to be. "I announced our marriage at the store this morning. Vernon wants us to throw a party so folks can congratulate us."

Jewel's first thought was to say no, but she supposed a wingding would be expected now that their supposedly secret marriage was exposed. "When do you want to have it?"

"I'd like to wait until Hicks leaves town. If he ever does."

"What's that mean?"

He filled her in on G.W.'s inquiries about land for sale.

"He wants to settle here?" She was appalled. She would be expected to be sweetness and light all the time if he were to build a home in the Grove.

"Not sure."

"I hope he doesn't."

"I agree. I'm not keen on having my publisher in town looking over my shoulder while I'm running the *Gazette*."

"And I don't want to have to be your wife all the time."

The low laughter that followed her response made her ask, "What's so funny?"

"Just you, sweetheart. Your determination is remarkable. You're not planning on laying down your weapons anytime soon, are you?"

"No." she said, chin raised.

"Then I'll have to work on disarming you."

"Thought you said you wouldn't force me?"

He reached into the wagon bed and pulled out the covered basket containing the food. "Who said anything about force? You'll come willingly."

"In your dreams, Eli Grayson."

"There, too, but I sense something's brewing between us, Jewel."

When she turned away, he smiled and grabbed the blanket out the bed. "Deny it if you want, but if I kissed you right now, you'd melt into your shoes."

"You are way too full of yourself."

"Maybe, but that doesn't change what I just said."

He was standing in front of her, close enough to make her aware of how inexperienced she was with this type of banter and with a man such as he, but she was determined to show him her best. "Let's see your money."

Reaching into the pocket of his trousers, he withdrew an eagle and held it up for her inspection.

"You sure you can afford to lose so much?"

"You're stalling, sweetheart. What are you putting up?"

With his hushed voice resonating inside, she took her handbag from the seat and brought out an eagle, too. In hindsight it came to her that maybe she should have kept her mouth shut, but she had too much Crowley pride to call off the challenge now.

"You sure you can afford to lose so much?"

"Now who's stalling?"

"Just giving you time to get ready."

"I'm ready. Kiss me."

The intensity that filled his eyes made her wish she'd kept her mouth shut yet again, but like before it was too late. His lips brushed hers ever so slightly, again, and then again, and it certainly wasn't the quick press of lips she had been expecting; this was lulling and warm, the pressure sweet and mind numbing. His mouth held magic, and as he kissed her in earnest the spell spread through her like honey warmed on the stove, and she had to back away or melt into her shoes.

When she broke the kiss, Eli was admittedly disappointed, but the passion lidding her eyes told all. "Pay up."

Without a word, she slapped her eagle onto his outstretched palm and stomped off toward the clearing. Standing there, he smiled, grabbed up the basket and blanket, and followed in her wake.

The stream that ran by the clearing added more beauty to the setting, so while she stood looking out over the water with her back to him, Eli spread the blanket, then set the basket on top. Out of the basket he withdrew a plate of still warm fried chicken, potato salad nestled in a pie tin of ice, collards, and biscuits. "Are you planning on eating?"

She didn't move.

Ever patient, he waited, all the while filled with amusement at her reaction. "Nothing wrong with having enjoyed a kiss, Jewel Grayson, and if you lie and say you didn't like it, lightning will strike you down."

"I paid up, didn't I?"

"That you did, so come and eat. I'm not going to tease you, if that's what's worrying you."

Jewel had been worried, and now, had only her own embarrassment to shake off. The kiss was still vibrating inside her like the fading note from a harp and she was mad at herself for not being worldly enough to remain unmoved. Her nipples were hard beneath her white blouse and there was a quickening between her thighs she prayed would abate soon. Having worked all day, she was very hungry, though, and with the fragrant smells of the chicken wafting her way it wasn't hard for her stomach to overrule her mind and send her over to the blanket where he sat waiting.

Without a word, he handed her a plate and let her fill hers first. Once she was done, he did his own.

"Thank you for the meal," she offered grudgingly.

"My pleasure, but thank Mother. She did the cooking."

They lapsed into silence. She avoided looking into his eyes, but Eli didn't mind. He was still buoyed by her response to his kiss. He'd been right, she did have a passion inside that was volatile and lightning sweet. Her body against his had been soft as summer rain. It didn't take a genius to know she wasn't happy about the outcome, but he was enjoying the many-faceted Jewel Crowley Grayson just the same.

She broke the silence by saying, "Making lemonade is going to be harder than I thought."

He held on to his smile. "Why's that?"

"Because. I didn't plan on any of this—this—"

"Kissing?" he voiced in an effort to be helpful.

"Yes."

"It's what men and women do."

"I know that, but—"

He waited.

"I never thought it would involve me."

"Why not?"

"Because," she said in a tone that supposedly made further explanation unnecessary. "I've been the only girl in my family most of my life. No one's ever explained these things to me."

"That's what husbands are for."

She sent him a withering look.

"I'm fairly well versed, I promise."

"I'll bet you are."

"Nothing wrong with having an experienced man."

Maddie had said pretty much the same thing, but Jewel had no plans to tell him that. "I shouldn't be this ignorant."

"Your inexperience doesn't matter sweetheart; besides, you did fine back there."

She didn't agree, after all she had lost the bet. "As I said, this is going to be harder than I thought."

Amused and finding her more endearing with each new breath, he went back to his plate. In reality, Eli had no idea what he was going to do with a wife. Accustomed to enjoying a variety of beautiful women, he'd nonetheless vowed to cleave to only one—one intent upon divorcing him as soon as she could arrange it, he thought sarcastically. He still planned to be faithful to his vows, even in light of her outrageous offer that he could bed others as long as he was discreet. He'd never heard of such a thing, but leave it to Jewel. He knew, though, and would be willing to bet, that if she were to catch him with another woman she'd probably fill his backside with birdshot. Looking over at her now, he liked the pleasing lines of her face, the full lips, and the dark fringe of lashes accenting her eyes. She was a beauty and, for as long as he could keep her, his beauty. Once again he thought the two of them could have fun in this unconventional marriage if she'd give it half a chance, but trying to convince her was going to be like teaching caterpillars to read the Bible. "What can I do to make this easier on you?"

"No more kisses," she answered bluntly.

"No?" he asked hoping his humor didn't show.

It did.

"This isn't funny."

"Never said it was, but the only problem with that request is, how you're going to feel having to eat crow?"

"And that means?"

"You're a healthy, beautiful, and apparently passionate young woman, Jewel Grayson. I'm not so sure that the part of you that melted back there is going to go along with that request."

"I know you're accustomed to women dropping at your feet whenever you cross their paths, but I'm not one of them."

"Did you or did you not just lose a bet?'

Her chin rose.

"That's what I thought, so okay, I won't kiss you again. If you want more you'll have to ask for them."

"Then I have nothing to worry about."

His eyes were filled with mirth. "Whatever you say."

"Again, you're way too full of yourself."

"It's well earned."

Refusing to rise to his bait, Jewel concentrated on her meal and wondered what she was supposed to do with him. Up until her marriage, she'd considered herself highly accomplished in most aspects of her life. Having run a household and taken care of her brothers and father since adolescence had given her a confidence most women her age didn't possess yet none of it had prepared her for a husband, especially one as complex as Eli. Who knew his kisses would make her come unglued. Who knew she'd want more of them. That unbidden thought shocked and appalled her.

Eli was watching her while he ate. "Penny for your thoughts."

"I don't have any."

"Thinking about kissing me again, aren't you?"

"No," she lied and set her now empty plate aside. "You're not the center of the world, Eli Grayson."

He simply smiled. Done eating now, too, he set his plate atop hers. "What would you like to do now. Want to take a walk?"

Jewel didn't trust herself to be around him for any length of time out of fear of succumbing again to his mind-melting kisses. "Since we're done eating, I think I'm ready to head home."

"Really?" he asked, eyes settling for a moment on the tempting curve of her mouth. "I wanted to lie back and look for shapes in the clouds."

The stunned surprise on her face made him ask easily, "What?"

As he laid back and looked up at the sky, she shook her head and again wondered what she was going to do with him.

"I'll bet you can't tell me the last time you did this."

"And you'd be correct."

"Then lie back and let's see what we can see."

"I'm not lying down with you, Eli."

The corners of his mouth lifted with bridled humor. "Why not?

"Because."

"That's very succinct." He turned his vision her way. "Afraid?"

"Of you?"

"My kisses and their ability to make you melt into your shoes."

"Thought you weren't going to tease me?"

"Just asking a simple question."

Sensing she wasn't going to win this, she moved the plates and joined him on the blanket. "Happy?"

"Immensely."

For the next hour they became children again, pointing out dragons, fish, hawks, and trees. Jewel even saw a cloud that looked like the Widow Moss, the Grove's resident crone. "See the nose?" she asked him.

It took Eli a few moments to hone in on what she was seeing, and when he did, the sight of the Widow Moss in the clouds was so surprising, he laughed so hard he had to sit upright to keep from choking to death.

Still prone, Jewel grinned.

Above her, Eli took in her beautiful smiling face and felt the loose ties between them begin to bind. "Didn't I promise you fun?"

"You did." And she'd had fun. Drawn to him even though she was fighting against it, she couldn't seem to turn away.

He slowly traced her full lips. "Promised you I wouldn't kiss you again, so let's get you home."

Singed by the fleeting touch, Jewel couldn't breathe or move, but knew that if she didn't sit up all would be lost, so she ducked away and got to her feet.

"I'd like to stop by my place first so I can put this food away. I don't want it to spoil."

"That's fine."

They gathered up their plates and silver, packed away the remaining food, and made the short trek to the wagon.

On the ride back through the meadow, Jewel was silent. In spite of wishing otherwise, she was becoming more and more attuned to Eli. In the past, he'd been a man of her adolescent dreams, dreams filled with schoolgirl fantasies and expectations. Now he was her husband. The fourteen-year-old Jewel would have been floating on a cloud at the idea of being kissed, and the twenty-four-year-old Jewel wondered what it might have been like had she asked to be kissed again. The first one had left her breathless. Even now the memory made her nipples tighten and the tingling between her thighs return. Just don't think about him, she chided herself but, lord knew, following that advice was difficult. He'd pledged not to do it again unless she asked so she considered herself safe, at least as far as she could see.

Eli's cabin was built on Grayson land and was a few miles away from the house Jewel shared with her brothers. It was a small structure made of wood and brick. The countryside surrounding it was filled with trees and open fields. There was a buggy parked next to the house when he and Jewel pulled up.

"Looks like you have a visitor," Jewel said.

"I don't recognize the buggy. Do you?"

"No." Most of the vehicles around the Grove

were well known to the residents. This one was black, and far more stylish than anything owned by the locals.

"I wonder who it belongs to?"

It didn't take long to find out. The elegantly attired woman who stepped out of his front door made Jewel stiffen. She was tall, beautiful, and not someone she knew.

"Eli," the woman trilled. "Where have you been?' she asked with a mock pout of her red painted lips. "I've been waiting forever."

Walking out to meet him, and after giving Jewel a quick dismissive glance, she added, "I've missed you, darling."

Eli cleared his throat, "Hello, Rona."

Jewel told herself that the vise tightening her breathing was a figment of her imagination, but had a hard time swallowing that.

"And who might this be?"

Stone faced, Jewel moved to leave the buggy. "I'll leave you two to visit," and she hopped down.

"Jewel—"

"I'll see you, Eli." She started up the road.

"Jewel. Hold on for a moment."

She didn't slow, nor did she look back.

"Dammit, Jewel! Wait."

But she didn't break stride.

Watching her walk away, her back stiff as a board, Eli's anger at himself was great.

Rona asked, "Who is she?"

"My wife."

"You're pulling my leg."

But the only thing being pulled was Eli's guilt. He'd forgotten all about his monthly visit from Rona Greer in the chaos of the last few days. He couldn't fault her for showing up, after all they'd been meeting monthly for some time. The fault rested solely on his own head. He continued to watch Jewel stride away and was haunted by the hurt he'd seen in her eyes.

"And when did this all come about?" Rona asked impatiently, bringing him back to the matter at hand.

"Yesterday. Sorry I didn't have time to wire you. Truthfully, I forgot."

"You forgot!"

His vision was focused on the small woman moving into the distance. "Yes. I forgot." Trysting with his mistresses had been the last thing on his mind. And now, the chances of his marriage with Jewel moving beyond this blunder were equal to him being able to walk on the moon. He cursed himself. "My apologies, but I can't see you anymore."

"You can't be serious about tossing me over for that. Why, she looks like she just stepped out of a schoolroom."

"She's no child."

Rona voiced bitterly, "Here I've been hoping to wrangle a marriage proposal out of you for months, and you up and marry, that." Her anger was plain.

"I never promised you marriage. We both knew the parameters going in."

"But, I thought—"

"You have my apologies."

She seemed to sense there was no point in further debating the issue; his jaw was firm, his eyes cool. "Then I'll leave you to your schoolgirl bride. Don't come whimpering to me when she turns out to be not what you want. I won't be available."

"Again, my apologies."

She stormed over to her buggy and drove off.

Eli wearily ran his hands over his eyes, then looked down the road for Jewel, but she was no longer in sight.

Jewel told herself she had no reason to be upset. Hadn't she encouraged him to keep his mistress? Hadn't she told him it was fine by her if he went to other women for his needs. But she was upset. Upset, embarrassed, and fit to be tied, truth be told. She also felt the burn of humiliation. The woman Rona appeared to be everything Jewel was not: sophisticated, worldly, confident with men. It was easy to see that she knew what she was about, and had apparently been in his bed long enough for the two to have an ongoing standing assignation. Jewel felt like a fool, but on the bright side the incident gave her a reason to resolidify the distance from Eli she'd been attempting to maintain. If the memory of her succumbing to his kiss ever plagued her again, all she needed to do was remember Rona.

By the time Jewel reached home, she had a handle on her emotions, but apparently they still showed on her face because the moment she entered the parlor where her brothers were gathered around the checkerboard, Abe asked, "What's wrong?"

"Nothing," she lied with as much false cheer as could be managed. "Who's winning?" She moved closer to the board. Jeremiah and Zeke were playing each other. By the number of kings stacked up on Jere's end of the board, Zeke's demise was imminent.

"How'd the dinner fare?"

"Fine," she lied again. "Eli's mistress was waiting for him when we drove up to his cabin, so I came home."

"What?" her brothers bellowed.

She shrugged. "Nothing to get upset about. I told him I wouldn't mind if he sought other women."

They stared her way as if she'd suddenly been turned into a six-point buck.

Jewel ignored that. "I'm going up to my room. I'll see you all later."

She left the parlor while her brothers gawked at each other in stunned amazement.

The next morning, Eli went in search of Jewel. Having found no one at the Crowley house, he headed to town. Her brothers were undoubtedly off to work, and because she'd mentioned putting in roses for Miss Edna, he planned to stop at the store. He expected a very chilly reception when he did find her, but he knew she was within her rights after yesterday's embarrassing encounter with Rona.

As he rode down Main Street he saw G.W. and Vernon in Vernon's wagon. Eli pulled his horse to a stop. "Morning, G.W., Vernon. Where you headed?"

"I have to go back to New York," G.W. explained, and he didn't look happy. "I received a wire last evening that the editor at one of my New York papers has disappeared, along with the month's take."

"That's not good news."

"No it isn't. Need to get Pinkertons on the man's trail before my money's frittered away on loose women and drink."

"If there's anything I can do–"

"You just get the *Gazette* office ready. I'll be back as soon as I can."

"Yes, sir."

"And take care of your lovely wife."

Eli nodded. "Have a safe trip."

G.W. waved and Vernon drove away.

Eli hoped G.W. would find the man, but his leaving was a blessing in a way. Now he and Jewel could have the wedding party the Grove was expecting. Unless of course she shot him on sight, and then a funeral would be in order.

When he entered the store, he greeted the customers inside and was told Miss Edna was out back with Jewel. Taking in a deep breath, he pushed open the door and stepped outside. Sure enough, there was Jewel kneeling in the dirt with Miss Edna standing over her. Both women looked up at his approach. Miss Edna smiled. Jewel did not. She held his gaze for a moment, then went back to positioning the plant she was working with.

"Morning ladies."

Edna asked, "And what brings you here?"

"I'd like to speak with Jewel privately, if I may."

She glanced down at Jewel who was still pretending as if he weren't there. "Of course."

She went back inside and left them alone.

"Are you speaking to me?"

"Why wouldn't I be?"

"You looked pretty upset when you left me last evening."

"Me? I wasn't upset. Did you and your lady friend have a nice visit?"

"I told her I wouldn't be seeing her again."

She looked up. "I hope it wasn't because of me."

Eli wasn't sure he liked this game. "Yes, it was."

"I told you I wouldn't mind, and I don't."

He stepped back.

"What's wrong?" she asked.

"When lightning strikes you I don't want to be hit."

She didn't speak.

"I'm sorry, he said."

"For what?"

"Embarrassing you."

"Why would I be embarrassed? I knew you had a mistress when you married me."

"Jewel, look—"

"Eli, I have work to do, so unless you have something of substance to discuss, I'd like to finish here before the sun starts to beat down."

Tight-lipped he held on to his temper. "We need to talk about this."

"No, we don't."

"What happened to making lemonade?"

"Decided I don't like the taste of it."

He studied her but she wouldn't look his way. "Okay. When you're done here maybe we can talk about the party."

"Just plan it and tell me when and where. It makes me no never mind."

He prayed for strength. "I'll come by and see you this evening."

"That's fine."

Filled with frustration and knowing he couldn't force her to talk to him, he turned on his heel and left.

When the door slammed announcing his exit, Jewel looked up. The fourteen-year-old inside herself was heartbroken, but Jewel the women paid the adolescent's pain no mind, or at least that's what she told herself.

# Chapter 6

Intent upon on following G.W.'s advice, Eli walked down to the *Gazette* office. First order of business was to remove the plywood covering the front window. Crowbar in hand, he vented his frustration on the nails securing it in place. He'd never met such an obstinate woman in his entire life. He'd always believed Adam Crowley to be the most stubborn person on the planet, but surely his daughter had him beat. Stubborn, hard-headed, maddening. For him, the divorce couldn't come fast enough.

"So, Jewel met your mistress."

Normally hearing Adam Crowley's gruff voice behind him would have sent a chill up Eli's spine, but not today. Today he'd had just about enough, and was in no mood for Crowleys of any size, name, or gender. "Yes, she did." That said, he turned to meet the steely eyes of the man who was both stepfather and father-in-law. "How'd you hear about it?"

"Boys told me this morning."

Eli went back to removing the nails. "If you've

come to give me grief, save it. Jewel doesn't need the help. I've tried to apologize. Even told her I sent Rona packing but I got nowhere."

"Being married is new to her, son."

"To me as well, remember? Things might be better if she stopped throwing up walls."

"Took me almost a decade to barrel through the walls your mother threw in my path."

Eli remembered. Adam married Abigail six years ago. Folks all over the Grove had followed with keen interest the volatile courtship everyone affectionately called The Battle of Abigail. He went back to the nails. "Mother cared for you. Jewel's only care is how soon the divorce can be arranged."

"If that were true, she wouldn't be so livid."

With Adam holding on to the now loose edge of the plywood, Eli started removing the nails holding the other edge. "According to her she's not livid at all. When I spoke with her a few moments ago at the store, she was maddeningly calm."

"The boys said she was chopping wood this morning before sunup. Usually that's a chore she leaves to them, so when she does it's always because she wants to chop someone's head off instead."

Eli met Adam's humor-lit eyes. "Really?"

"Oh yes. She's mad. Guess all that nonsense about you seeing other women reared up and bit her on the behind."

Eli ruminated on that. Was she really simmering over her outrageous offer?

"And if she's that worked up, she's caring about more than a divorce. The boys think she's jealous."

Eli stilled. Jewel jealous? He thought pigs would ride horses first.

"You know, Eli, I told your mother years ago that if she had married me first instead of that bounder, you'd be my son. You've always been special to me, even during that mess with Cecile."

Eli studied the face of the man he'd always wanted to be his father. Growing up, Eli had had his Uncle Absalom, Nate's father, to help guide him, but there'd been something special about the Crowley family. "I envied your sons." And he had. It was plain to see how much Adam Crowley cared for his boys. They all hunted together, fished together, celebrated together, and Eli had wanted to be a part of that, but he'd never known Adam's true feelings until now.

"You were at the house so often I should have given you your own bed."

Eli smiled. The memories of those times were good ones.

They both went silent thinking back on what might have been had fate dealt a different hand, then Adam said, "I know I was against the idea of you and Jewel marrying when you first proposed it, but I'm hoping you two can find common ground. She could do a lot worse."

"Thanks."

Adam patted him on the back. "In the meantime, I'll help however I can."

"Has she told you about the house she wants built?"

"No."

Eli filled him in.

When he finished, Adam chuckled, "So, once she gets her divorce she figures the house will be hers? Not a bad plan."

"No, but you'd think she'd wait until the ink dried on the wedding certificate before she started planning her life without me. I have to admit, the Colored Casanova of Cass County is feeling a bit bruised by all this disdain."

Adam's laugh made Eli's lips lift with a smile.

"Bible says: humility is good for the soul. You know, though, a better place for a house would be that land of yours that faces the lake."

As a descendant of the Grove founders, Eli owned a large tract of open land and he paused for a moment to think about the suggestion. Adam was right. From the slope of it to the small lake nearby, it was perfect. "But the house is for her, not me." He pried out the last of the nails and they set the plywood against the brick façade.

"The house *I'm* building will be for the both of you."

"Good luck getting her to agree."

"She doesn't have to. Jewel may be a force of nature but she can't build her own home. And since I'm her father I'm going to build it where I deem best. It'll be my wedding present."

"She's not going to be happy."

Adam shrugged. "If she kills me, I know your mother will give me a decent burial."

The two men who had always craved being in each other's life grinned.

"Now that we've settled that," Adam said, "what are you doing with this window?"

"Putting the pane back in." Eli looked into the shadow-filled interior and wondered out loud. "Be nice if I could expand the place a bit. What do you think? Hicks seems to have big plans for the *Gazette*."

"I think you're going to need my help."

Eli agreed. So they began to plan.

Up at the store Jewel put the final touches to Miss Edna's roses and then went to the pump to wash off her grimy tools and clean herself up. She'd shower when she returned home but, for the moment, settled for washing her face and hands. Drying off with a small clean towel Miss Edna had left earlier, she placed all of her implements and tools in the bed of the wagon and prepared to leave. Just as she climbed up on the seat, Miss Edna stepped out.

"Jewel, I hear your father's over at the *Gazette* office. Will you tell him I can have those nails he wanted early next week."

"What's he doing at the *Gazette*?"

"Not real sure, but the Patterson twins said he and Eli are talking about expanding the place."

"Really?" She wondered when Eli had decided on that. "Okay, I'll let him know."

"And thanks for the roses, Jewel. Your mother named you well."

The praise warmed her heart. "Thanks, Miss Edna."

Driving the horse and wagon up Main Street, Jewel girded herself to face Eli again. The whole marriage business was far more complex than she'd envisioned, and she hoped the fourteen-year-old Jewel who'd fantasized about gaining his attention, marrying him, and someday bearing his children was satisfied now that the wish had come true, because Jewel the woman certainly was not.

She waved to a few people who greeted her from the walks, and when they called out congratulations and asked about the wedding party, she smiled falsely, called back her thanks, and promised to let them know soon. Shaking her head at small-town living, she drove to the newspaper office to relay Miss Edna's message.

Why her father wasn't in Niles overseeing the homes he and her brothers were constructing was beyond her. She spied him standing out front studying something at the base of the building, and huddled with him were the Patterson twins, Vernon Stevenson, and a few other men she recognized. Eli was there as well, and her eyes swept over him, even though she didn't want them to. Like all of the Grayson men he was tall, his build lean and strong. She was willing to concede that she hadn't been the least bit cooperative during their conversation earlier, but to admit she'd been hurt and embarrassed to find herself face-to-face with his mistress would be to admit that she didn't want him seeing other women, and because she couldn't, wouldn't do that, pretense was all she had. "Hey, Pa."

He looked up and gave her a fatherly smile. "Hey there, Jewel. Did you get Edna's roses in?"

She felt Eli's eyes on her as vividly as a touch but kept her attention trained on her father. "Yes, and she told me to tell you she'll have those nails you need next week."

"Thank you. How about you and Eli having dinner with me and Gail tonight?"

Her attention swung instantaneously to Eli, who was watching her with a knowingness that made her quickly turn back to her father. Over her racing heart she replied, "Uh. Sure, Pa. What time?"

"Five okay?"

She nodded and Eli wondered affectionately how one woman managed to stay so dirty. The worn blue cotton shirt she was wearing was mud streaked as were the legs of her denims, yet all the grime somehow served to magnify the clear beauty of her small brown face.

"How about we ride over together after I'm done here?" he asked her, knowing she'd probably prefer to drive herself. He was betting she wouldn't put up a fuss, though, not with her father and the others looking on.

He was right.

"That's fine," Jewel responded quickly. In spite

of this morning's chilly encounter she sensed a heat emanating from him that seemed to touch her everywhere. Fighting off the undertow his attention was causing, she nodded to the men with an ease that was pure pretense, then signaled her horse and drove away.

Eli watched her retreat for a few long moments, then with a smile on his face went back to the plans they were making for the *Gazette*.

As he dressed for dinner later that evening, Eli thought back on the conversation he'd had with Adam about Jewel's reaction to Rona. He had no problems accepting the theory that she was mad, but he was having problems accepting Adam's explanation for the reason. Jewel jealous? Surely that couldn't be. Could it? The idea that the answer might be yes, made him grin at his reflection in the mirror as he put his brush to his hair. If she was indeed green-eyed that meant she felt something for him, which also meant maybe good things for their marriage. He wouldn't mind scaling her walls now, especially if on the other side waited a woman even remotely open to his husbandly overtures. The thorn-shrouded Jewel Grayson was well on her way to being plucked, he thought to himself. Putting down the brush, he went out to hitch up the buggy.

Jewel was having problems reconciling her inner feelings for Eli with the logic she should be applying to this so-called marriage. She didn't want her heart to race whenever he looked her way, nor did she want to be warmed by the heat his presence seemed to bring. More than anything she wanted to be cool, distant, and emotionless, but that didn't seem to be working.

Dressed now in a clean long-sleeved blouse and a flowing black skirt, she did her bangs, then braided her thick hair into a single plait and let it hang free. She didn't want him to think she'd taken extra care with her preparations; his head was swelled enough. She slipped into her shoes and told herself that she needed to be aloof. Of course, she had no idea how that might be accomplished, seeing as how he was so much more experienced at this than she, but she was as determined as she'd been the evening they'd married to come out of this with her heart and feelings intact.

Looking at herself in the mirror, she wondered if maybe she should give in a little, then reminded herself that the last time she'd decided to make lemonade, she'd choked on his mistress.

She fished a pair of hoop earrings out of her small jewelry box and hung them in her lobes while wondering how many more of Eli's women would magically appear to remind her that she was just a country girl in a marriage way over her head. There were no answers, of course, at least not at the moment, and she realized that in spite of being able to hold her own in a house filled with men, she was unsure about succumbing to her husband's kisses and all that might follow. The talk she'd had with Maddie proved Jewel knew next to nothing about the physical side of married life, but how would she? Abigail and Miss Edna had guided her when her menses began, and the only other information they imparted was that she was old enough to bear children so be careful around the boys at school.

Unlike the girls in the big cities, she hadn't had close girlfriends to gossip with or giggle over boys with while growing up, mainly because there hadn't been many Grove girls her age. The few friendships she did manage to make always ended when the families moved on for reasons that were sometimes economic and other times personal.

So that left her father, but he was a man, of course, and whenever she had questions, he sent her straight to Abigail, Miss Edna, or their good friend Anna Red Bird. Not because he didn't care enough to answer, but because anything pertaining to women things embarrassed him to no end.

On the other hand, Eli professed to know everything, and his boasting brought heat to her cheeks, especially when she remembered the potency of yesterday's kisses. In the end, she decided to keep her fists up, because that was something she did well.

He arrived at the house at a bit past four-thirty, dressed casually in a clean shirt and trousers. She noted that he could have worn a flour sack and fishing boots and still be the most handsome man around. After informing her brothers that she was leaving, she let him escort her to the buggy. When he handed her up, the unnerving warmth spread over her fingers and up her arm. As always she tried to ignore but failed miserably. Everything about him seemed to draw her in, in spite of her wishes to the contrary.

As they drove off, Eli looked over and saw that she was sitting so far away she seemed to be clinging to the outer edge of the seat. "Somebody driving by would think you were looking for a chance to jump out. I'm not contagious. I promise."

Jewel smiled but kept her gaze averted.

"Would it hurt you to sit a bit closer?"

"Depends."

"On?"

She shrugged. "I'm fine where I am."

"And if I asked you very nicely to please sit closer?"

Jewel sensed a trap but wasn't sure where it was hidden. Seeing the signatory amusement in his gaze didn't help matters. "It bothers you that I'm immune to your charms, doesn't it?"

"Nope," he tossed back easily. "Mainly because you're not."

"Sure I am."

He snorted.

She raised her chin defiantly. "You may believe what you want."

"So can you but we both know the truth. Didn't you lose a bet yesterday?"

She didn't want to remember that. She scrambled

for a rejoinder. "That was before being introduced to Rona."

"She doesn't have anything to do with you melting into your shoes. And if you say you didn't, my winnings say you're wrong."

Jewel folded her arms and fought down the memories of how dazzling the kiss had been.

"Cat got your tongue?"

The leveling look she sent him only broadened his grin.

"I could kiss you right now, Jewel Grayson, and you'd melt just like before. I won't even take your money this time."

"You're supposed to be driving."

"And you're running scared."

"I am not afraid of you."

"You are of my kisses, and I can prove it."

"Drive."

"Coward."

"You're trying to bait me but I'm not biting."

"Coward."

She socked him in the arm. Hard.

Chuckling, he rubbed at the small sting. "Punching coward."

She turned to keep her smile hidden.

"I want to kiss you, Jewel."

The soft, honey-toned declaration slid through her defenses like smoke, and almost made her jump from the buggy for real. "We're going to be late," she pointed out in a voice far less commanding than she'd planned.

He pulled back on the reins, and when the

horse stopped, he studied her. "Yesterday's wasn't nearly long enough."

"I thought you were going to make me beg?"

"Hell will freeze over first."

Jewel swallowed her laugh.

He reached out and gently raised her chin so that her chocolate eyes met his. She felt herself grabbed by the shakes but prayed they didn't show.

"I can only imagine how embarrassing it must have been for you yesterday with Rona and everything. I'd never knowingly cause you pain. Ever."

Jewel wanted to deny she'd been wounded, but because she was so completely mesmerized by his nearness, the only words that would come were, "I won't be another notch on your bedpost, Eli."

He leaned his head down and kissed her with such slow and tender passion she immediately began to smolder. "From now on, the only notches on the bedpost will be ours," he whispered—hotly.

Jewel melted right down into her shoes. She couldn't help it. The timbre of his voice, the spell of his lips conspired to render her breathless. Mindless, too, and even though she swore to herself that she wanted to back away, she couldn't. His mouth tempted her to taste the sweet fire she'd only gotten a sample of yesterday in the meadow. This version was longer, fuller, and far more wonderful than anything she'd ever experienced. Yesterday's kiss had been her very first in life, and in spite of the logical mind that usually ruled her thoughts, a woman she did not know was being born inside who didn't care for logic. All she wanted was more of the promises flowing from his lips.

The realization made her draw back in order to keep from losing touch with her true self. Every inch of her body was humming like she'd been strummed. Her nipples were standing up inside of her blouse, and there was a damp fullness between her legs she wanted to assuage. "What are you doing to me?" she whispered before she could stop the words and take them back.

Eli ran a slow finger over her gorgeous, kiss-swollen mouth. "Seducing you, I think."

"You think?"

He gave her a lopsided grin. "Yeah. It wasn't anything I'd planned, though." But after the tantalizing interlude it was all he and his manhood could think about. "Had planned on this marriage being built on friendship and respect, but now, there's something else going on here." Although her kisses were virginal and untutored he'd tasted a heat in her that he wanted to coax into full bloom. He leaned in and kissed her again, slowly, fervently. "So what do you think?"

Jewel wanted to be argumentative and in control but couldn't muster the emotion. He was right. There was something happening between them, and it had her body and senses opening like a spring rose. Feeling his warm lips against the curve of her jaw, she purred in response. "I think you're right."

He pulled back and noted what an alluring sight she made with her glittering eyes and passion-parted lips. Unable to resist he ran the tip of his finger over the sultry curve and wondered how mad Adam would be if they didn't show up. Being with her had gone from duty to desire, and he didn't know why, how, or when.

In those few seconds, Jewel managed to drag a small portion of her mind back from the fog. "I'll still want a divorce," she stated, although the words were far softer than she'd been aiming for because her world seemed to be spinning.

"That is your choice, of course," he conceded, but his gaze matched his tone when he asked, "But, do you really want to deny yourself this . . . ?"

Again, slow kisses blazed a meandering trail down her jaw to her throat above the frilly high collar of her blouse. Hands hot as a stove in winter cascaded at a snail's space down to her waist and then back up to her arms. She swore her blouse had burned away and that he was moving his hands over her bare skin.

"I want to notch our bedpost, Jewel," he husked out against the shell of her ear, and all she could do was tremble.

"We're going to be late." Her blood was pulsing in rhythm with her heart.

Eli knew she was right. "But I'm going to seduce you first chance I get. Just so you'll know."

"Thanks for the warning." Jewel wondered

how long it would be before she'd be able to think clearly again, and if the heat between her thighs would abate before winter returned. Nothing in her life had prepared her for her body's response to his skilled caresses. She was in need of a very frank discussion with Maddie first thing tomorrow. Sensation had her pulsating and throbbing everywhere. "I'm assuming you know how good you are at this?"

He gave her a small grin. "I am."

"Modest, too. I see."

"I won't deny my manly experience, nor how much I seem to want you." And he did, totally and unashamedly.

"And how many times have you used that old saw?"

He shrugged. "Two, three times?"

She snorted. "Drive before Pa comes looking for us."

He leaned over, gave her another quick kiss that left her breathless yet again, then he picked up the reins and did as he'd been told.

The house Adam and Abigail shared was one he'd built for her as a wedding gift. It was half the size of the huge sprawling home he'd lived in with his family, but Abigail had insisted on a place she could maintain without hiring help. Jewel had always loved its gabled roof and gingerbread trim and now that she'd decided to have a house of her own she wanted to incorporate some of the same decorative features.

Abigail greeted them at the door. "Come on

in. Adam's out back with Anna Red Bird seeing to the pheasants on the spit." She paused for a moment, and Eli saw her taking in Jewel's kiss-swollen lips and slightly lidded eyes. Turning her attention his way, she gave him a look of mild surprise but he kept his face impassive in response. "Lead the way, Mother. I'm suddenly very hungry."

Outside, Jewel was delighted to see Gail's old friend, Anna Red Bird, a Napowesipe of the Sturgeon Clan. Her tribe called themselves the People and were among the area's original residents. Like the Native clans all over the country, most of Anna's people had been forced off their land by the government, but a few families remained in the Grove.

The stout Anna stood and embraced Jewel warmly, saying, "Congratulations on your marriage."

"Thank you." Jewel returned the strong hug not only because of the congratulations but because, after her mother died, Anna had been one of the women looking after her, too, and Jewel loved her very much.

Anna, arm still around Jewel's waist, turned to Eli. "I expect you to treat her well."

"I will." And the knowing look in his eyes made Jewel's heart pound so hard she had to look elsewhere.

As they ate, Adam asked Anna how her Lakota relatives were doing out west.

"Things have gone from bad to worse, and it

doesn't matter if you are Napowesipe, Lakota, or Apache. They have penned our families in like cattle. The buffalo are gone, as is the land."

It was a sad tale. The U.S. government seemed intent upon wiping out a people and a way of life that had existed far before Jamestown or the docking of the Mayflower at Plymouth Rock. According to the last newspaper story Eli had read, the Lakota Chief Tatanka, more commonly known as Sitting Bull, had had his youngest son surrender the old chief's rifle to the army at Fort Buford in Montana because he wanted to be remembered as the last man of his tribe to surrender his gun. "Did Tatanka get his reservation near the Black Hills?"

Anna shook her head sadly. "No. He and his men are jailed at Fort Randall as prisoners of war."

"A war they didn't start," Abigail pointed out tersely and they all agreed.

# Chapter 7

After dinner, Jewel and Anna helped Abigail gather up the dirty dishes and leftover food and take it back into the house. "I'll wash everything up later," she told them. "Right now, we need to plan your wedding reception, Jewel."

Inwardly Jewel sighed. Outwardly she smiled falsely. "Sure."

They decided to hold the event on Sunday after church, which only gave them a few days to get everything ready. Gail said, "We don't need big doings, but people can come by, eat cake, and pay their respects."

Jewel was hoping only a few friends of the family would attend, but because she knew that small-town folks jumped at any occasion to socialize and get together with their neighbors, she envisioned everyone in the Grove showing up.

Gail was scribbling details on a piece of paper. "I'll ask Edna to make her punch and since it's the Sabbath she'll have to forgo the bourbon she always adds. Adam's not going to be happy but I'm sure he'll survive."

Anna and Jewel shared a grin.

For the next few minutes, Gail listed all the people she planned on asking to contribute to the festivities: from the small band Vernon commanded, to getting Jewel's brothers to level out the horseshoe pits. Once she was done, Jewel was tired from just listening to all the things her stepmother had planned. No big doings indeed. "Are you sure we can get all of this ready in time. Today is Thursday, Gail."

Gail waved her off. "Of course we can. How long does it take to bake a cake or make sandwiches? I'll let all the ladies know what they are to bring at the meeting tomorrow night." She was referring to the monthly meeting of the Female Intelligence Society of Grayson Grove.

"Okay. So what shall I bring?" Jewel asked. She supposed she could contribute her prize-winning pound cake.

"Nothing my dear. For once you are going to let someone else do the work."

Jewel started to protest only to have Anna weigh in. "Listen to Gail. Your job on Sunday is to look beautiful for Eli, nothing more."

Jewel mentally rolled her eyes. "Whatever you say."

Once Abigail was done, the ladies went back outside to join Adam and Eli. The two men were hunched over something Adam was penning on paper. Peering over his shoulder curiously, Jewel had seen enough similar drawings to recognize the diagram as a building plan for a house.

Adam looked up. "Your brothers and I are going to build you and Eli a home. I've decided to put it on that land he owns near the lake."

"But—"

He cut her off. "The lay of the land, the water. It's a perfect spot."

It wasn't what she'd planned.

"Problem?" he asked.

Jewel shook her head. "No, Pa." If he was determined to build on Eli's land she could argue with him until she turned blue and it wouldn't make a whit of difference. "Eli's land is fine."

Eli asked, "Do you want a sitting porch on the front and back?"

Her eyes brightened. "Yes. Like the ones Pa built for Viveca."

Under Adam's direction, the men of the Grove had built Nate and the doc a new home after an arsonist set fire to Viveca's small cabin. Jewel had always coveted Viveca's sitting porches. The thought of having her own overrode her disappointment at not having the house built where she'd originally wished.

She studied the drawing with interest. "Everything on one floor?"

Adam nodded. "For now. I want to get it built and you two in it as soon as possible. We can always add another floor and more rooms next spring."

Eli thought the plan a sound one. By Adam's estimation, if the Crowley's could work on the house full-time, it could be ready for occupation in a month's time, providing the weather cooperated. Eli also noted the excitement in Jewel's eyes when he'd asked about the porches. Who knew being able to please his thorny rose would give him so much pleasure in return.

They spent a few more minutes further discussing the matter, then Adam folded the drawing and stuck it into his shirt pocket. "We'll start clearing land this weekend."

Jewel had to admit she was pleased and excited. Although Eli's land was on the far side of the Grove, it was still close enough for her to continue keeping house for her brothers.

Anna Red Bird left shortly afterward, promising that she and her son Isaac would be on hand for Sunday's reception. As Adam and Gail walked their good friend out to her wagon, Eli and Jewel were left alone.

"So?" Eli asked while wondering when he'd get a chance to kiss her again. "Are you pleased with the plans?"

"I am."

"Adam picked a good spot."

"It's not my first choice, but he's the experienced one."

"I'm glad there was no fight."

"I saw the look in his eyes. He wasn't going to be moved."

Eli got the impression that she had moved a few inches closer to being a true wife and that pleased him as well. "How about we drive over and look at that land before I take you home?"

The inner parts of Jewel that wanted more of the passion he'd planted in her rose like a seedling in the sunshine. "That would be fine." *I want to notch our bedpost.* The memory of his voice continued to echo in her blood, and desire flared anew. She supposed she could try making lemonade again but she'd sip slowly this time so she wouldn't choke.

After Eli and Jewel made their goodbyes to their parents, they took a slow drive through the countryside. The peace of their passage was broken only by the clop of the horse's hooves against the hard-packed earthen road. In spite of everything swirling around in her life, the quiet was calming and Jewel sighed with contentment. She loved the Grove; glad she'd been born there and hoped her children would grow up there, too. Thinking about children had come out of nowhere. Granted, it wasn't the first time she'd contemplated motherhood, but because she'd been unmarried for so many years, it was not something she'd deemed attainable, so she'd stowed it away with all the other life wishes that would never be, like seeing her mother one last time. Now, however, as she glanced over at Eli holding the reins, she wondered if things might change. Certain she didn't want to proceed any farther down such a slippery slope, and because she was still planning to divorce him, she set the musings aside and took in the beauty of the land. "I wonder what the Grove looked like when your grandparents first settled here."

"Far more trees since there were no Crowleys about yet."

She knew he was poking fun at her family's lumberjack roots but she didn't mind. He was correct, though. The virgin forests of beech, oak, and maple must have spread far as the eye could see. Game had probably been more plentiful then as well. Yet even though the state's forests were being leveled by the lumber companies faster than anyone would have ever thought possible when the first French explorers set foot on Michigan's shores, the land still held a spirit a person could feel in her bones.

"I don't think I'd want to live anywhere else," Eli told her truthfully.

"You might if Hicks makes you and the *Gazette* famous."

He shook his head. "Not even then. The Grove's in my blood."

"And in mine."

"Good to hear." Eli wondered if quiet talks like this were common in a marriage. As he'd told Adam, being married was unfamiliar territory and he had no idea what to expect or anticipate. Lord knew he'd never planned to take a wife, but now that he had he wanted to be a good husband, even if she did have her sights set on divorce. He told himself that her plans to dissolve the marriage didn't matter, but that was a lie. The whole idea stuck in his craw like a fishhook. Admittedly some of his reaction stemmed from vanity. He'd never had a woman publicly state that she'd be kicking him out of her life just as soon as it could be arranged. The Lothario in him was unaccustomed to being dismissed so out of hand. Humility was good for the soul or so it was said, but he wasn't so sure. He who'd sampled beauties from Detroit to Chicago had been brought to his knees by a rose-planting woman with a mouth sassy as a firecracker and sweet as summer peaches.

And it was that mouth that would change the balance of power, he knew. He wasn't called the Casanova of Cass County for nothing. He'd tasted the passion beneath her thorns waiting to be set free. He doubted she knew the depths of her sensual nature, but he did, and once he finished teaching her all she needed to know, she was going to have trouble *spelling* the word *divorce*, let alone pursuing one.

They reached their destination a few minutes later. Eli guided the buggy up the slight slope and came to a halt in the tall grass in the center of the bluff overlooking the shimmering blue water below. The view was spectacular. His grandfather had named the lake after his wife, Dorcas. A few years back, the state had given it a "proper" name, but the locals still referred to it as Dorcas Lake. In a state known to have thousands of lakes, the one he and Jewel silently gazed out over now wasn't very big but was more than deep enough to boat on. It was also teeming with fish. "I almost sold this lot back when I was drinking."

"I'm glad you didn't," she said softly and looked over to find him watching her.

"Those were ugly times for me."

"I can imagine."

Eli could still feel the shame of what he'd done. Turning away, he stared out unseeing for such a long while, she touched his back with sympathy. "Let's go look around."

The bleak eyes slid into a melancholy smile. Taking her hand, he solemnly kissed the tips of her fingers. "Lead the way."

Hand in hand they walked the land that would be their home, and Jewel realized there was a darkness inside of Eli that she'd not been aware of. He was usually so playful and full of teasing, it gave her pause to realize he was brooding inside. She'd been very young in those days; too young to be interested in scandal, but as she'd grown older she'd heard the stories of his great sin and the drunken years that followed. "If I remember Pa's drawing correctly, this is about where he wants to put the house." She didn't want to talk about the sorrow she felt in him.

Apparently he didn't either. "I think you're right."

The spot was far enough away from the edge of the bluff to be sheltered from the fierce westerly winter winds, but close enough for the lake to be seen from the front porch. "Pa's right. This is a much better piece of land."

"Jewel admitting she was wrong? The devil must be freezing," he voiced with mock surprise and awe.

She punched him in the arm. "I can admit I'm wrong."

"Since when?"

"Since I've decided I like the taste of lemonade again."

"You just want more kisses."

Another punch and a smile. "Your head is so swollen it's a wonder you don't topple over."

Laughing he grabbed her around the waist and swung her around until her skirt billowed and she giggled with delight. Then time slowed and he was kissing her, and Jewel lost touch with the world. Her arms rose to hold him closer and his did the same to her. His mouth was warm, inviting her to let him teach her all she needed to know, and she surrendered willingly. His tongue played lazily against her own and his hand slid up and down her ribs. Virgin wary, she tried to keep her mind on where it might journey next because she wasn't sure good women were supposed to allow such liberties outside of the bedroom, but the lure of him and the way her body purred in response made her not care.

Eli transferred kisses to her jaw and the trembling edge of her throat. He tasted heat, smelled roses and was surprised by the fierce call of his desire. Her lips parted and her rising sighs drew him back to her mouth like a desert nomad to an oasis.

Jewel had no idea being with a man could be so powerful. His open palm teased over the tight points of her breast causing her to ripple and moan. She'd never been touched this way before. She felt storm-tossed and so out of control, all she could do was drop her head back and will herself to breathe.

"You're a beautiful, beautiful woman," he murmured while continuing to learn the lines and planes of her body, a body so buffeted that when he dropped his head and bit her breast gently through the thin fabric of her white blouse, the earth shattered and she cried out as she flew apart.

Eli recognized the sound of an orgasm when he heard one and he was pleased. His hand continued to dally with her breasts, all the while wanting to undo her buttons and bare the twin temptations to his touch and kisses. "Did you like that?"

Jewel couldn't answer the hushed question. With his hands still teasing her she found it difficult to express herself, but she'd liked it immensely even though she wasn't sure she was supposed to.

Devouring her with his eyes, Eli wanted all of her then and there. "The French call it *la petite mort*. The little death." He brushed his magic mouth against her tingling lips once again. "It has many names."

Jewel was having trouble recalling her own name in the wake of her body's shattering and his continuing caresses. "Does it happen every time—you—we . . ." Having never broached such an intimate question before, she felt an uncharacteristic shyness taking hold, but she forced herself to meet his eyes.

The innocence he saw in them made Eli even harder. "If we do it right."

"I did like it."

The pleasure in his gaze made her look away, lest she melt like wax again.

He coaxed her chin back up so he could savor her beautiful face. "Then let's make sure we do it right—every time."

Her shyness caused her to look down at her shoes. Only after she'd calmed herself a bit did she lift her vision again.

He brushed a finger over the alluring bow of her bottom lip. "Once your body becomes more attuned, the little death won't happen so quickly, but for an innocent like you, it's normal."

"Are good women supposed to enjoy the marriage bed."

"If her husband teaches her right."

"Then I am in good hands?"

"Oh yes."

Jewel didn't know what to think, do, or say. As she'd noted previously, what little she knew of relations would fit on the head of a pin, but from what she'd read, a woman's participation in the physical sides of marriage was strictly duty, and good women did their duty because they were supposed to. It never occurred to her that there might be more to it, or that she would enjoy herself.

"I will never force myself on you, or ask you to do anything that won't bring you pleasure in return. I promise."

Jewel wasn't real sure what he was alluding to, but the sincerity in his promise was touching. Not trusting herself to speak, she nodded.

Eli found her reticence endearing, too. Just as he'd hoped, he'd found a way to disarm his warrior wife, at least temporarily, and he was looking forward to fully exploring the depths of her sensuality. "Are you ready to go home."

"Yes."

He eased a finger down her silken cheek and thrilled as her eyes shuttered closed. Bending low, he pressed his mouth to hers in a tender farewell, then walked her back to the buggy.

Dusk had fallen and the moon was rising when he pulled the buggy to a halt in front of her house. Reins in hand, Eli looked her way and gave her the soft smile that had been melting women since the day he was born. "Sleep well, Jewel."

Drowning in his smoky eyes, she doubted she would after all that had happened, but replied, "You, too." Her gaze dropped to his lips and the memories of the pleasures it had bestowed made her want more. Scandalized, she dragged herself together. "I'll see you tomorrow. I can get out on my own."

Finding her more irresistible with each passing moment, Eli acknowledged her exit silently. He didn't want her to leave. He hadn't gotten nearly enough of his rose of a wife but he'd cut through the first layer of thorns, and he'd have to content himself with that, at least until next time.

Anticipating the future pleasures to come, he waited for her to disappear inside before he drove off. Whistling contentedly, he pointed the horse and buggy toward home.

# Chapter 8

The next morning, Jewel fixed breakfast for her brothers, and after they left for work, she fed the chickens and checked the fencing on her gardens. Were it not for the fencing, rabbits, deer and other critters would turn her emerging vegetables into their personal dining hall, but as she walked the perimeters, she saw no signs that her defenses had been breached.

Pleased, she went into the barn and grabbed her fishing gear. She had a taste for trout, and wanted to catch a string for dinner. First, though, she had to pay a visit to Maddie.

Driving her old wagon down the tree-lined road, Jewel hoped Maddie hadn't already gone into town to tend to the lending library. Eli's face flitted across her mind and all Jewel could say was, *Lordy.* It had taken her a long time to get to sleep last night. Tossing and turning as if she had a fever, all she could think about was him. Him and *la petite mort.* She'd never dreamed such a thing possible and it made her shake her head with amazement. Who knew? She certainly hadn't. The scandalous memory of him gently biting her nipple and the way her body had shattered in response threatened to send her spinning once more. *Lordy,* was right. He'd promised her that she'd become more accustomed to the sensual assault as time passed, but she wasn't convinced. He'd left her body at such sixes and sevens that when she slipped between her sheets last night to go to sleep her nipples had puckered from just the pressure of the lightweight coverlet. And she didn't even want to think about the yearning fullness between her thighs. Surely this couldn't be normal, could it. She had no answers but knew Maddie would.

Maddie's tragic childhood was well known. In spite of Dorcas Grayson's mandate that the settlement's school be open to both boys and girls, Maddie's father, Meldrum refused to let her attend. Not being a Grove native, he saw no value in his young daughter having an education, even though she was one of the brightest children by far, so he beat her every time he caught her reading. She wasn't deterred. With help from Eli and Nate, she kept up with her schooling. Abigail helped her hide her books. When she became old enough the Grayson family even offered to financially support Maddie's desire to take the woman's courses at Oberlin, but when she asked her father's permission, he blackened both of her eyes and his strap put stripes on her back that would have done a slave overseer proud. So the next day she ran away with an itinerant peddler who'd convinced her of his love. Instead, he put her to work on the streets of Chicago peddling her body. She'd been fifteen years old, and with no one to help a young girl so far away from home, she'd had no choice.

The fates were kind, however. A wealthy White man named Pierce entered her life. Enamored by her beauty and her intellect, he took her away from the peddler, set her up in a small house of her own, and for the next decade she entertained only him. Upon his death she was bequeathed enough wealth to never have to work again. Only then did she return to the Grove.

Jewel thought about how much courage it must have taken Maddie to carve out the life that she had, and to come out of the experience whole inside. She had brass, too, and showed it when she came home to the Grove: she promptly opened a whore house on the outskirts of town. She named it Meldrum's Emporium, much to her father's fury, but kept the doors open until the day he died, then closed the place and retired to her books and her beloved hunting dogs.

The aforementioned dogs greeted Jewel's arrival with a chorus of barked greetings. She scratched necks, rubbed backs, and affectionately said good morning in response to their happy welcomes.

Maddie, dressed in her signature buckskins, stepped out onto the porch. "Quit spoiling my dogs!" But she was grinning.

Jewel told Blue, Maddie's oldest and best loved,

"She's just mad because I didn't say hello to her first."

Blue barked in agreement and a smiling Jewel walked up on the porch.

Maddie gestured to the old sofa on the porch. "Have a seat. How's married life?"

Jewel sat and in response to the question ran her hands over her eyes. "I'm not sure. Did you hear I met his mistress?"

"No," Maddie responded, an eyebrow raised. "Was it Rona?"

Jewel nodded.

"I hope he sent her packing."

"He did, and I pretended not to be upset."

"Pretended? What happened to you not minding him seeing other women?"

Jewel's lips tightened.

"Ah. The truth hurt, did it?"

"It did."

"Figured it would, but I wasn't going to be the one to tell you."

"Thanks." Blue came up on the porch and lay at Jewel's feet. She lowered her hand to scratch his neck.

"So will Rona be back?"

"He says no." And Jewel believed him, especially in light of the sincere apology he'd given her on the bluff. Their time together there had been wonderful.

"So how are things with you two otherwise?"

"We're getting better, I guess. Pa's going to build us a house."

"Are you happy about that?"

"I am. My idea was to have him build it on my land, but he's putting it on Eli's plot overlooking Dorcas Lake instead."

"Pretty spot."

"Complicates things, though."

"How so?"

Jewel told her the reason why she'd wanted the house on Crowley land.

At the end of the explanation, Maddie shrugged. "After the divorce, have Adam build you another house. One that's all your own."

Jewel wondered why she hadn't thought of such a reasonable solution, probably because Eli's mind-numbing kisses had her brain all muddled, she thought to herself. "But there's another problem."

"And it is?"

She had no idea how to politely broach the subject, so she wrestled with it silently for a few moments, trying to put words to what she wanted to say.

Maddie peered into her face. "I'm known for a lot of things, Jewel, but mind reading's not one of them."

"Sorry. Okay. I'll just spit it out. *La petite mort.*"

Surprise lit Maddie's dark eyes. "Well. Tasted the little death, have you? Didn't like it?"

"I did like it. Very much," she admitted. "That's the problem."

"You don't want to be attracted to him?"

"I'm going to divorce him."

"Ah. Having trouble remembering that, are you?"

"I had trouble remembering my name."

"Passion can do that."

"There has to be something I can do to keep me from going to pieces."

"Not that I know of."

"Are you sure?"

"Positive."

"I'm sorry for asking all these questions, but I feel so ignorant."

"You are a well-raised woman, Jewel. That's nothing to be ashamed of."

"But where do I get the knowledge that I need? I don't even know what comes after kissing. I mean, I know a man cleaves to his wife, but what does that really mean?"

Her look was so earnest, Maddie reached over and patted her shoulder in sympathy. "I have some paintings and pictures that will show you, but I don't want you to be so shocked you wind up not wanting him to touch you. Genteel ladies aren't supposed to view things like this." Then she added in an aside, "But many do."

Maddie went into the house and returned a few moments later carrying a large book. The binding appeared very ornate and decorated with motifs of gold. Jewel took it from her hand, and as she viewed the foreign-looking nude man and woman on the cover, her eyes widened like plates. The couple was seated facing each other and their bodies were linked by the man's . . . Jewel turned to Maddie with shock all over her face. "Where'd you get this?"

"In Bengal, on one my visits years ago with Mr. Pierce. It's a reproduction of the *Kama Sutra*. The drawings inside show hundreds of positions a man and woman can achieve."

Jewel blinked. "Hundreds?"

Maddie grinned. "Hundreds. The dogs and I are going for a walk. Give you some privacy. If you have any questions I'll answer them when I get back."

As she left the porch and called the dogs, Jewel watched them leave, then opened the book with shaking hands.

To say that she was given an education was an understatement. In all of her sheltered years in the Grove she'd never seen anything remotely close to the drawings on the pages. Each portrayed couples in a different position: sitting, standing, or lying down. Some of the renderings were tame, while others were so outrageous she covered her mouth to stave off her shocked giggle. She studied couplings she was certain only a contortionist could accomplish, and a few that required her to turn the book this way and that in order to get a true view. Amazement had her shaking her head.

The pictures were stimulating, too, she honestly admitted. The embers still smoldering from her sensual encounter with Eli were once again glowing, so she set the book aside. Leaning her head back on the old sofa, she drew in a deep breath then slowly exhaled. Would he want to do those things with her? Would her agreeing make her wanton? The book had provided far more knowledge than she'd needed, to tell the truth, but the horse was already out of the barn. *Lordy!*

Maddie and the dogs returned a short while later. "Well?" Maddie asked stepping up onto the porch.

"I'm in big trouble."

Maddie chuckled, "You think so?"

She nodded.

"But you're in good hands."

"That's what I'm afraid of." Because Eli's hands were so very good there'd be no telling what kind of shameless woman she'd be when it was all said and done. "Do people actually do those things?"

"That and more."

Jewel ran her hands over her eyes. "I'm going fishing."

"You want company?"

"No. I know you have things to do and I need to think."

Jewel stood and met Maddie's humor-lit eyes.

"Jewel, it's a part of life. Men and women have been coming together since Adam and Eve. And if that Eli is as well versed as I hear he is, you're going to be smiling. I promise."

"But I'm supposed to be divorcing him."

"There is that, but you'll figure it out."

Jewel supposed she would. "Thanks, Maddie. For everything."

"You bet. If you need anything else, just let me know."

"I will."

Maddie watched her young friend climb up on the wagon seat. When she drove away, Maddie picked up the book and with a knowing smile carried it back into the house.

Eli and a small crew of men spent the morning dismantling the slats that made up the back wall of the *Gazette* office. Adam had promised to stop by after work to oversee the initial construction of the addition, but the wall had to come down first. The volunteer crew removed the wood as carefully as possible with the hopes that some of the pieces would be reusable, either in the new building or somewhere else in the Grove.

By noontime, they'd made good progress. Most of the wall was down, leaving the rear of the office open to the sunshine. Eli covered his ancient printing press and the rest of the equipment with tarps to protect them from the elements and to ready them for transport to the store's cellar where they would rest in peace. With nothing left to do for the moment he called it a day. His helpers drifted off, leaving the very pleased editor alone to walk around inside and dream about the possibilities.

As the editor of the *Gazette,* Eli continued a tradition started by Samuel Cornish and John Russwurm, who'd founded the nation's first Black newspaper, *Freedom's Journal,* back in 1827. Until that time sympathetic Whites had carried the standard for the race and been the voice for both slave and free. Although the *Journal* ceased publication two years later in 1829, the seed took root. Newspapers like the *Colored American*, the *Boston Observor*, and Detroit's *Excelsior* rose to pick up the mantle. Now, all over the nation, Black newspapers did their best to keep their subscribers informed and to beat the drum for the justice and equality owed America's darker citizens. Papers like the *People Advocate* in Washington, D.C., the *Colored Citizen* in Fort Scott Kansas, and the *Freeman*, published in New York were only a few of the monthlies and weeklies that continued to speak to not only the oppressive conditions its readers faced, but celebrated the successes of the race. The national papers owned by Pulitzer and the like were more inclined to highlight the race's crimes and foibles while omitting news items that were uplifting or showed Black people in a positive light.

But for the small Black newspapers, keeping the presses going with limited finances was an uphill battle—yet the editors and publishers persevered because without papers of their own, the race would again have no voice, and men like Eli refused to let the clock be turned back. His dream was to have the *Gazette* be the newspaper of choice for all of the state's Black citizens, so for now, he'd settle for getting it back in print. G.W.'s wealth and influence would handle the rest.

Eli drove his wagon down to the store, and with the help of some of the men inside, moved the printing press into the store's cellar. When that was done, his work for the day was completed. Now, to search out his wife.

*Jewel.* As he drove away from town the thought of her made him smile. She was as multifaceted as a brilliant gem; hard one moment, soft as butter cream the next. He hadn't planned on wanting her so intensely yet he did, in every way. Usually courtship took place before the marriage but in their case it was going to have to be the other way around. Not that he minded. In the past, he'd always eschewed virgins. Who wanted to waste time with a woman who knew nothing about the dance of love, but for some reason, Jewel's inexperience aroused him, made him want to spend the rest of his days showing her, pleasing her, notching their bedpost. He'd have to ask Adam to build them a big fine bed because he wanted her first time to be in their bed. If the truth be told, however, he wasn't sure he could hold off long enough for the Crowleys to get the small house up and ready to occupy. Personally, he was going to have trouble not making love to her when he found her today! After yesterday's interlude on the bluff, all he wanted to do was pick up where they left off and show her just how ripe she was for pleasuring. Realizing he was making himself harder by the moment, he tried to put thoughts of her aside but had a hell of a time doing so.

When he reached the Crowley place, he saw her old beatup wagon parked by the house and assumed she was inside. It was too early in the afternoon for her brothers to be home, which pleased him immensely because he could visit without a crowd looking on.

He called to her through the screened front door. "Hey, Jewel. You in there?"

Jewel looked up from the fish she was preparing. Eli. Taking a deep breath to calm her nerves, she rinsed her hands then went to the door drying her hands on the white butcher-type apron tied around her waist. The sight of him made her heart race.

For a moment neither spoke because they were both remembering last night. He was recalling the smell of roses on her heated skin and she the little death.

"May I come in?"

She nodded and pushed on the door so he could enter.

"I'm in the kitchen."

He followed the sway of her denim-clad hips through the quiet well-furnished house. As they entered the kitchen he took up a position by the door and she went back to the fish and began to salt them.

"How's your day been so far?" he asked, fighting the urge to fit himself against her and hold her close so he could smell the subtle rose fragrance on her neck.

"Fine. I went fishing."

"Nice-looking catch."

She nodded.

Eli usually preferred elegant sophisticated women, but Jewel had her hair pulled back in a loose tail and her bangs looked frazzled from the day's heat. He also spotted two silvery fish scales sparkling like odd jewels in those same bangs and it made her all the more captivating. "Once the house is built you'll be able to walk down to the shore and fish."

"Yep." Jewel knew she was answering inanely but she couldn't help it. Memories of the *Kama Sutra* drawings were floating across her mind and she kept seeing herself and Eli as the entwined couples.

"Something wrong?"

A quick shake of her head. "No."

"Then may I have my first kiss of the day?"

Her knees went weak.

"Yes? No?" he asked quietly.

Unable to meet his gaze because she was so overwhelmed, she finally gave him a quick peek over her shoulder and an even quicker nod. She tried to convince herself that sharing a kiss wouldn't present much of a problem, but as he closed the distance between them she began to shake with anticipation. When he slipped his arms lightly around her waist and brushed his lips softly against her neck, her eyes closed in shimmering response. The fit of his body against hers, his clean smell and possessive hold, turned her brain into mush.

"I missed you today," he murmured.

Deep down inside, she'd missed him, and lifted her lips for the aforementioned kiss.

And it was sweet, so sweet that she soundlessly turned her body to him so they could feast slowly and in earnest. His mouth was firm and beguiling; his tongue against the edges of her parted lips, tempting. Desire pulled her deeper and deeper into the maelstrom, and as he left her lips to lazily brand her throat and the shell of her ear, she could hear her own ragged breath against the silence. His lips captured hers again, and an urgency took hold. He kissed her everywhere: her mouth, her cheeks, the edge of her jaw, and she kissed him back, thrilled by the fire-tipped seekings of his tongue and the hands moving over her so beguilingly.

She was so lost in the kissing, she didn't know he'd undone the buttons on her shirt until she felt his hot mouth burn across the bare skin above her white camisole. Had she known she was going to be doing this she might have worn something more feminine but it didn't matter because he was pulling the undergarment down to bare her, and she felt her orgasm rising and gathering like clouds of a summer storm.

He took a straining bud into his mouth and the sensations shot through her like small bolts of lightning. "Lordy!" she whispered softly. Staggered by her body's reactions, she braced herself against the edge of the counter to keep from sliding to the floor like a spilled pot of honey.

Her whispered exclamation made him smile

and his manhood stretched and pulsed, but he forced his mind away from his own pleasure because her pleasure was his main concern. *God, she's gorgeous.* Her sable-tipped breasts were like silk in his hands and the nipples twin aphrodisiacs. Gifting her with licks that set her afire and soft suckles that made her gasp and moan, he wanted to make love to her then and there. The male in him didn't care if it was on her kitchen floor, but the husband in him knew she deserved better her first time, so he set aside his manhood's hunger and raised his mouth to recapture the bliss of her lips. "Soon as the house is finished, I'm going to spend a month making love to you in every room."

The hushed promise echoed through her like thunder, and in her mind's eye she saw them coupling like the man and woman in the drawings, but then, after he again lowered his mouth to her damp, ripe nipples and dallied so magnificently, her vision fled. Feelings overrode sight—his warm mouth, his hand sliding over her hips, her body calling and crooning for more. The roaming hand came to rest between her denim-covered thighs and began to tease. Her legs parted of their own volition so he could play, and a few moaning moments later, the orgasm grabbed her up and carried her away.

Her legs instantly locked on his hand. She came arching and curving, eyelids closed, mouth open, and he watched her with glowing eyes. His desire to tug down the denims and touch the damp lush spot in all the ways he craved was so strong he almost succumbed. Instead he leaned in and kissed her mouth until she slowly returned to earth.

She opened her eyes to his soft smile, and upon seeing his pleased male look, said, "You are so scandalous."

"I'm not the one standing in the kitchen half dressed like an emperor's concubine." He gave her a suggestive little rub between the thighs and she playfully slapped at his hand. "Stop that."

He saw the humor in her face. "You sure?"

She backed away from his hand. "Yes. You're as bad as Maddie's pictures." Shock filled her. Had she said that aloud? A wail went up inside. She hadn't meant to, but he had her so befuddled.

"What pictures," he asked, curious, his attention caught.

Knowing that if she looked in his face she'd instantly die of embarrassment, Jewel kept her eyes low and worked on righting her clothes. "It was nothing."

Eli grinned and reached out to coax her chin up. "Did Maddie give you some naughty pictures to look at, Jewel?"

She backed away. "I need to get this fish ready for dinner."

"Jewel?"

"No, she didn't." Heat burned her cheeks.

"She did," he countered, sensing the truth. She looked so embarrassed he almost laughed aloud. "Well, now."

"Go home, Eli." Hoping he'd do what he was

told, and knowing he wouldn't, she avoided looking at his grin as she pulled a skillet out of the cupboard and set it on the stove, all the while trying to keep her own grin hidden.

"Did you see anything you want us to try."

Jewel took down the lard jar and using a long-handled wooden spoon scooped out a fat white mound and slapped it into the cast iron skillet. "I'm not talking to you."

Eli was so filled with curiosity and amusement, he couldn't resist prolonging the conversation. "Then I suppose I'll just have to ask Maddie."

Spinning to him, spoon raised like a weapon, she promised, "If you do I will shoot you."

He began to laugh. The humorous fire blazing in her eyes offered him little choice. "Oh, sweetheart. What am I going to do with you?"

"You are going to leave my kitchen, Eli Grayson."

"In a minute." Arms crossed, he studied her. The realization that his virgin bride had viewed what had to be some of Maddie's collected erotica made him hard all over again. "Those must have been some pictures."

She huffed back around to the skillet.

He laughed softly. Walking up behind her, he fit himself against her back and held her close. He inhaled the rose scent rising from her so sensually and placed a soft kiss on her neck. "I'm supposed to be meeting Adam in town later to go over the plans for the *Gazette*. I'll come get you after your meeting and take you home."

In spite of acting bad tempered, she knew she wasn't, and he did, too. "And suppose I don't want to be taken home."

"Then how about we go by Maddie's and look at those pictures."

She smacked him across the shoulder with her spoon. "Out!" she pointed, grin peeking out for him to see. "Take your smile and your kisses and leave me in peace."

But of course he didn't. Instead he turned her to face him and gave her a kiss that was so deep and sweet and filled with such arousal the spoon slipped from her hand and clattered to the floor. Only when he was convinced that she'd melted completely and totally into her shoes did he reluctantly break the kiss. "See you tonight," he whispered, and he was gone.

Breathless and brainless, the pulsating Jewel Crowley Grayson stood against the stove with her eyes closed for a very long time.

The monthly meeting of the Female Intelligence Society of Grayson Grove was called to order promptly at seven that evening. The society was named after the Female Intelligence Society of Boston, which in 1832 made history when it sponsored a speech by Black female abolitionist Maria W. Stewart at Boston's Franklin Hall. Stewart's appearance marked the first speech given by an American woman of any race to an audience of both men and women. In those days, it was thought unseemly for a woman to lecture to a promiscuous, or mixed gender, gathering.

The Grove's meeting was presided over by President Abigail Grayson. Vice President Jewel Crowley Grayson was in attendance, as were Secretary–Treasurer Miss Edna Lee, and Sgt.-at-Arms Maddie Loomis. Local members like the Quilt Ladies and the Widow Temperance Moss, wearing the same black weeds she'd been wearing since her husband Emery's death thirteen years ago, were joined by various women from Calvin Center, Dowagiac, and Niles in the chairs set in a circle in the back corner of the store. The meeting's location varied from month to month, and this time it was Miss Edna's turn to host. There were twenty-five women on the official rolls but twelve had shown up for that evening's gathering.

First order of business was the secretary's report. Edna read the minutes from the April meeting, where they'd discussed, among other things, seeking out similar women's clubs to align themselves with in order to add more weight to their voice. Next came a recap of their ongoing campaign to provide books and other supplies for the Grove's school.

Once the minutes were approved, Edna put on her other hat and gave the treasurer's report. Just like last month, they had very little money. Pledges were on target but the Society spent it as fast as it came in on their charity work and other projects. They were having a fund-raiser at the end of June, their annual Sweetheart Dance, and hoped to make a significant profit.

The history of Black women banding together for the good of the race began in the United States as far back as the seventeenth century with benevolent societies that benefited the sick, the dying, and the poor. Many started as outreach groups of their churches. One particularly active group was the Female Benevolence Society of St. Thomas, founded in 1793 in Philadelphia at St. Thomas, the first African Episcopal church in the nation. Free Black women living in Newport, Rhode Island, formed the African Female Benevolent Society in 1809, because they could neither vote nor hold office as members of the community's male society. Daughters of Africa, a New York group, was another cornerstone. Two hundred members strong in 1821, the Daughters, working as domestics and laundresses by day, pooled their extra pennies to loan money for funerals, pay doctor bills and death benefits, thus becoming one of the nation's first insurance companies.

All over the nation women of the race counted themselves as members of societies that looked after orphans and folks unable to look after themselves, and fostered literacy. Black woman also supported suffrage and were as ready for the vote as their White counterparts. Black abolitionist and feminist Frances Harper put it best when she said, "The world cannot move without women sharing in the movement," but with the White organizations limiting the seating of Black women at their conventions and other suffrage groups prohibiting attendance altogether, working for the betterment of women everywhere was being hindered by the friction.

One of the new items to be discussed at the evening's meeting was whether to send representatives to a national suffrage convention being held in the fall in Chicago. Like most Black women, the females of the Grove supported the National Woman's Suffrage Association spearheaded by Susan B. Anthony and Elizabeth Cady Stanton, in spite of both women having campaigned against the ratification of the Fifteenth Amendment. They and their supporters were angered by the thought of Black men being given the vote before White women.

Gail took the floor to voice her support for the measure. "Even if they do choose not to admit us, I say we go. If for principle alone."

Jewel agreed. As women of the race, they were forced to hurdle the double-edged barrier of racial bigotry and female discrimination, and they knew neither would be banished if they didn't make themselves heard. "I'm with Abigail. If they don't wish to seat us, they'll hear what I have to say about their hypocrisy, even if I have to stand on the roof of the convention hall and shout it to the world."

They all smiled because they knew how committed she was to the vote. At the age of fourteen, she'd accompanied Maddie, Gail, and Miss Edna to the county seat where the older women were determined to vote in the 1872 elections. Nationwide, women of all races had been encouraged by suffrage leaders to go to the polls, and the call had been answered. Among the most prominent were Susan B. Anthony, who'd been arrested in Rochester, New York, and fined $100 for what the court called, "knowingly and unlawfully voting." Sojourner Truth, residing in Battle Creek, Michigan, also tried to vote, but her demands for a ballot fell on deaf male ears.

Upon hearing Jewel's declaration, Edna drawled, "Make sure Adam knows you're going so he can begin gathering his funds to pay your fines."

An embarrassed but smiling Jewel dropped her eyes, then came to her own defense. "I made the local newspapers and I received many letters of congratulations for my daring."

Gail offered wryly, "That's not what your father called it. He chewed my backside when he came home from bailing you out. Made me promise to never take you on an excursion like that again."

When the voting clerks refused to give Miss Edna, Maddie, and Gail ballots, and no amount of arguing would change the men's minds, Jewel sat down in the doorway of the courthouse and refused to move. For over an hour the officials asked, cajoled, threatened and begged, but she didn't budge. The police were finally called. They removed her but she didn't go quietly so she was arrested and charged with assault and disturbing the peace.

Maddie said, "Well, I'm with Gail and Jewel on attending the meeting in Chicago, and if they won't let us in, I'll be raising hell right along with Jewel, and I have money to pay the fines for both of us."

So it was agreed, Gail, Edna, Maddie and Jewel would attend the suffrage meeting.

When the remaining business items were taken care of, Gail turned the conversation to the reception planned for Sunday to celebrate Jewel and Eli's marriage. When she asked for contributions, everyone eagerly volunteered to bring food except the Widow Moss. "I find it deplorable that your father would approve such a marriage. I'm sorry, Abigail, I know he's your son, but no daughter of mine would marry an adulterer and a fornicator."

Before Gail could reply, Jewel replied coolly, "Then you are more than welcome not to attend."

The widow, who always looked like she was sucking on lemons, turned even more sour and stood. "If the meeting is adjourned, I'll take my leave."

Gail's dark eyes were blazing. "The meeting is adjourned."

The Widow Moss sailed out.

Maddie muttered, "Old bat."

That brought on smiles. With their moods lightened, the remaining members refocused their attention on the reception.

The meeting broke up an hour later and by then it was dark. Those who lived too far away to make the drive home would be staying overnight with the Quilt Ladies. As the women shared their goodbyes and the store began to empty, Jewel, Maddie, and Gail stayed behind to help Edna place the chairs back in the storage room and clean up the dishes they'd used for their cake and punch so everything would be cleared away when she opened the store in the morning.

It was easy to see that Gail was still simmering over the Widow Moss's denunciation of Eli, and in truth, Jewel was as well. "Wouldn't it be nice if the widow suddenly inherited a fortune and moved to China?"

Gail chuckled in spite of her temper. "That would be nice, wouldn't it?"

Widow Temperance Moss was the bane of the community. She considered herself even more of a moral force than the Quilt Ladies and over the years her acidic tongue had lacerated everyone.

Maddie folded a wooden chair. "Personally, I think Magic's prank on her was the best of all time."

Before Nate Grayson married Dr. Lancaster, he made the mistake of hiring the widow to be a governess of sort to his adopted daughter Majestic, or Magic as she was affectionately known. Magic had been ten years of age in those days and she'd hated the widow in ways only someone that age could because the woman constantly berated the child's manners, deportment, and parentage. Magic fought back by playing pranks.

Chuckling, Gail said, "The day she sewed Temperance's drawers together I thought I would keel over I laughed so hard."

"Put snakes in her bed, too, as I remember, and the next day rotten eggs in her Sunday bonnet," Edna reminded them.

They were all grinning now.

Edna added, "But I know which incident Maddie is talking about. Everybody around heard about Magic putting cow manure in the widow's slippers."

Gail could barely speak for laughing. "When she put them on they were already occupied."

They all howled as Gail continued, "Magic couldn't sit for a week after the whipping Nate gave her, but the widow refused to teach her any longer so I believe Magic won."

Jewel did, too, and in solidarity she picked up her half-filled punch cup and raised it high. "To the feisty, give-no-quarter women of the Grove, of all ages!"

"Hear! Hear!" the others declared, raising their own cups. They drained the contents and went back to cleaning up.

Once they were done, Maddie looked over at her friends. "I should be getting on home before Blue comes looking for me."

They knew she was serious because on more than a few occasions her dogs had come to find her when she'd been late getting home. "They're worse than a maiden aunt. Good thing I don't have a man." She waved and strolled out.

Abigail and Jewel left right behind her so that Edna could lock up and retire to her rooms above the store. Outside, the night breeze felt good and the stars were like diamonds in the sky overhead. All of the businesses were closed, but Jewel assumed Eli and her father were still working on the *Gazette* because down the street she could see lights from the lanterns they were working by. She looked over at her stepmother who was now also her mother-in-law. "Are there a lot of people still holding bad feelings for Eli?"

Abigail leaned on her cane and looked out at the night. "I'm sure there are, but unlike Temperance, most have the decency to keep it to themselves." She went silent for a moment then said with soft pain, "He's been trying so hard to repair his name and done a magnificent job, I think."

"He's never going to please everybody."

"I tell myself the same thing, but . . ."

For a moment Jewel waited for her to continue, but when nothing was said, she asked quietly, "But what?"

Gail shook her head regretfully. "Just wish it had never happened. I spent a lot of years blaming Cecile, but in the end, Eli knew right from wrong. He made a choice and it's one that will shadow his life for as long as he lives here."

"You want him to move away?"

"Of course not. He's my only child, but I,"—she sighed and shrugged—"I just wish it had never happened."

Jewel remembered the darkness she'd sensed in him the day they'd driven to the bluff. She slipped an arm around Gail's waist and gave her a tiny squeeze. "He's a good man. Even I know that."

"I think you'll be good for him."

Now it was Jewel's turn to stare out into the night. She thought of the way they'd parted earlier that afternoon and allowed herself an inner smile. "Why?"

"Just a mother's feeling." She looked down into Jewel's eyes. "Give it a chance."

"I'm keeping my mind open."

"That's all I ask."

Adam drove up out of the darkness and called out, "You women done plotting to take over the world for one night?"

They grinned and Gail tossed back, "Yes, but I've decided to run for president."

He pulled hard on the reins and the shock on his face was plain to see in the moonlight. "What!"

Gail said to Jewel, "Your father is so easy to get." To Adam she called, "It's a joke, Adam, so pull your tongue out of your throat and let's go."

"Abigail," he said warningly, realizing he'd been had yet again.

Smiling, she ignored the tone. "I'd like to get home before the sun wakes up." She turned to Jewel. "One of the boys coming to take you home?"

"Paul drove me in, but Eli's supposed to be meeting me."

Adam answered. "He's on his way. He's putting the lanterns away."

As if one cue, Eli drove up in his buggy. "Sorry I'm late."

Jewel's heart sang at the sight of him and her nipples stood up shamelessly beneath the old shirt she was wearing. She had no intentions of letting him know, though. His head was swelled enough.

Eli was glad he hadn't missed her. He like everyone else in town knew just about what time the meetings usually adjourned, but apparently they'd met later because he'd truly expected her to be gone already. "Can I still see you home?"

His soft invitation made Jewel feel fourteen all over again. No matter how hard she tried to be on the outside, inside she was soft as lemon curd. "I suppose."

Jewel saw Adam and Gail watching with interest. "You two can go on," she said. "We'll be fine."

Adam turned the wagon around and the parents waved in parting. They disappeared into the darkness, and in the silence that followed Eli got out of his buggy and walked over to where Jewel stood in the breeze.

He teased a finger down her cheek and she wondered if she'd ever be immune to what he made her feel inside. As it stood now, she rippled every time he touched her and it didn't matter the time or place.

"How'd the fish turn out." he asked.

"Fine."

Without a word, he leaned in and pressed a soft kiss on her lips. That done, he took her hand and walked her to the buggy.

# Chapter 9

Silent, they drove through the night. Under the pale moon the trees lining the road resembled eerie specters and for Jewel the sight stirred up a long forgotten memory. "Do you remember the night I got lost playing Moonlight Hide and Go Seek?"

"I do. You couldn't have been more than, what, seven or eight?"

"Eight. I waited for somebody to come find me, but no one did."

"The way I heard it, you were supposed to be in bed."

"Well, yes," she admitted. "But when the boys were talking about playing after supper, I asked if I could join in and they all said I was too little, including Pa."

"So how did you expect to be found if nobody knew you were a player?"

"Noah knew. In fact, he helped me slip out of bed while Pa was chopping wood out back, and I hid in the barn until it got dark. I stuffed some pillows under my bedding so Pa would think it was me, then when it got dark, I went and hid."

He chuckled. She'd been a force of nature even back then. She and his niece Magic had similar personalities. Both had needed full-time keepers while growing up. "You must have been scared after so long a wait."

"Not really, because I knew every inch of the Grove and I wasn't afraid of the animals. My mistake was falling asleep."

Eli had been sixteen and drafted as a member of the hastily assembled search party. Men all over the Grove were awakened that night by Crowley sons banging on their doors and relaying the frantic Adam's need for help. She was found the next morning asleep in the hollow of an old oak on Crowley land. "Did Adam punish you for sneaking out?"

"Nope. Didn't switch Noah either after he confessed to helping me. I think Pa was so glad to see me he didn't have the heart and he didn't want me to tell Mama about my adventure. She and Gail were away at a suffrage rally in Battle Creek and I'm sure he didn't want to have to explain to her how he'd come close to losing her only daughter. More than likely she heard about it soon as she returned, though. There aren't any secrets in the Grove."

No there weren't, Eli mused. Back then he'd been trysting with Cecile and was as devoted as any lap dog; that hadn't been a secret either. He wondered what ever became of the woman he'd willingly waded into hell for. Not that he cared, but he was curious as to whether she was still ruining lives or if she'd turned her life around like he'd been trying to? He certainly didn't miss those years or the ones that followed.

Jewel gave him a glance. Because he'd gone so silent she felt compelled to ask, "You all right?"

"Just thinking about what I was doing in those days."

She sensed the darkness rising and remained silent. If he wanted to talk about it she'd let him, but it would be his choice.

"How much of the story do you know?" he asked.

"That you committed adultery with Nate's wife."

"Again and again and again," he admitted in hushed bitter tones. "Even after he returned home from the war, broken from being buried alive by the Rebs at Ft. Pillow, I kept seeing her. Nothing mattered but Cecile."

The memories inside Eli rose, bringing back the haunting shame. "When Nate found us together, he beat me almost to death. I didn't fight back. I'd hurt him more than the Rebs, and I'd deserved it."

"But the two of you are better now."

"Thank God for Viveca. Had she not come to town and served as a bridge, Nate and I might never have found each other again."

"I'm glad you did."

"So am I. Did you know he once saved my life?"

She hadn't heard that story. "When?"

"I was nine, so he would have been eleven. We were swimming one afternoon and a cramp crippled my leg. Had he not swum to my rescue I would have drowned," he added darkly. "And I repaid that blessing by sleeping with his wife."

To Jewel it was obvious that he hadn't forgiven himself, or made peace with his perfidy. She felt sorry for him and wanted to mover closer and offer what sympathy she could, but knowing he didn't want her pity or anything resembling it, she stayed put.

"I brought shame on my family, my name. My mother," he whispered emotionally. "And not a moment of it can be changed."

He was right of course, but if Nate could see the way to settings things clear between them, Jewel hoped Eli would somehow find the means to salve the pain he was carrying inside.

He glanced over. "So now you know all of it."

"I'm not sure I'm supposed to say thank you to something like this."

He gave her a small smile. "Perfect response."

"It's the truth."

"And one of the many things I like about you, Jewel Grayson—your honesty."

"You enjoy calling me that, don't you?"

"I do. Like the way it feels in my mouth."

She immediately thought of the way her nipples

felt in his mouth and wondered if he'd phrased his response specifically for that reason. "Are you trying to be scandalous again?"

"I think so. Am I being successful?"

"Way too full of yourself, Eli Grayson. Way too full."

"I'll take that as a yes, then."

Amusement made her wonder if she'd ever win one of their bantering battles, but she didn't hold out much hope. As she'd noted before, what she knew about these matters could fit on the head of a pin—although Maddie's drawings had greatly expanded her knowledge. "Maddie did show me pictures."

"I gathered that."

"The *Kama Sutra*."

"Ah, the Holy Grail. Remind me to get her something special."

"Eli!"

"Sorry."

"No, you're not." She was laughing. "This is very embarrassing."

"Sweetheart, nothing we're going to do together is going to be embarrassing, at least not after the first time." He circled an arm around her waist and gently urged her closer. "I keep telling you I'm not contagious."

Jewel didn't put up a fuss and let herself be held close while he guided the reins with his free hand. She liked being cuddled against his side. His solid strength gave her a peace and contentment she never would have thought possible the evening the reverend pronounced them man and wife. "Your mother said she didn't want big doings for the reception on Sunday, but she has half the women in the county bringing food."

"Let's hope that'll be enough, because more than likely everybody in the county's going to show up."

"I'm not looking forward to it, truthfully." She felt his shoulder tense in response, so she sought to reassure him. "Not because of why we're having the reception, but because I'm not one for a lot of hoopla." When his shoulder relaxed she smiled inside, glad she'd clarified her meaning. "I don't even enjoy going to parties for other people."

Eli gazed down into her shadowy face. He'd thought she'd been protesting the marriage again and was glad to hear differently. "You just need to learn to let your hair down. Have some fun."

"I do fun things."

"Such as?"

"I toss horseshoes with my brothers. We play chess, checkers, and baseball."

"But most of the time, you work."

"Because there's work to do. I am the only female in the house, Eli. I also have my roses and my committee work. Having too much fun would put me behind."

"Would that be such a terrible thing?"

Jewel raised up. "Let's see how much fun you make time for once the *Gazette* starts publishing again."

"Touché, Mrs. Grayson."

"That's what I thought."

He squeezed her with all the affection he felt inside. "You are something."

"And you'd do good to remember that."

He squeezed her again, "Keep sassing me and I'll make you melt into your shoes. Again."

Jewel smiled against his arm.

"Awful quiet."

"I'm not denying it."

"Denying that you're quiet or that you like my kisses?"

"Both." She looked up and met his smile.

"Well now. That's good to hear." His voice was soft

"I knew it would be."

"Liking that lemonade, are you?"

She nodded. "I am."

He let the reins go slack and the horse stopped. The breeze sweeping over them rustled through the trees like a whispered song, the chorus of nocturnal insects accompanied by the rhythmic chirping of the crickets its music, while Jewel's thumping heart added a steady cadence of its own.

Eli used the moment to glide a finger slowly down her cheek. He was filled with what the future could hold for them if they would just give it a chance. He wanted to tell her that but was unsure if he could find the right words. "Let's see if we can make a life together, Jewel. Here and now. Do away with all the reasons and the whys, and see where we end up."

"I'd like that." And it was the truth.

He leaned down and pressed his lips to hers, then brushed her ear, "I will provide for you, protect you, and make love to you, for as long as you wish to stay. . . ."

Jewel couldn't breathe. The promise in his words and in the lips placing humid fleeting kisses on the edge of her jaw, throat, and trembling mouth stole her soul. Never in her life had she imagined a man whispering to her this way. The short fervent kisses ignited her senses. The hot pass of his hands making the old flannel shirt slide silently against her skin and over the tight tips of her breasts made the spot between her thighs awaken and pulse. When he eased her onto his lap she didn't protest, she was too busy soaring.

Eli had no idea why he wanted this woman so much; all he knew was that he did, badly. From the sweetness of her mouth to the way her nipples rose under his touch, he felt possessed. Placing licks and kisses against the bare skin of her throat framed by her open collar, he filled his hands with her shirt-covered breasts, lowered his head and bit them possessively while she moaned. Buttons were undone, and then he stopped. Chuckling and amazed by what she was wearing beneath the shirt he drew back, then played with the buds he couldn't wait to taste. "Why are you wearing a man's union shirt?"

Jewel couldn't believe he wanted her to talk. The space between her thighs was on fire and there was a wanton rhythm infecting her hips that she couldn't seem to control. "It belonged to Noah," she finally managed to whisper, "He'd outgrown it."

Taking a moment, he undid the tiny buttons running down the front and then pushed the halves aside. "No more wearing your brother's underwear, Jewel Grayson. . . ." And to make certain she remembered he lowered his head and gave the dark-tipped twins such a sultry tongue lashing her hips rose in sultry response. "You hear me?" he whispered hotly. He reprimanded her for a few wanton moments more, then raised his mouth to her ear. "Say 'Yes, Eli,'" he commanded in a voice brimming with both passion and humor.

She played along. "Yes, Eli."

On the wind came the sound of horses galloping on the road behind them. A dazzled and panicked Jewel hastily did up the buttons of her shirt and tried to leave his lap but he kept her there. "We're married, remember?" he told her with a smile. "You're fine right where you are. I promised that nothing we do together is going to be embarrassing after the first time. Consider this one of those things."

Jewel supposed she could look at it that way although she'd expected such moments to apply only in the bedroom. She also reminded herself that if people were to believe that she and Eli had been secretly married for some time, being seen out here sparking in the dark would go a long way in support of the ruse. Nonetheless, she was embarrassed knowing whoever was coming would find her seated on his lap, but in reality she was still reeling from his expert loving and that overrode all.

When the two riders got close enough, she and Eli recognized James Wilson, the Grove's mill operator. He was also the man Adam Crowley had nearly come to blows with over his disparaging remarks abut Jewel and Eli. He and her father butted heads often.

On the horse beside him was his son Creighton, the only man in the Grove who'd ever courted her.

The elder Wilson pulled back on the reins. "Evening, Eli. Jewel." He scanned them slowly. "Nice night."

"Yes, it is," Eli responded easily. "How are you Jim? Creighton? Creighton, are you home for a visit?"

Creighton nodded a response but everyone could see that his eyes were focused solely on Jewel. "Back home for good," he said. "The job in Detroit didn't work out. How are you, Jewel?"

"Doing fine, Cray. You?"

"Kinda sad when I heard you and Eli were married, but I'll survive."

Jewel's lips tightened ruefully. One of the reasons their strong-willed fathers didn't get along was because James was convinced that Adam had run Creighton off because he didn't want Creighton courting his only daughter. In reality, Creighton had been so scared of her father he couldn't talk. At the time, she'd regretted that he'd stopped coming around, but now that she'd been with Eli, she was convinced that had she married the quiet, steady Creighton she would have been insane inside of a week. "I'm sure you'll find someone, too."

He nodded, lips terse.

James pulled on his horse's reins and grumbled, "We'll leave you two in peace."

"Have a good evening," Eli replied coolly. Wilson was a competent manager and the Grayson family had no complaints about the way he ran the mill, but on a personal level, Eli didn't like the man. Wilson exuded an arrogant smugness that rubbed him the wrong way.

The Wilsons rode off leaving Jewel and Eli alone in the night once again. Jewel cracked, "I'm sure he'll be telling anybody who'll listen what he saw first thing in the morning."

"He saw my wife sitting on my lap and that's all. Any embellishment and he'll wish he had stuck to the truth."

"Then we'll sic Pa on what's left of his body."

Eli agreed, but he had a question. "Did you know Creighton was sweet on you?"

She nodded. "I did. He came to the house a few times, but nothing ever came of it."

Not even the shadows had been able to mask the yearning in Creighton's eyes. "When was this?"

"A couple of summers back. You were gone most of that summer trying to drum up advertisers for the *Gazette*."

"Ah." In his search for supporters he'd traveled all over the state and then down to northern Indiana and over to Chicago. Even though he'd traveled for weeks, it turned out to be a fruitless venture. "Why'd he stop coming around?"

"Pa scared him so badly, all he could do was shake—couldn't even talk. The boys thought it was the funniest thing they'd ever seen, but were decent enough to hold the laughs until he left the house."

"I can't see you married to him. Too tame."

"I thought the same thing."

"Have I spoiled you?"

"I believe you have."

"Good."

For a moment they stared at each other, then he kissed her softly. After a few passion-filled minutes, he reluctantly broke the seal of their lips. "Let's get you home."

Jewel didn't want to leave his lap or his kisses, but whispered, "Okay."

When they reached the house, he pulled back on the reins to halt the horse. "Here you are."

"Thanks." An uncharacteristic shyness took hold. "I'll see you tomorrow."

"And the next day and the next, and the next."

"Sleep well, Eli."

"You, too, Jewel Grayson."

Her nipples tightened. Ignoring the shameless reaction as best she could, she hopped down and started up the dark walk. When she reached the porch, she turned and gave him a wave. She disappeared inside and the pleased Eli drove away.

* * *

Eli was still in bed the next morning when a stout rapping on his front door pulled him awake. Hoping whoever it was would go away, he rolled over intending to return to his dream where he'd been making love to Jewel, but the noise grew louder. Cursing, he yelled, "Give me a minute, will you?"

He grabbed his robe and stumbled to the door. Snatching it open, he barked, "What?"

Abigail sniffed. "You used to be such a polite son."

Chagrined he opened the screen so she could enter. "Sorry. Come on in. What brings you out at such an ungodly hour."

"It's nearly seven. I assumed you'd be up by now." She looked around at his cluttered front room and shook her head. "Is there furniture under all these papers?"

The place was filled with newspapers and sheets of the writing paper he used to pen his editorials. Even though the *Gazette* was closed he continued to compose editorials and letters to the editors of papers across the country. "I think so."

He removed a large pile from one of his old chairs and she took a seat then set the cane against the arm.

He scratched his head sleepily and sat on his small worn sofa.

"What I came to discuss won't take but a moment. Here." She handed him a set of papers tied with twine.

"What is this?"

"Open them."

He did as instructed and discovered a sheaf of bank documents. He looked over at her curiously. Some had his name across the top of them. "Mother?"

"Your inheritance."

His confusion deepened. He mentally shook off the cobwebs of sleep. "What inheritance?"

"The one I've been keeping from you."

Stilled, he studied her. "Why?"

She didn't respond, but the set of her face and the love hiding behind her stern eyes gave him the answer. "You didn't trust me to have it."

"No, I didn't."

"I haven't touched a drop in years, Mother."

"I know, but I needed to be sure."

He scanned the papers silently, wondering if he should be angry or grateful. "This is quite a sum."

"It's your portion of the rents, profits from the businesses, and what the family has earned from various investments, including the ones I asked Viveca's mother, Francesca, to make on our behalf in California. And you are correct, it is quite a sum."

Eli looked up from the documents. "I could have used this when the *Gazette* went under."

"I know," was all she said.

"Yet you didn't offer it then?"

"No."

"May I ask why?"

She didn't hesitate. "Because if and when I have grandchildren I wanted them to be able to eat something besides news print, and drink something besides ink."

"In other words, you thought I'd sink it all in the newspaper."

"Yes." Then she added, "Your paper is very important to us, Eli, and I want it to thrive just as much as you, but yes, you would have sunk all of your money into it, leaving you to struggle to support any family you might have had in the future."

"And if I hadn't married Jewel?"

"I would have turned it over to you at this point anyway because of the way you've handled yourself since the paper folded."

"You were waiting to see if the disappointment would make me start drinking again?"

"Yes."

He sat back and met her level gaze. Another force of nature, he thought to himself. "I'm trying to decide if I'm angry."

"That's fair."

"I am grateful, though, so thank you."

"You can curse me after I leave."

He smiled for the first time. "Never that."

"Don't lie." She stood, leaning on her cane.

The grin spread across his face. He stood too and placed a kiss on her cheek. No matter how he felt about her decisions, one thing would never change. "I love you."

"But I love you more."

As he walked her to the door, she asked, "What are you planning today?"

"I'm probably going to drive down to Niles and see if I can find Jewel a wedding ring now that I have some funds." In reality he had more than some. The investments by the doc's mother alone had netted thousands. "Maybe I'll see if she wants to go with me."

"Excellent idea. She works much too hard. She needs a holiday."

"I agree."

Abigail's eyes held his. "I'll understand if you're angry at me for what I've done, but try and look at it from where I stand. I did it for you."

He nodded. Considering all the shame and heartache he'd caused her, he knew that he had no right to be angry at her for anything, ever.

"Have a good time in Niles, and remember the reception is tomorrow. Everyone is expecting you two to be there."

"We won't disappoint you."

She stepped down from the porch and called back over her shoulder, "And don't let Jewel tell you she can't go because she has to help with the reception. Her only role is to show up."

"Good to know." He watched her reach her buggy and get in. After she drove off he closed the door.

Taking a seat he studied the documents again and was outdone by the numbers they held. He could pay off all of his creditors and still have enough remaining to start his life with Jewel on a solid financial foundation. He still wished his mother had offered him at least a portion of the funds to deal with the *Gazette*'s fall. The thirty-two-year-old man inside wasn't happy knowing she'd treated him as if she were doling out the allowance of a twelve-year-old. However, the son inside him understood, and not knowing how to balance the two opposing views, he decided to simply let it go. He was no longer poor as a church mouse living on the scraps he called his savings, and for that he was grateful.

Leaving his seat, he set the bank papers aside and returned to his room to dress and start his day. He wanted to ride over to the Crowley's and find Jewel before she headed off somewhere to play in the dirt.

And that was exactly what she was doing when he walked up. Dressed in her signature denims, an old shirt that had probably belonged to one of her brothers, and wearing a pair of well-worn brogans on her feet, she was kneeling in one of her vegetable gardens pulling weeds. She was placing them in a short barrel beside her. Since there were only a few weeds in the bottom of it, he assumed she hadn't been at the task very long.

She looked up and gave him a smile that filled his heart with sunlight. "Morning."

"Morning."

They grinned at each other for a few long moments remembering last night's pleasure-filled drive under the moonlight, then she stood and clapped her grimy gloved hands together to get rid of some of the soil clinging to them. "So where are you off to all dressed up." He had on his brown Sunday suit, a high-collared shirt and tie.

"We're going to Niles."

She raised an eyebrow. "We?"

"Yep. We'll be back this evening."

"And the reason *we* are going to Niles?"

"To get you a wedding ring."

She stared, frozen.

He enjoyed making her speechless. "So hurry and get dressed so we can go."

"But I have chores. I have . . ."

He folded his arms.

Seeing that, her argument trailed off and a twinge of guilt rose. "This is what you were talking about last night, wasn't it? Me being too busy to let my hair down."

"You said it, not me. The weeds aren't going anywhere."

"But they'll be larger."

"If you don't want a ring just say so."

"But I do," she said more earnestly than she'd intended. A ring—for her? It was yet another one of those things she'd never imagined in her life. "I just—" then she stopped. "Okay. I'll go. Write this down, Mr. Editor. I am eschewing weeds to take a trip to Niles. I am turning my back on the large number of chores I had planned today in favor of fun."

"Duly noted."

Jewel was pleased. "I won't be long." She started toward the house.

"Jewel?"

She stopped and turned back. "Yes?"

The happiness in her face made his heart swell. "Thank you."

She nodded and hurried off to get ready.

The ride to Niles took a little over an hour and the closer they got to the city limits the wider the roads became and the more people they passed. Niles wasn't a large place by any means, but it was large enough to have a train station, which made it a metropolis when compared to the Grove.

Jewel had to admit she was enjoying herself. For the first few miles she'd bemoaned all the chores she'd left behind, but then put them out of her mind. As Eli noted, the work wasn't going anywhere, so she decided not to fret anymore and to just relish the freedom of the journey and his company.

As they drove down Main Street, passing stores and businesses, she saw people of many races on the walks and driving down the street. "Where are we going first?"

"Jeweler friend of mine named Jake Adler."

She didn't know Mr. Adler or how to deal with the idea that they were here after a wedding ring. The wearing of a ring to show a woman's married status had become popular after the war. Now it was all but expected, but again, she'd never thought she'd be wearing one.

Eli turned down a side street then stopped the buggy in front of a small storefront with a sign above the door that read, Adler's Fine Jewels and Stones. He came around to help her down, then escorted her inside.

The indoor electric lights that were all the rage back east hadn't made their way to the small towns of the Midwest, so the store's interior was shadowy and dim like most stores its size, but the light from the smile of the thin-boned man who walked out from behind the counter upon their entrance could have lit up the entire town.

"Eli!"

"Afternoon, Jake. How are you?"

The two men shared a handshake of greeting then Adler looked down at Jewel. "And this is?" he asked.

"My wife. Jewel."

"Beautiful name for a beautiful woman. Honored to meet you. Welcome to my establishment, Mrs. Grayson."

"Thanks. A pleasure to meet you as well."

Jake turned to Eli. "Please tell me you're here to get her something."

"I am, and to give you something." Eli reached into the inside pocket of his suit coat and pulled out the bank draft he'd written that morning.

Jake took it, scanned it, then studied Eli. "What is this?"

"What I owe you." Jake had been one of the friends who'd lent Eli money when the *Gazette*'s finances began to spiral out of control, and he was pleased to be able to repay the debt. "I'm on solid ground now, so thank you."

"You sure?"

"Positive."

And when Jake seemed satisfied, Eli said, "Now. Jewel needs a ring."

For such a small shop, there was a wide selection of styles; some too elaborate for Jewel's liking, and some just right. Picking up one of the latter, she tried it on and looked at the beauty and simplicity of the gold band on her finger. "This one."

"Sure you don't want something more showy?"

"I'm sure. It's simple and plain, like me."

Eli didn't think her simple or plain at all. To him she was as fine as the rarest stone, but he knew what she meant, so he didn't argue with her choice.

Adler went to write up the sale, and when Jewel began to remove the ring, Eli gently stopped her with his hand on hers. "You can keep it on if you like."

"You sure. I thought I should wait until tomorrow."

"If you want to wear it now, be my guest. It is yours."

She held out her hand to survey the ring on her finger, and the smile on her face made his heart skip a beat. "Thanks, Eli."

Raising herself up on her toes, she gave him a soft kiss on the cheek. "It's beautiful."

He thought she was, too.

After waving goodbye to Jake Adler, they walked back outside. Jewel, feeling as if she were glowing, asked, "Now where to? Home?"

"Nope. Not yet. We have to get you something to wear besides your brothers' hand-me-down underwear."

"Eli!" she whispered, scandalized that someone walking nearby may have overheard him.

"Don't Eli me. You're a woman, Jewel."

Keeping her voice low, she defended herself. "Why should I waste a perfectly good undershirt? It isn't right to throw them out just because they're too small for the boys."

He shook his head and chuckled. "You have a husband now, Mrs. Grayson, and when he undresses you he doesn't want to be reminded of your brothers."

The next shop was a short drive away. The storefront was whitewashed and the curly blue lettering on the sign read: Fine Women's Clothing. Jewel didn't want to know how he knew about this place.

A bell over the door tinkled daintily to announce their entrance. Inside was a tasteful display of women's day wear, shoes, and gowns. A tall well-dressed woman appeared from the rear of the store and her beautiful golden face lit up like Adler's had at the sight of Eli. "Eli Grayson, what are you doing here? I haven't seen you in a dog's age?"

"How are you, Sally?"

"I'm well." She seemed to notice Jewel for

the first time. "And who is this gorgeous young woman?"

"Sally Lyle. My wife, Jewel Grayson."

She blinked. "Your wife?"

Jewel saw dismay flash across the woman's eyes, but it vanished quickly and was hidden behind her smile. "I'm pleased to meet you, Jewel."

"Same here."

Sally turned back to Eli. "What can I help you with today, Eli, or did you just stop by to introduce Jewel?"

"Jewel needs a trousseau."

"Really?" she asked with genuine interest. "Then let's see what we can do. Eli, you go do something somewhere else and come back in an hour."

"What?"

"Leave. This is women's work."

"But—" He looked to Jewel who was a bit caught off guard herself.

Sally waved. "Goodbye. She's in good hands, I promise."

He stood for a moment as if torn, then finally acquiesced. "Okay." He reached into his inner pocket and extracted some of the bills he'd withdrawn from the Grove bank that morning and handed them to Jewel. He saw her eyes widen at the large sum, so he cautioned with amusement, "No frugality allowed. Treat yourself."

Her stunned eyes raised to meet his.

"I'll be back later." With a smile on his face he exited with a tinkling from the bell.

Silence settled over the shop and Sally said, "I'll bet Rona blew her bustle when she found out about the marriage."

Jewel looked up from the startling amount of money in her hand and, upon seeing Sally's grin, decided she was going to like Sally Lyle after all.

She followed Sally into one of the back rooms where the torso mannequins were outfitted in items obviously designed to catch a man's interest. Gauzy, lacy camisoles, some so thin they ruffled when the awed Jewel walked by, were posed next to daring, nearly transparent nightgowns held together by tiny ribbons. Some of the gowns were long and flowing, others only waist high. Everything in sight was far finer than the plain cotton items folded neatly in her wardrobe drawers back home.

"See anything you like?" Sally asked.

Jewel glanced around at the sensual confections. She realized she was in over her head and wished she had Maddie or Viveca with her to help with selecting. "I'm not sure. To be honest, I don't wear this sort of thing."

"It's never too late to start. Will you let me guide you?"

Jewel studied the kind angular face. "Sure."

With Sally's help, Jewel soon had a small trove of gossamer items. Sally seemed to know what would fit best and what to overlook. Most of the selections left Jewel embarrassed at the thought of Eli seeing her in them, but she swallowed her discomfort and let Sally continue the choosing.

Sally held up an ankle-length, long-sleeved gown made of black lace that Jewel couldn't help but gawk at. It was made of silk, and there were no closures or fasteners. It was designed to hang loosely on the shoulders and the scalloped edged halves would gently billow with each step. Sally said, "If I may be so bold, your husband will adore this."

Jewel fingered the expensive fabric. "You think so?" She thought it was as beautiful as it was sensual.

"I do."

Jewel turned her attention from the gown for a moment. "May I ask you a question?"

Sally nodded and replied, "Yes, Eli and I were lovers. It was years ago and it didn't last very long."

A bit floored that Sally had read her mind, Jewel asked. "How'd you know I—?"

"I saw you watching my reaction when he introduced you as his wife. My mask slipped, didn't it?"

"Yes it did."

"It was quite a shock."

"Did you break it off or did he?" Jewel knew it was a nosy and personal question, but being Eli's wife, she claimed the right to be nosy and personal. Sally didn't have to answer if she didn't want to.

"I broke things off. I have a fairly high opinion of myself," she admitted proudly, "and I don't like to share."

Jewel responded with a quiet, "Good for you."

Sally's eyes were sad but still sparkled with light. "I'm betting you aren't the sharing type, either."

"No."

"I knew that the moment I looked into your eyes. And good for you, too."

"Thanks."

Sally folded the gown and laid it on the counter with the other choices Jewel had made and continued the conversation. "I was selfish enough and, yes, arrogant enough to believe I should have been enough for him, but he was of a different mind." She paused for a moment and stared off unseeingly as if remembering the past. The silence lengthened until she said, "He's a good man, though. Funny, attentive, generous. Not many women would have the fortitude to ask the questions you have."

"Not many women would have the graciousness to answer." Jewel stuck out her hand, "Pax?"

Sally nodded, her smile soft. She clasped Jewel's hand in response. "Pax."

Jewel never thought she'd make peace with one of Eli's old mistresses, but she had with Sally, and now, on the way home, packages filling up the boot in the buggy, she thought about the day. First a wedding ring and now a wealth of gowns that she might be too modest to wear. She'd made a conscious decision not to relay the conversation she'd had with Sally out of respect for Sally's kindness and for the sadness Jewel sensed she carried. Eli didn't need to know.

She looked his way, taking in his sure hands holding the reins. Sally had described him as funny, attentive, and generous. Jewel could only agree. "Thank your for the purchases, but did you rob a bank?"

The smoke-black eyes held hers. "I wondered when you'd bring that up."

"It's not every day somebody fills my hands with so much money."

He told her about the visit from his mother and the whys and reasons surrounding his newfound wealth. "You're married to a fairly wealthy man."

"Better than a fairly poor man, I suppose."

"Having been a fairly poor man as recently as yesterday, I can only agree."

Smiles met and they went back to enjoying the drive.

Jewel kept thinking about Sally and wondered if after the divorce the memory of Eli would haunt her the way it seemed to haunt the other woman. Three days ago, had someone asked Jewel if she'd ever pine for Eli, she would have laughed in his or her face. Now she wasn't sure. Being with him was enjoyable. He kept her on her toes with both his banter and potent kisses and she would be the first to admit that she now cared for him in a way that she hadn't when she'd been just plain old Jewel Crowley. Her fourteen-year-old self aside, what seemed to be blossoming inside now were the feelings of a grown woman for a man, and that was a bit unsettling, only because she didn't want to give him her heart and maybe end up second-guessing her decision to go through with the divorce. However, she was honest enough to admit that a portion of her heart was already his. There wasn't a woman born who could resist Eli's charms—but she kept seeing Sally staring off into the distance. Jewel didn't want to be that woman so she planned to keep the rest of her heart hidden away.

"How did you and Sally get along?" he asked.

"Fine. She has some beautiful things and I treated myself, just as you suggested."

"She's an outstanding lady. She's also a former mistress." He looked her way. "You need to know that."

"Oh."

"She called it off when I wouldn't agree to see her exclusively. I was real stupid back then."

Jewel's soft chuckle fell between them. "Do tell."

"Yeah. Contrary to popular belief, my swelled head is much smaller now than it was in those days. I'm surprised I didn't topple over myself."

He went silent as if he were remembering, too, then said, "I want you to know about my past so that you can't be hurt by it."

The sweetness of his words was moving. "Forewarned is forearmed?"

"Something like that."

"Thank you, Eli."

"You're welcome."

And as Jewel went back to admiring the country she felt another piece of her heart become his.

# Chapter 10

As Jewel rode to church with Eli Sunday morning, she looked down at the gold band gleaming on her finger and smiled. She had no idea what being married was supposed to feel like, but for some reason she did. Maybe it had to do with the ring or with the fact that she and Eli were getting along so famously. Whatever the reason, she was content being Mrs. Eli Grayson.

"This will be our first Sunday at church as man and wife," he pointed out, interrupting her musing.

"I know. I just hope we aren't assaulted by a slew of impertinent questions. It would be very unchristian of me to have to shoot someone during the reverend's sermon."

He flashed a smile. "Yes it would, so let's hope everyone behaves themselves." Eli was content, too. He was proud to be her husband. The rough patches that had plagued their union initially seemed to have smoothed over. Now they could concentrate on enjoying each other.

The Grayson Grove African Methodist Episcopal Church was packed. Usually such crowds were reserved for the first Sunday of the month, but on this, the second in May, the small whitewashed church with its new steeple was filled to capacity and Jewel assumed they'd all come to see her and Eli.

Seated up front in the Grayson-family pew beside Eli, Abigail, and Adam, she saw the smiles on the faces of people like Maddie, Miss Edna, and Vernon Stevenson. In contrast was the burning disapproval of people like Widow Moss and James Wilson and his family, but she forced herself to ignore them and concentrate on the reverend's sermon.

Before being married, Jewel's seat in church had been on the Crowley pew with her brothers. Now that her status had changed she wasn't sure she liked sitting so close to the pulpit. The reverend, although a fine man, wasn't the best preacher. Known for being long-winded, he sometimes lost his place in the sermon and therefore had to preach longer in order to get back to the message he was originally trying to impart. In the past if her mind began to wander, her former seat in the middle of the church kept her from being overtly noticed, but up here on the Grayson pew she had to pay attention, or at least pretend to because not only could she be seen by the entire congregation, the reverend standing right above her could see her as well. However, that didn't seem to deter her father. He habitually drifted off to sleep just as soon as the reverend began to speak. Gail countered by jabbing him in the side with her elbow, startling him awake as if silently reminding him that if she had to listen to the sermon, so did he.

After the reverend finally wound down, the rest of the service seemed to go quickly, and a short while later, she and Eli and the rest of the congregation were out in the sunshine heading to their buggies and wagons for the drive to the Crowleys and the reception—everyone except the Widow Moss and a few others like the Wilsons, who got into their vehicles and drove off in the opposite direction.

Jewel wasn't sure how the reception would go. It was obvious that some of the attendees had come strictly to be nosy, like Mrs. Rumble, the former Sunday-school teacher, who stopped Jewel on the way to the food tables and asked, "Is it true you and Eli eloped in the middle of the night?"

"Yes ma'am," Jewel lied without batting an eye.

But to Jewel's surprise she had a good time. There were spitted pigs, fried chicken, lemonade, pies, and ice cream among the many food offerings. Children ran here and there playing tag, glad to be outside in the sunshine after being cooped up in church all morning. The men threw horseshoes and talked politics, while the women saw to the food, played croquet, and shared the latest news. During the first hour, Eli never left her side. The two of them went from group to group thanking folks for coming and graciously accepting congratulations on their marriage.

Later, while he went to play a few rounds of horseshoes, she drifted through the celebration, pausing here and there to talk to family friends and neighbors. She spotted Abigail and Anna Red Bird seated under the shade of a big elm and waved to them as she walked by. The salacious gossip that had caused her marriage in the first place seemed to be a thing of the past, now that she was wearing Eli's ring. The change in attitude didn't make her feel any better about the sullying of her name, but because the day was so perfect, she chose not to dwell on it.

She found Maddie dishing up ice cream.

Maddie greeted her appearance with a smile. "Enjoying yourself?"

"I am," Jewel replied as she took a seat on the bench. Maddie stuck the big spoon in a pot holding water and sat down next to her.

"That's a fine ring."

Jewel looked down at it and nodded. "It is, isn't it. Eli and I went to Niles yesterday to buy it."

"Still enjoying your lemonade?"

"I am—more than I ever thought I would."

"Then I assume you're going to be moving to his place sometime soon?"

Jewel quieted. The thought had crossed her mind. "I was going to wait until the house was built, but I don't really have to, do I?"

"No, and it will make the marriage look more real, if you know what I mean."

"I do." The idea of living with Eli made her a bit breathless even as it set off an uncertainty she wasn't sure she could name.

A few children ran over to Maddie and asked for ice cream. While Maddie set about the task, a still-pondering Jewel rose to her feet, gave Maddie a smile, and moved on.

The wooden swings her father had built for her and her brothers during their childhood had been taken out of the barn and hung from sturdy branches. The children on them were happily swinging away while a line of their peers anxiously awaited their turns. She stood there for a moment remembering how much fun swinging had been when she was their age, then saw Creighton Wilson watching her from a short distance away. He nodded emotionlessly. Unsure about whether to approach him, she settled for nodding in return, then went to seek out Eli.

He was at the horseshoe pit watching her father go against one of the Patterson twins, and when she walked up he smiled. "Hello, Mrs. Grayson. Would you like to accompany me to the punch table?"

Her brother Noah called out. "Getting the pants beat off of you tends to make a man real thirsty."

The men laughed and Eli smiled.

He and Jewel began to walk away and once they were out of earshot, he said, "Missed you."

Jewel's heart pounded just as it did each time

he told her that, and she didn't know how to make it stop or whether she even wanted it to. "You'll always know where I am."

He responded with a look so intense it seemed to reach into her soul. "As will you."

Jewel hooked her arm into his and let him escort her to the table.

Doing duty at the punch table were Miss Edna and Lenore Wilson, daughter of James and sister of Creighton. Jewel and Lenore had been fast friends growing up and had shared a schoolgirl adoration of Eli. However, as they grew older, they drifted apart because Jewel was focused on keeping house for her father and brothers and Lenore was focused on gossip, fripperies, and landing a husband. She'd chased after every eligible bachelor in town including Jewel's brother Noah, only to come away bitter and empty-handed.

"You want punch, I suppose?" Lenore asked tightly.

Miss Edna shot her a look.

Jewel kept her tone light. "Yes, please."

Lenore splashed some of the liquid into two cups and handed them over. "I'd offer congratulations but it's a sin to lie on Sundays. I heard what you did to get him."

Jewel shot back mildly, "Was this before or after Noah told half the town he wouldn't marry you because he had boots more intelligent?"

Eli spit punch.

Miss Edna turned away and smiled.

Lenore's eyes blazed.

Jewel's were sardonic. "Thanks for making the punch, Miss Edna."

"My pleasure."

"Ready, Eli?"

"Oh, yes, ma'am."

As they threaded their way back across the crowded grounds, Jewel told him, "If I hear she's spreading lies, she's going to need new teeth."

An amused Eli put his arm around her waist and gave it a loving squeeze.

The final event of the gathering was the jumping of the broom contest, a tradition made popular in the southern contraband camps during the war. Its origins were murky, but many people were convinced it had either African or Native roots because of the trickster element involved. The contest was to decide who would wear the pants in the family—the husband or the wife. It was all good-natured fun, but neither the bride nor the groom wanted to lose.

The length of wood serving as the broom was held by Jewel's brothers; Paul on one end and Abe on the other. Everyone was crowded around calling out encouragement to the contestant they were supporting—women for Jewel, men for Eli. It being a Sunday, no gambling was allowed, otherwise people would have been challenging each other to put their money where their mouths were.

As everybody in attendance eagerly waited for the game to begin, Adam stepped forward. In his hand he held a coin. He flipped it in the air. "Call it!"

"Heads!" Jewel yelled.

It hit the ground. Heads. Jewel would take the first jump.

Eli bowed graciously. "Ladies first."

Jewel nodded regally and turned her attention to the wood held up by her brothers. It was about three feet off the ground, a height she doubted she would have trouble clearing. Confidence high, she moved back a few steps and took off at a run. Her supporters were yelling and cheering. She cleared the wood and they roared their approval.

"Not bad," Eli told her as she joined him on the starting line again. "Not bad."

He took his turn. He had no trouble jumping the wood either and this time his side cheered.

The bar was raised incrementally higher as both Eli and Jewel continued to clear it. Then it reached four feet.

"You're in trouble," Eli told her as the crowd looked on and laughed.

Jewel didn't deny it. The height of the bar was now above her waist and she was going to need wings to stay in the competition. She gave it a try anyway. Backing up, she raised her skirts to the tops of her half boots and flew toward the goal, but as she reached it she stopped short. It was too high. She couldn't make it. Her supporters groaned. She gave a mock pout and stomped back to the starting line where a smiling Eli waited.

"It's those short legs of yours," he teased. "They're pretty legs, but they're short."

"Long enough to kick you to Kalamazoo. Take your turn."

Chuckling at the light in her eyes, he eyed the bar, took a short run and would have cleared it if Abe and Paul hadn't suddenly raised it over their heads, which brought him to an abrupt halt.

"Foul!" Eli called over the erupting laughter of the crowd.

Clapping her hands happily, an ecstatic Jewel ran up and gave each of her brothers a big kiss on the cheek while Eli threw up his hands. "I want an *apisaci*!" he demanded with mock outrage.

*Apisacis* enforced the rules during a lacrosse match, but since this was not lacrosse, there was no one on hand to judge his complaint.

Adam stepped up and declared, "It's a draw. No one wears the pants in this family!"

People fell over laughing.

"Adam!" Gail yelled scandalized.

Jewel shook her head at her father's antics. A happy Eli put an arm around her waist and squeezed her tight and said for her ears only, "I say we have a rematch. Kisses this time."

"Think you can win that one?"

"Are your brothers cheats?"

She grinned.

The reception was now officially over. The pleased crowd began to gather their families and belongings for the ride home. Before leaving, however, they all made a point of telling Eli and Jewel how much fun they'd had and wishing them well in their marriage—all except for Lenore

Wilson, who'd left before the broom jumping began.

After everyone's departure the Crowleys and Graysons cleared the fields of the tables, chairs, and other leftover items. Once the grounds were pristine again, they toasted the clean-up effort and the marriage with chilled tumblers of the last of the lemonade.

They then took seats on the wide Crowley porch.

Eli looked to his cheating brothers-in-law and promised, "I will get you two."

Chuckles followed, and Noah said, "I wish you could have seen the surprise on your face."

"Bunch of cheaters," Eli grumbled with amusement. "And to think I'm related to you all."

Jewel grinned over her drink. "You could do worse."

Adam cracked, "And so could you, so go up and pack some clothes. You're going home with your husband."

Jewel spit lemonade.

Smiling, Abigail handed her a napkin.

Eli waited and watched, eager to see how this would play out.

She met his eyes but he kept his face expressionless.

Jewel turned to her father and, upon seeing his arm-folded stance, said with mock humility, "Yes, Pa."

Keeping her smile hidden, she went into the house.

After she left, Adam said, "That was easy."

Eli drawled, "Maybe for you. I'm the one taking her home."

That brought on a few smiles and nods of agreement, but everyone knew this was for the best.

Jewel did, too. Upstairs in her room, she had no problem with her father's edict because she'd already made up her mind. True, she hadn't intended to be moving so soon, but going to live with Eli wasn't anything she was averse to. In fact parts of herself were giddy at the prospect, but she was also nervous and a tad uncertain. Setting all that aside for now, she finished her packing and went outside to join the others.

The only person on the porch was Eli. "Where's everybody?"

"They thought you might come back with your bird gun, so they scattered."

She laughed. "No bird gun. Just a valise. I'll retrieve the rest of my belongings later."

"You sure you want to do this."

She gave him a nod. "Yes."

"Would you have agreed if I'd asked you earlier today."

"Yes."

He was surprised. "Really?"

"Maddie and I talked about it, and I'm ready."

"Good," he voiced softly while trailing a finger down her satiny cheek. "Be warned, though, the place is pretty cluttered. I'd have cleaned up had I known I'd be bringing my wife home."

"I live with five brothers remember. I won't be shocked."

"Can you put that in writing?" he asked, thoroughly captivated.

"Whatever you like."

"I'd like to go home with my wife."

"Then lead the way."

She walked with him to the buggy. He helped her in then stowed her valise. As they drove away, Jewel looked back at the sprawling house she'd lived in her entire life and saw her father watching the departure from the porch. As her eyes met his, he gave her a nod of satisfaction, and her heart was so full, tears stung her eyes.

Eli's small cabin was made of brick and wood. Surrounded on all sides by large trees, it was plain and unadorned. He pulled back on the reins to stop the horse. "Well, we're here. You promised not to be shocked."

"Unless you're hiding dead animals inside, I'll be fine."

He came around to help her down and Jewel fought off a rising case of nerves. She didn't know anything about taking on a husband, a panicked voice inside wailed, but calming herself, she waited for him to grab her valise, then followed him to the door.

The interior made her stare around in awe. Papers were everywhere. Her surprised eyes met his and he shrugged. "Told you."

She took a hesitant walk deeper into the room.

Newspapers were stacked on every flat surface. There were piles set against the walls, and piles beside the chairs; or at least she assumed they were chairs. It was hard to tell with everything covered. Portions of the floor were carpeted with writing tablets while more mounds of newspapers lined the surface of the brick mantel. "Nice place you have here, Eli."

He grinned ruefully. "I knew you'd like it."

"When can I start cleaning?"

He draped his arms around her waist and gazed down at her small face. "I didn't bring you here to clean."

The intensity in his eyes and the deep tones of his voice caused her heart to pound. "Are you sure? I could be done by Christmas," she tossed back as his nearness flooded her senses.

"I have something more wifely for you to do."

"What's more wifely than cleaning?"

"This . . ."

The slow fervent kiss he placed against her lips singed her from the soles of her feet to the top of her head. It was so sweet she didn't remember moving closer, but found herself flush against him, aroused by every hard inch of his tall, lean-muscled frame. The kiss deepened and he ran a possessive hand up to the back of her neck to bring her even closer to his masterful mouth. She was drowning, weightless, and shimmered as his kisses moved to her ear. "I want to make love to you, Jewel. . . ."

Overcome by all that he was and the riot of sensations he was making her feel, she trembled in response to the husked-out request.

"Let me teach you, show you . . . pleasure you," he breathed in a voice that made her core ripple and come alive.

Under the play of his hand, her nipple strained and hardened, and when he lowered his head and bit her gently through the thin cotton of her white blouse, she gasped with pleasure. He treated its twin to the same wanton salute until her legs went weak.

Eli thought this was far better than cleaning; she was gorgeous, vibrant, and beautifully formed. The soft weight of her breasts drew him into the web of desire he felt caught by, and he wanted her bared so he could love her as ardently as she deserved. Alternating between capturing her passion-parted lips and undoing the buttons of her blouse, his blood pounded with need. Beneath the blouse she was wearing a thin lace-edged camisole that moved seductively over the buds under the impetus of his warm hand. He dragged it down while savoring the scent of roses on her skin, then took the nubbin into his mouth.

Her answering moan of pleasure made his manhood throb and harden. He loved her slowly, fully, enjoying her as if she were his own personal candy until their ragged breaths filled the silence.

Jewel didn't know which was more masterful, his mouth or his hot hands. In reality it didn't matter. She just wanted it to continue.

He didn't disappoint. While he continued to make her nipples plead, the hand moving over her skirt-covered hips tempted her with its lazy wanderings then slid scandalously between her thighs. The *little death* crackled through her like summer lightning and the echoing thunder shook her entire being.

A smiling Eli continued to ply that warm damp place, watching the pleasure play across her face. He wanted to take her there and then, but not on a carpet of newspapers, so, before she came back to herself, he hoisted her gently into his arms and walked them into his bedroom.

Jewel knew she was being carried but didn't care where. Her body was pulsating from her orgasm and the only solid things in her hazy world were his strong arms. Moments later she felt the bed beneath her and she slowly opened her eyes. He was above her, and the passion in his gaze touched her like a hand. He traced a finger over her kiss-swollen lips.

"I know this is your first time, so we'll go slow. Promise."

There was a virgin's nervousness hovering beneath her desire, but Jewel wanted whatever came next, so she sat up and after raising herself on her knees kissed him with a fervent invitation that made him groan and pull her closer. "Lord, woman," he murmured, not sure how he was going to keep himself from taking her as vigorously as his manhood longed to. Kissing her back down onto the bed while his hands kept her nipples tight and ready, he explored her slowly and possessively. He thought her small form perfectly made, and his hands moved over the satin skin reverently.

She whispered, "What should I do?"

He leaned over and touched his lips to hers. "Nothing, this first time will be all for you."

And it was. He removed her blouse and, while she held his eyes shyly, her skirt and slips. Lying next to him wearing nothing but her camisole, drawers, and dark cotton stockings, she felt the nervousness return, but as if sensing her hesitation, he ran his hand gently up and down her torso and asked softly, "Do you know how beautiful you are, Mrs. Grayson?"

Jewel couldn't respond because she was too busy spiraling from the caresses touching her everywhere, especially the ones wantonly teasing the damp vent between her thighs. Touches that had her breathing harshly and infected her hips with a rhythm that coaxed her to part her legs even more.

She was so lush and open, Eli had to force himself not to lean down and pay her the ultimate lover's tribute. Deciding to forgo that gifting for another time, he drew back, and while she lay on his bed with her eyes closed, he removed his shirt and undid the placket on his trousers. He was bursting with need and all he wanted was to slide into her dampness and let the little death carry him away. As hard as he was, he knew it wouldn't take long, but he wanted her to be ready.

So he began again and worked his way sensually down her body from her lips to her hips. Her soft breaths and the untutored caresses she gave him in response drove him to the edge. She let him remove her drawers and as she lay there watching him he moved his palm over the warm soft hair crowning her thighs. "This may hurt sweetheart, but only this once."

And it did at first, so much so that the pain showed in her face. A sympathetic Eli would rather cut off his arm than cause her injury so he touched her mouth softly. "It won't last long," he promised while he throbbed in the tight virgin channel and forced himself to remain still.

Jewel didn't want to do this anymore. She hurt, and having him inside of her body felt foreign, strange, but as he began to move back and forth slowly and invitingly, the pain slid away and she could feel the desire return. It bloomed deep within and rose with each new stroke. Soon she was matching his rhythm and all the hurt was forgotten.

When Eli felt her body open to receive him, he knew she was no longer in pain, and that pleased him immensely. He kept his pace slow, however, even though her answering responses were bewitchingly sensual. Reaching out, he grabbed a pillow and placed it under her hips.

The added height increased the pleasure.

"Like that?" he asked.

"Oh, yes."

Further words were eschewed; their joined

bodies communicated in the language of passion, and Jewel thought she might lose her mind. Sensations became her world, and when he reached down and teased the tiny bit of flesh from which all pleasure emanated she danced the dance of the little death once again. She came, arching, filling the room with the cry of his name.

That did it for Eli, the orgasm roared over him like wildfire and he stroked her with a controlled ferocity that left him shuddering.

Jewel came back to herself with him lying beside her atop the disheveled bedspread. She felt limp as pudding. Turning her head she met his eyes, then smiled. He responded in kind. Noting the sunlight outside from the cabin's small window, she said, "I thought married people were supposed to have relations at night."

"At night, at dawn, in the middle of the afternoon."

"You're something."

"So are you. Are you sore?"

She nodded. "Yes, a little bit."

"Then we'll wait for your second time."

"I'd no idea it would be so moving."

"It gets better."

At her surprised face, he laughed softly and brushed a finger over her cheek. "Just you wait."

On the heels of his response the pictures in Maddie's Kama Sutra rose to mind and Jewel wondered if all of the positions she'd seen could really be done. A desire to find out claimed her, but she put the shameless thoughts away.

"Penny for your thoughts," he inquired quietly.

"Just thinking about Maddie's pictures."

The delight in his eyes was plain to see. "And what about them?" His finger tempted her nipple with a slow circling. As the bud tightened he leaned down and took it softly into his mouth.

Jewel groaned sweetly. "I can't think if you do that."

Desire rising again, Eli pleasured the chocolate tip until she arched sensually. He wanted her again, now, but didn't want to make her more sore, so he raised his head and said into her eyes. "Good, because thinking is not allowed in our bed."

His words thrilled her and so did the slow deliberate pleasure that he began to conquer her with, and this time she orgasmed while brazenly riding two of his well-placed fingers.

Later after being coaxed into yet another orgasm she finally sat up and looked around the small bedroom for the first time. To her amazement it was as cluttered as the front room, but with books. "You have enough books in here to start a lending library."

Like the newspapers, the books were everywhere: piled on chairs, on the floor, on the dresser, and atop his dusty wardrobe. She turned to him questioningly and again he shrugged. "I enjoy reading."

"Are you sure you didn't marry me just to get someone to clean this place?"

He gave her a kiss. "Possibly."

As his kisses dazzled her, she forgot all about the clutter. When it ended, she fell back onto the bed. "Lord, you're good at that Eli Grayson."

He chuckled. "Why, thank you." He took hold of her hand and gently pulled her up. "Come, let's get washed up. I'm starving."

Having been raised in her father's well-appointed home, she was a bit taken aback by his outdoor facilities. The shower or what passed for a shower was little more than an enclosed wooden stall with a large cooper's barrel on a platform above the bather's head. When you wanted water, a tug on the rope attached to the barrel's bottom opened a small plug that let the water drain down. If you didn't wash and rinse quickly, the barrel would empty before you were done.

A skeptical Jewel was scrutinizing the series of pulleys used to raise the barrel from the ground. "Has the barrel ever fallen on your head?"

"No, Jewel."

"Not trying to offend you, Eli, but are you sure?"

"I've been here eight years, Jewel, and it's never fallen."

"Could probably kill a person if it did."

"No doubt, but it's safe. I promise you."

She looked around at the space. "Do you heat the water somewhere?"

"Not usually."

She stared. "So what do you do in the wintertime?"

"Wash inside."

"Ah."

"And don't worry. There will be a true washroom in the new house, just like you had at home."

"Thanks goodness."

He grinned. "Do you want me to go first?"

She shook her head, saying, "I should be fine, and quick," she added giving the barrel another skeptical glance. "Let me go back inside and get some clothing."

As she hurried away, Eli looked up at his shower and couldn't imagine what she found wrong with it. Personally, he thought the rigged-up contraption quite clever, and as a bachelor it suited him just fine.

Jewel had to admit the shower did work; of course she'd had to wash and rinse herself at lightning speed so that she wouldn't run out of water, but as he'd predicted the big barrel did not fall on her head.

Later, after they were both clean and in fresh clothing, they sat on a blanket underneath the spread of trees and ate sandwiches and pieces of the pie left over from the reception. Because it was early May, the blood-thirsty mosquitoes weren't about yet, which allowed them to enjoy the evening in peace.

"Do you mind if I start cleaning the place tomorrow?"

Smiling at her persistence, he said into her eyes, "Do I have a choice?"

She shrugged. "It's your home."

"Our home."

"Then I'll start cleaning *our* home tomorrow."

"Thank you for giving me a choice."

"You're welcome." Her tone turned serious. "I know how much you must value your things, so I promise not to throw anything away without your approval, but we have to be able to come in the door, Eli."

He chuckled softly. "I understand."

"Then first thing tomorrow."

"Okay."

After the short meal, he took her hand and pulled her to her feet. "How about we ride over to the bluff and watch the moon rise."

"Is this more of Jewel needs to have more fun?"

"No, this is Jewel needs more of her husband's kisses."

And to prove his point he eased her closer, touched his lips to hers, and kissed her until her knees turned into applesauce. "Am I right?" he whispered.

"Bull's-eye," she managed to reply.

"I'll get the buggy."

The drive was a short one. When he halted the buggy in the clearing, they saw that just as Adam had promised, some of the surrounding trees had already been felled. Jewel stepped out of the buggy and walked with him to the lip of the bluff that towered over the blue waters of the river below. Standing beside him while they took in the beautiful scene, she could feel her connection to the land slowly rising. At the moment, the tract was as wild and as undeveloped as the Good Lord made it, but before the summer ended, a home would fill the clearing—her home, Eli's home. The thought gave her goose bumps. Home had always been her father and brothers and at its heart the memory of her mother. Now, in a few months time, she'd be in a place where new memories would take root and grow, and she found herself looking forward to it with anxious anticipation. Once again, she thought about the unexpected turns in life. Never in her dreams had she thought hers would take this road. Never.

He spread the blanket out and leaned back against a tall maple. "Come sit," he invited softly.

Jewel settled herself on his lap and let him wrap his arms around her gently. "I never watched the moon rise like this before," she confessed.

He kissed her hair. "I should hope not." Eli couldn't believe the contentment he felt. Truth be told, he was enjoying this husband business more and more. "If I could give you three wishes, what would they be."

"To have an unlimited number of wishes."

He jostled her. "Smarty pants. Be serious."

"I am. An unlimited number of wishes."

"You are no fun, Mrs. Grayson."

"That isn't what you said in your bedroom earlier today."

"Sassy woman."

Smiling, she asked, "So, what would your three wishes be?"

"Not sure." He knew that one would be that they be able sit this way for eternity, but he kept that to himself.

She raised up. "Then why'd you ask me?"

"Wanted to see what you would say."

She resumed her position. "I'll let you know when I figure it out."

"Fair enough. I'll do the same."

The moon rose in all its glory and Eli found his wife just as glorious. "Will you sit with me like this after the house is built?"

"As long as the house comes with a real washroom and shower."

He laughed. "You don't have a romantic bone anywhere in that sweet little body, do you?"

"I beg your pardon." She raised up and, imitating the way he always touched her, used a finger to slowly trace his lips. Upon gaining his full attention she kissed him with such warm invitation he drew her closer to receive all she had to offer.

One thing led to another and she wound up with her blouse undone, her camisole rucked down, her skirt rucked up and his hands and mouth everywhere.

He husked out, "The first night we move into the house—you, me, on the porch in the moonlight."

She drew away. "The porch?"

He slid a tantalizing finger between her thighs. "The porch, the buggy, the kitchen table."

Jewel's breath stacked up in her throat as that same finger impaled her and her body arched for more. "Oh, lord, Eli."

"What Mrs. Grayson?" he asked heatedly. "Having fun?"

His wicked ministrations made her part her legs scandalously. "Yes." The night breeze played over her nipples, which were now hard and damp from his loving. No matter where her mind went, there was pleasure. Thought fled, though, as the magic increased and she began to croon and arch and moan. Then little death rose, rocking her, claiming her and when it broke, she turned her face into his chest to keep from screaming loud enough to be heard across the Grove.

Eli's second wish was to watch her in the throes of orgasm until death do they part. The sight of her riding out her pleasure so uninhibitedly made him as hard as the tree trunk his back was braced against, but he'd promised himself not to take her again until tomorrow and he'd keep the vow, even though his maleness hungered for relief.

In the silent aftermath, Jewel was as boneless as a rag doll. No man had the right to be so masterful, but because Eli was, the woman she'd become smiled contentedly.

# Chapter 11

The chirps of birds greeting the dawn roused Jewel from her sleep. Because of her barely awake state, her surroundings were at first unfamiliar, but Eli's softly snoring in the bed beside her put everything into focus. What a day they'd had. Her body was stiff and tender from all the loving, and the memory of the scandalous interlude they'd shared in the moonlight made her cheeks burn. She wondered if all married couples had such a good time, but it was not a question she'd get an answer to, so she set it aside. More than anything she wanted to burrow back under the lightweight bedding and cuddle against Eli and return to sleep, but it was Monday morning, and morning meant chores. Easing herself quietly out of bed, she tiptoed over to her valise and picked it up. Looking over at her husband with regret, she slipped from the room and dressed in the hallway. She'd get a proper shower when she got home, but for now, she needed to hurry if she wanted to get to the house and cook breakfast for the boys before they headed to work.

A little after dawn, Eli slowly awakened. Smiling sleepily at the memory of Jewel falling asleep in his arms, he reached out to ease her warm little body closer but she wasn't there. Thinking she was probably up tackling the clutter, he drifted back into sleep. Thirty minutes later he awakened again and this time sat up and dragged himself out of bed. He'd never been an early riser, but to make love to his wife, he'd get up at dawn.

But she wasn't there—not in the front room, not in the shower, not anywhere in the house or on the grounds. He pondered that for a moment wondering if yesterday had been a dream, but his remembrances of watching her taking her pleasure in the moonlight made him as hard now as he'd been last night; it had to have been real. "So where the hell is she?" he asked out loud.

It came to him then where she might be. Tight-lipped he went to wash up and get dressed.

She was where he knew she'd be, in the kitchen of her brothers' home. Apparently they'd already left for the day because when he walked into the house the place was otherwise empty.

At his entrance, she looked up from the dishes she was washing and called merrily, "Mornin', Eli. Sleep well?"

"I did until I woke up and found my wife gone."

Jewel studied his features in an attempt to gauge his mood. "I came over to cook breakfast."

"So I see."

"Is there a problem?"

"Maybe."

Because she had no idea what this was about she raised her chin. "And it is?"

Paul walked in. "The problem is, you don't live here anymore little sister."

She turned. "What are you talking about?"

"Jewel, you're Eli's wife now. You should be cooking breakfast for him."

"I didn't notice you complaining about me being here when you were helping yourself to fresh biscuits earlier, and besides, he doesn't have a stove."

Paul hid his smile, "That isn't the point."

She glanced over at Eli and found him watching her with amusement. "How am I supposed to cook you breakfast when you have nothing to cook on?"

"As your brother said, Mrs. Grayson, that isn't the point." Eli admitted to being somewhat jealous of the bond she had with her brothers. He'd wanted her to wake up in his arms, not eschew him in favor of frying up a bunch of eggs. Eyes still trained on his beautiful wife, he said to his brother-in-law. "Do me a favor and hire a housekeeper."

"Already looking into one."

"Thank you."

Jewel was trying to decide if she was mad or not. She'd cooked breakfast there every morning for at least a decade. How was she supposed to know that being married changed things.

Paul grabbed one of the last aforementioned biscuits from the plate on the stove. "Now that that's settled, I'll leave you two alone. We'll be over at the bluff building your house if you need us."

"Thanks, Paul," Eli said.

"My pleasure. Bye, Jewel."

She gave him an exasperated look that he of course ignored, then he and his half-eaten biscuit left the house.

In the silence that filled the kitchen after his departure Jewel didn't know what to say. For the moment, she concentrated on putting the remaining washed and dried dishes back into the cabinets. "If you want an apology there won't be one. I didn't do anything wrong."

A grin played around the corners of his mouth. "No, you didn't, and I'll admit to not being happy that you chose bacon and eggs over me."

She looked his way and confessed truthfully, "I wanted to remain in bed with you, Eli, but this is what I do every morning—cook breakfast."

He walked over to where she stood and draped his arms around her waist. "I know, sweetheart. I'm just a man with a bruised ego."

"That wasn't my intent."

"I know that, too."

He kissed her softly, "Good morning, Mrs. Grayson."

Jewel kissed him back just as softly, and when the contact broke, she wrapped her arms around him tightly and laid her head on his chest. "Apparently there are a lot of things I don't know about being Mrs. Grayson."

He kissed her hair. "That's okay, because there are a lot of things I don't know about being a husband."

"You did pretty good last night," and heard the rumble of amusement against her ear.

"You think so?"

"Oh, yes."

"Good."

He leaned back and looked into the face of the woman he wanted to awaken with for the rest of his days. "Your brothers are lucky to have someone as loyal as you looking after them."

"I agree."

"Modest, too, I see."

She shrugged. "Can't argue with the truth."

"Are you done here?" he asked, indicating her kitchen duties.

She nodded.

"Then let's go home."

"But what about the laundry and supper and my garden?"

Eli chuckled in the face of her dedication. "Jewel, didn't your brother say he was looking into a housekeeper?"

"Yes, but he didn't say he'd hired one."

"Your brothers are big boys. I'm sure they can take care of themselves until then."

"And in the meantime, we eat where?"

He paused. "Well?"

She waited.

He replied finally, "There's mother's, and then there's Miss Edna's and the Quilt Ladies'."

She stared confused. "Is that where you eat your meals?"

He nodded. "They feed me like the stray that I am."

Grinning, she looked up at her oh-so-charming husband. "I am not a stray and since I am perfectly capable of providing meals for the both of us, how about we eat here until the house is built? Better yet, you're a wealthy man. Let's buy a stove."

Eli smiled. "A stove."

"Yes, a stove. You know, you cook on it."

He mockingly warned, "Keep sassin' me and you'll find yourself with your denims down and screaming my name on top of that table over there."

She looked so surprised, he barked a laugh, then told her, "Better yet, let's go to Niles and buy a table. That way you can scream as loud as you like."

Her nipples tightened as if they couldn't wait for his kisses. "You are so outrageous!"

"Yep. Do you want to go to Niles or not?"

She couldn't suppress her laughter. "No."

"No?" he asked as he ran a slow finger down the vee of skin framed by the open collar of her shirt. Her pulse rippled in response. He pressed his lips to the spot just long enough to make her feel as if she were drowning, then backed away, saying, "I promise it will be worth the trip."

The blaze in his eyes and the soft heat in his voice were her downfall. "Let me get my handbag."

For the next week, Jewel spent the daylight hours cleaning up Eli's cabin, and her nights making love. Finally, the house was clean enough to bring in the table they'd purchased in Niles, and just as he'd promised her, the end result was well worth the trip.

Wearing her widow's weeds, Cecile stood on the platform of the Detroit train depot, trying to pick out her next pigeon. She had no idea if Pinkertons were on her tail, but it had been almost three weeks since she'd left Bethany Briles lying in a pool of her own blood, so she assumed there were.

Now she was out of money, and without the assistance of a benefactor, further flight could become problematic. The depot wasn't very crowded for a weekday. She assumed most were waiting for the afternoon train to Chicago. From beneath the black curtain of her veil, she kept her eyes low as she pondered which of the men standing on the platform might become her next knight. She settled on two likely candidates. Both men were traveling alone, but there was an obvious difference in their social stations. The younger man's cheap clothing and gregarious manner all but shouted small town, while the fashionably dressed older man with well-kept muttonchops appeared to have a fatter wallet.

Having lived by her wits for many years, she'd learned that men both young and old were susceptible to a woman in distress. The older types were more inclined to buy her a train ticket and sometimes provide her a meal as well, but the younger ones often wanted to raise her skirts in exchange. Cecile had no desire to be pawed by a penniless bumpkin, so she stepped out from under the depot's wooden awning and peered down the track, as if looking for the train. Seeing nothing, she edged back into the crowd.

The change in her position placed her close enough to muttonchops to begin her act. Nodding at him politely and receiving a silent nod in response, she opened her handbag and began to look through it. A few seconds later the search began more frantic. Her shrouded face filled with alarm, she knelt and dumped the contents of the handbag out onto the depot floor.

Sensing she had his full attention, she began sifting through the papers and ticket stubs. Quickly getting to her feet, she hastily patted the pockets of her skirt, then dropped her shoulders in a sign of weak resignation.

Right on cue, he asked, "Is there something wrong?"

She knelt and slowly stuffed the contents of her handbag back inside it. "My ticket and coin purse appear to be missing."

The concern on his face almost made her smile beneath the veil. "I know I had them both when I left Philadelphia. What am I going to do?"

He said nothing for a moment, and she could see him visually evaluating her. He asked, "Is there someone you can wire for more funds—a family member perhaps?"

She shook her head. "Unfortunately, no. I am all I have."

"Where are you heading?"

"A small town called Grayson Grove."

His face brightened. "Why, that's where I'm headed as well."

"Really?" Cecile stilled, not sure if he was a good choice now or not. "That's quite a coincidence. Do you reside there?"

"Not at the moment, but I may in the future. May I ask your name, widow?"

"Cecile Green. My husband died a few weeks back. I lived in the Grove many years ago and I thought I'd visit with a few old friends on my way south to evaluate some property my husband owned down there, but now, with no ticket or funds, I may be forced to stay here until I can figure out what I should do."

"Let me assist you. My name is George Washington Hicks. I'd be honored to buy you a new ticket."

She shook her head. "I wouldn't want to impose. You don't know me."

"No, but I do know that it is my duty to help a woman in distress. You are grieving the passing of your husband. It shouldn't be made more difficult by being stranded here with no funds."

Cecile could have kissed him but kept her enthusiasm hidden beneath her persona of the dignified widow. "You are a godsend, Mr. Hicks."

"Come, let's see the agent about a new ticket."

Cecile took his offered arm and let him lead her to the ticket counter.

To Jewel it appeared as if everyone she and Eli knew was helping her father and brothers build the new house. The frame was complete and the walls were going up. The Patterson twins were hammering nails; Reverend Anderson and some of the men from the church were using mules and draft horses to remove the stumps of the felled trees; even Miss Edna and Maddie were on hand, adding to the hive of people swarming over the site like ants.

Jewel was sanding the porch rocker she'd been building for the past few days. It wasn't a fancy creation; flat slats mostly, but she'd cut the wood and nailed the pieces together herself and she was proud of it, even if it rocked a bit crookedly.

Abigail, who'd been supervising the lunch wagon, sauntered over with the aid of her beautiful cane. "How's the rocker coming, dear?"

Jewel pushed the chair back and forth. "Almost ready to stain. One of the rocker bases is still uneven, but I think I can fix it."

"It's very lovely," Abigail offered, eyeing the unvarnished wood with admiration. "Not many women have such skill, Jewel."

"When you grow up in a house with lumber

beasts and carpenters, you don't exactly learn dressmaking." She rocked the chair again, then knelt down to determine which of the two curved pieces on the bottom was the problem.

"Have you seen Eli?" Gail asked looking around at all the people.

"He and Pa took some logs to the mill. They should be on their way back by now."

"Good. Vernon got a message from Calvin Center. Mr. Hicks is at the depot in Niles."

Jewel looked up. "Is Vernon going to go fetch him."

Gail nodded. "I just wanted Eli to know."

"I'll tell him."

"Thank you. Now that lunch is done, I'm going to drive over and check on Anna Red Bird. She hasn't been feeling well. I'll be back in a little while. Let your father know, if you would."

"I will and you tell Anna I send my love and hope she feels better."

"I will."

Jewel watched Gail's departure, then went back to inspecting the rocking chair.

Eli and her Pa returned an hour later hauling lengths of newly milled oak in the back of a flatbed work wagon. The oak was scheduled to be laid over the rough-hewn subfloor that was temporarily serving as the home's main floor. She hoped Mr. Wilson hadn't given them trouble and she was glad they'd made it back safe and sound.

Remembering Gail's messages, she walked

over to relay them while a small group of the volunteers helped unload the boards from the wagon.

Eli saw his saucy little wife coming his way, handed his board off to one of the others, and walked out to meet her. "Hello, Mrs. Grayson."

"Hello to you, too. How'd it go at the mill? Mr. Wilson give you any problems?"

"Yes. Tried to make us come back tomorrow, said the place was too busy, but when I politely reminded him of the name on the front of the building and that that same name signed the bank drafts that paid him, he suddenly found an opening in the schedule."

"Nice man."

"Your father thinks so as well. Anything happen while we were away?"

"Just work. Your mother's gone to visit Anna Red Bird, and Vernon went to the Niles depot to pick up your Mr. Hicks. Guess he's back."

Eli was elated. "Now I can see to the *Gazette*."

"I knew you'd be pleased."

He pulled a pocket watch out of his old shirt and consulted the time. "If Hicks came in on the afternoon train, they should be here in an hour or so." He began to mentally list all the things he needed to do first. Now that the additional space had been added to the *Gazette*'s office, there'd be room for the new printing presses he hoped G.W. would help him invest in. Having his own money to put into the paper now made all the difference in the world because he could expand his dreams in ways he hadn't been able to do before.

"Eli?"

He came back to the present. He'd been so deep in thought he'd forgotten she was there. "Did you say something?"

Her eyes filled with humor. "Yes. Don't you hear Pa yelling?"

"What?" A confused Eli stared, then heard, "Grayson! This house isn't going to build itself! Jewel! Stop distracting my workers!"

"Yes, Pa!" She grinned at her husband. "You'd better go."

"I think you're right. See you later." He stole a quick kiss and was gone.

Jewel's wobbly rocker was fixed with a couple passes of a plane, so she spent the rest of the afternoon staining the chair and watching her house take shape. She found it very exciting and the glimpses she got of her husband were even more so. Marrying Eli had been a good thing, she realized. He made her feel special in ways she'd never dreamed possible and just the sight of him made her heart skip and her nipples bloom. Pushing her mind away from the scandalous thoughts, she went back to work.

She was soon joined by Maddie, Miss Edna, and Gail, who reported that Anna Red Bird was feeling much better. They were in the middle of talking about the next Intelligence Society meeting when they all saw Vernon drive up with Hicks and a veiled woman in widow's weeds seated beside him.

"I wonder who the woman is?" Gail said.

Jewel paused with the varnish brush in her hand and watched the wagon approach. She wasn't sure where Eli was, so she thought it only polite that she welcome his mentor back to town. "Let's go find out."

Setting the brush down, she wiped her hands on a clean rag, then on her denims, and threaded her way through the workers to intercept the wagon while the others followed.

When she neared, she greeted Vernon, and Hicks tipped his hat, "Mrs. Grayson. How are you?"

Jewel swore the veiled woman flinched, but the movement was so slight, she decided it had been her imagination. "Doing well, sir. Welcome back."

"Thank you. This is Mrs. Green. I met her in Detroit. She has friends here."

By now, Eli had drifted over as had her father. Jewel could see Maddie and Miss Edna looking on with a casual interest.

Eli, now standing beside Jewel, addressed the widow. "Welcome to the Grove, Mrs. Green."

"Thank you, Eli," she said and slowly removed her veil.

Jewel heard Gail gasp and saw her clutch Maddie's arm to keep herself upright. Jewel's eyes snapped back to the woman in black and saw the sugary smile. Maddie let out a curse.

Eli stared at Cecile dumbstruck, then asked coldly, "What are you doing here, Cecile?"

Upon hearing the name Jewel understood everyone's shocked reactions. She'd been very young when Cecile was married to Nate and so hadn't recognized her.

Cecile eyed him slowly, then Jewel. "My doctor suggested I take a trip to the country to restore my nerves, and where is more country than Grayson Grove."

"Get back on the train."

"Surely you can be more polite after all we shared."

Hicks looked out at the angry faces flanking the wagon. "What's going on here, Grayson?"

Maddie snarled, "You've brought the serpent back to the garden, Mr. Hicks."

He stiffened and stared at Cecile, then at the granite set of Eli's face. "Grayson?"

"She's my cousin's former wife, and not wanted here."

"Why? Because I remind you of the adultery we committed," she asked calmly.

Jewel stiffened and anger rose inside.

Hicks's eyes widened.

Cecile turned to Hicks, "Yes, he and I committed adultery, but I've changed my life. It's one of the reasons I came back. I'm here to make amends. If I can." She then met Jewel's eyes. "You're his wife?"

Jewel nodded.

"I hope the two of you are happy. I truly didn't

return to cause trouble." She looked around, "Where's Nathaniel? Is he here?"

Eli's voice hadn't warmed. "He's out of town with his wife and children."

"So, he's remarried."

Eli didn't respond.

Cecile smiled a bit sadly, "I can't undo the past, but I am here on an honest mission. I lost my husband a few weeks ago, and I loved him very much. I'd hoped to come here and gather myself before moving on with my life."

Maddie shook her head, "You do that. I'm going home to hide the silver." She stalked over to her wagon and drove away.

Eli wanted to do the same. Instead he said, to G.W., "Welcome back, sir." He then turned to his father-in-law. "Let's get back to work, Adam."

Adam led the men back to the house.

Jewel met Cecile's eyes and Cecile smiled ruefully. "Guess it won't be as easy I as thought it would be."

G.W. said to Vernon, "Take us to town, Mr. Stevenson, if you would please."

Vernon didn't look happy, but he snapped the reins and headed the team toward the road.

Everyone at the construction site watched until the wagon rolled from sight, then resumed their work.

Later that evening, after the crews had left for the day, Jewel and Eli sat on the edge of the house's floor and looked out over the bluff.

"Do you believe she's here to make amends?" she asked.

He shrugged. He'd been thinking about that all day. "Anything's possible, but truthfully, no. My question is how did she happen to be in G.W.'s company?"

"You'll have to ask him, I suppose."

"He's such a moralist, he'll probably pull out on our deal now."

"It'll be his loss, then."

He turned his head her way and smiled. "Did you believe what she said about changing her ways?"

"No."

"You say that with such conviction."

"Even though I never knew Cecile, I trust Maddie's instincts, and if she says hide the silver, I start digging."

"What could she be after, though, after all this time?"

"Hopefully, it isn't you. I'd hate to have to shoot her."

"You'd shoot her for me?"

"Right between the eyes."

He put an arm around her shoulder and eased her close. He gave her a kiss on the brow. "Thanks."

"You're welcome."

That night as Jewel lay in bed, she realized that she had no intentions of letting Cecile affect her marriage. She and Eli had just gotten everything straightened out between them and there would be hell to pay if Cecile was intent upon tangling things again. Because her father had worked Eli and the other men like mules, Eli was already asleep. Listening to his even breathing, she lay in the dark, her eyes focused on the ceiling above. Why had Cecile come back? It was a question being asked all over the Grove by now, she'd be willing to bet. As Eli noted when they first married, small towns took their amusements where they found them, and this business with Cecile was going to be like the circus come to town.

The following morning, Eli was in the mayor's office looking over the mail and transferring the rent payments from the tenants into Nate's ledger when a knock on the open door caught his attention. Looking up he saw Hicks standing on the threshold. "Morning, G.W."

"Eli," he responded with a chill in his voice. "May I come in?"

"Certainly. Have a seat."

He sat and from the tight set of his lips, Eli assumed something was wrong. Cecile, no doubt, so he decided to get it all over with. "Sir, if you would rather pull out of this partnership, I won't hold it against you."

"Who said anything about pulling out?"

"You seem very cool this morning."

"It's because I'm having a bit of a dilemma."

"About what?"

"Who and what to believe."

Eli understood. "You have my sympathy."

"I don't want sympathy, I want the truth."

"As we all do, sir."

Hicks seemed to think on that for a moment. "I was taken aback by the blunt reaction of Miss Loomis yesterday."

"Maddie doesn't bite her tongue."

"That was very apparent." He added, "May I be blunt as well?"

"Sure."

"I came back with the intention of attempting to get to know her better."

"Maddie?"

"Yes."

Eli stared, searched G.W.'s face, and asked again, "Maddie?"

"She isn't married is she?"

"No." Eli studied Hicks. "It's just—" Eli was very confused. What had happened to Cecile? "No one's ever courted her before, at least not anyone in the Grove."

"Do you think she'd be amenable to the interest of a short squat man like myself?"

He shrugged. "I can't speak for her." Eli didn't have the heart to tell the man that Maddie's past would probably send him running to the hills; he'd leave that to her. "How about you come have dinner with me and Jewel, and we'll invite Maddie."

"When?"

"Say, tomorrow?"

Hicks smiled. "That would be agreeable."

Eli nodded and hoped Maddie would feel the same way. In the meantime there was still the matter of Cecile to set straight. "How did you happen upon Cecile? Did you know her previously?"

G.W. shook his head. "Met her on the platform at the Detroit depot. She'd somehow misplaced or lost her ticket and her coin purse."

"Ah. I see."

"You sound skeptical."

"My apologies. It's not my place to judge. I was as guilty as she back then."

"Would it be improper to ask you what happened."

"No, since you're bound to hear the story anyway."

So Eli told him. Everything.

When he finished, Hicks met his eyes. "That's quite a tale. I saw her at breakfast. She thanked me for my assistance this morning and said she planned to spend the day doing some visiting."

"I can't imagine who'd she'd be wanting to see. We were both pariahs in those days."

"You keep saying *we*."

"I was young, G.W., but I knew what we were doing wasn't right. I've accepted my role in the matter."

"And your cousin, Nathaniel, has he forgiven you?"

"As much as he can."

"And have you forgiven yourself?"

"No."

Hicks nodded as if he understood. "And you haven't seen her in all the years since?"

"No, which is why everyone is wondering what she's after."

"She said she's turned over a new leaf."

"If she has, I applaud her."

"But you don't believe her."

"Honestly, no."

"Well, let's leave that subject for now. I saw you added more room to the office while I was away."

"Yes, sir. I've also been studying the types of presses we may want to purchase."

"We?"

"Yes. It seems my mother had funds that were mine and she just transferred them to me. It gives me some breathing room."

"Good. Let's see what you're considering."

Eli opened a desk drawer and took out the pictures of the various presses he'd sent away for and the notes he'd penned on them. "I'm partial to these new Curtis and Mitchell's," he said.

G.W. nodded. "They're out of Boston, aren't they?"

"Yes, and with this model you can pause it if you need to feed in more newsprint."

"I like that idea."

They spent the rest of the morning discussing the advantages and disadvantages of other models Eli had on his list, but in the end, decided on the Curtis and Mitchell. Eli was pleased. "I'll wire them tomorrow and hope we can get the press here by the end of the month."

"In the meantime, I want you to do an editorial for the papers in my syndicate."

"Any particular subject?"

"The madness being perpetrated in the South. That is of most concern right now."

Eli agreed. Death and anarchy were marching hand in hand across the nation's southern states, trampling the lives and rights of its newest Black citizens. He had a few drafts on the subject already started at home. "When would you like to see it?"

"As soon as you can complete it."

"Okay." He then studied Hicks for a moment before asking, "Are you truly interested in Maddie?"

"Unlike any woman before, even my late wife."

"And Cecile?"

"What about her? I've no interest in her in that way. I have arranged to pay the bill for her room at the Quilt Ladies' until the end of the month. After that, she'll need to make other arrangements. I'd hate to think I'm being taken advantage of, though."

Eli didn't respond.

"From your silence, I'm assuming you think I am."

He shrugged. "Time will tell. I'd be interested in knowing her true motive for coming back. She hated the Grove when she was married to my cousin. Complained day in and day out about the slow pace and the weather." And night in and night out, he'd shared her bed.

"Yet she's here."

"Yep." Bringing back memories he'd rather not have.

"She's an attractive woman."

"Not nearly as much as my Jewel, though."

G.W. smiled. "On that, you and I are in agreement."

Then Eli was curious about what had taken G.W. back east." Did you find the man who took your money?"

"Thanks to the Pinkertons, I did." He paused for a moment, then asked, "Do you think a wire to the Pinkertons might be in order on the widow?"

"That's up to you, sir. I won't influence your decision either way." But he did think it was a good idea because he was interested in knowing as much as he could, not for his sake but for Jewel's. He didn't want her to be hurt in any way. He'd kill Cecile himself if she was back to stir up trouble.

"Maybe it won't provide any answers at all, but I plan to mull it over for a while, anyway. I hate to be made a fool of." He stood. "Thanks for your time, Eli, I'm going to look at some property with Miss Edna. Still considering living here."

"Hope you find something to your liking."

He departed, leaving Eli alone with his thoughts. How does a man forget the first real woman he ever coupled with, he wondered. As if it were yesterday, he had no trouble recalling how it felt to be in Cecile's bed—the texture of her lips, the softness of her skin—but the desire he'd had for her in his youth was now as cold as the winter winds of January. The man he'd grown up to be was about as interested in starting up with her again as he was in making love to the Widow Moss. Would G.W. really contact the Pinkertons? Eli had to admit that it would be one way to get a definitive answer. If Cecile were up to no good, the detective agency would know; and if she had indeed changed her life, it wouldn't matter. He'd still want her on the first train out of town.

# Chapter 12

After completing the town business for the day, Eli left the office, locked the door, and headed up the street to the Lending Library. Maddie usually opened the place around ten, and since it was half past that now, he assumed she'd be there.

And she was. When he walked inside the small converted store front with its wall-to-wall books, small polished tables, and comfortable, old, upholstered sofas, she was dressed in her buckskins and sweeping the wooden floor.

"Morning, Maddie."

"Eli. Anybody find Cecile dead yet?"

He grinned. "Not that I know of. Are you ready to confess?"

"Maybe." She stopped in midstroke and asked bluntly, "What in the hell is she doing back here?"

"Wish I knew. Thought about killing her myself, I have to admit."

"If Nate comes back and finds her here, he's going to save everybody the trouble."

Eli hadn't received a letter from his cousin in over a week. He hoped Nate and the doc weren't on their way home. Nate didn't need to be reminded of the sins committed against him, or the pain.

Maddie was sweeping and muttering, "Talking all mealy-mouthed about how much she's changed. It's a wonder lightning didn't strike her for lying."

"Suppose she has changed?"

"If she's changed, I'm a virgin."

He laughed. "Do you know how much I love you?"

"You Grayson men are always professing to love me, but when it comes to proposing you find somebody else." Maddie had been sweet on Nate since they were all youngsters. She'd finally given up hope after he was bowled over by his love for Viveca. The two feisty women were now best friends. "I came to extend a dinner invitation."

"Where and when."

"Tomorrow at our place. I'm having G.W. over, too. Just so you know."

"Just so you're not playing matchmaker."

"Me? I know better."

"Okay. What time?"

He told her five, hoping Jewel didn't have other plans because he hadn't talked to her about any of this yet.

"Five's fine. Should I bring anything?"

"Nope."

"Okay. Thanks for the invite."

"You're welcome."

He made his departure and wondered how the dinner would turn out. He couldn't see Maddie and G.W. making sparks, but he hadn't seen Jewel in his future, either. Thinking about her made him realize they hadn't made love in nearly a week out of respect for her monthly, but he was pretty sure that had passed. Smiling, he walked down to his wagon and set off for home, wondering if he might interest her in a nice hot helping of his always fulfilling Jewel's Delight.

Jewel had spent the morning cleaning out Eli's barn. There were old saddles, boxes of dried inkpots, clothing mice had nibbled on, and various pieces of rusted machinery she guessed were parts of discarded printing presses. There was barely room to turn around in the small barn, let alone space for all the piled-high junk. Although she didn't think any of the items or clothing were useable, she stuck to her promise of not tossing anything away until he'd gone through it all.

As she dragged out a rotted barrel of weather-ruined newsprint, she thought about Cecile. No matter how much she tried not to, her mind kept filling up with thoughts of his former love. He certainly hadn't acted overjoyed about seeing her again, but Jewel wondered if the flame would be re-kindled? Nate's former wife was very beautiful. Her clear dark skin and well-formed figure would have little trouble ensnaring any man, but the only man that concerned Jewel was Eli. Parts of herself knew she had nothing to fear. Hadn't he plainly stated that that part of his life had ended under Nate's thundering fists. And didn't he still carry the shame inside of what he'd done? In truth, he'd given her no reason whatsoever to be concerned, but Cecile represented all of the worldly sophisticated women he'd spent his bachelor days chasing after, and Jewel didn't fit the mold at all. Deciding she was going to make herself insane if she didn't stop obsessing over a problem that wasn't there, she turned her mind back to sorting through Eli's junk.

When she was done for the day, she was covered with dust, cobwebs, dirt, and splotches of ink that had been leaking from one of the pots. Her first thought was to jump on her horse and ride to her brothers' home and take a real shower; she was still wary of Eli's rigged-up barrel contraption, but truthfully, she was too tired to ride all that way, so she opted to use the facilities where she was.

As always, she washed and rinsed herself at lightning speed, grateful the water didn't run out, and that the barrel didn't tip over on her head. In the house, dressed in an old but clean skirt and blouse, she looked around the small front room glad to be able to see the furniture and the rugs. Speaking of which, she thought the rugs should probably be taken outside and beaten, since they hadn't been done in over a week, but decided she wanted lunch first.

She'd just taken out the bread and some of the turkey they'd had for dinner yesterday and transferred the items to the table when Eli entered the kitchen.

"Hello, Mrs. Grayson."

"Hello, yourself. Did you get everything done at Nate's office?"

"Yep. Had a talk with G.W. about the presses, too. He wants me to compose an editorial to run in his papers on the violence down south."

"That's quite a coup, congratulations. I'm making a sandwich. Would you like one?"

"Yes, ma'am."

But there was something he wanted more, so he moved up behind her while she was slicing the bread and slipped his arms around her waist. "I've missed hearing you scream the last few nights."

She chuckled. "And I've missed screaming."

He placed his lips against her neck, and Jewel's mind began to melt. "I'm supposed to be making sandwiches."

"I'm not stopping you."

What he was doing, however, was undoing the buttons on her blouse. "You smell like roses and your neck's damp. Did you just shower?"

Her blouse was open, and after tugging down her camisole, he filled his hands with her soft silky flesh.

"Yes," she finally whispered. Turning her to face him, he leaned down and took a pleading nipple into his mouth, and after a dazzling few moments transferred his wanton attention to the other. Jewel could barely stand and had to brace herself against the table's edge.

He husked out, "I think I'm going to come home this time of day more often."

Jewel was soaring, and when his hands worked her skirt up her legs she rippled everywhere. His hot touches found her already ripe and open. Her stance widened, her head dropped back, and were it not for the table behind her she would have been unable to remain upright. He took her drawers from her without a word and returned to his play. Employing dallying caresses that coaxed and seduced, he soon had her running with love.

Eli, his manhood hard as it always was when he was around her, planned to take her on the tabletop, but she looked so fetching half dressed and with her beautiful brown legs parted so provocatively, he lowered himself to his knees and flicked his tongue against her. She gasped, tightened, and tried to back away.

"Where do you think you're going?" he asked hotly with a half-smile, his fingers plying her boldly. He leaned in and put his mouth to her again, teasing her with well-placed licks.

Jewel could not believe this was happening. Scandalized, breathless, and not wanting him to stop, she grabbed the table and held on for dear life. She groaned, "Eli."

"Can't talk now sweetheart. I'm busy."

And he was, busy making her lush, mindless,

and his. He'd never loved her this way before. Even though she'd seen the drawings in Maddie's book, Jewel hadn't believed they were real, but they were—so real that after only a few moments of his breathtaking devotions the orgasm ripped through her with such force, she couldn't have stopped the scream if her life had been in the balance. Wave after wave of powerful sensations buckled her, shook her, and tore through her so deliciously she wanted it to last forever.

"Much better than a sandwich," he echoed, smiling and watching her dance the little death.

When it was finally over, Jewel was so overcome, all she could do was slide to the floor. Her very pleased husband stood above her to undo his belt and remove his trousers. Then he was beside her and she was astride him in the middle of the kitchen floor. Her initial thought—once she was able to think again—after his slow, carnal slide into her body was how glad she was that she'd mopped and waxed the floor last night, but as he began to thrust and she began to ride him, all thoughts fled.

They'd made love in this position before and she found it much to her liking. Not only could she take in as much of his magnificence as she wanted, her being on top gave him sweet access to all that made her woman—her breasts, her lips, her core. And he took full ardent advantage; suckling, touching, making her moan.

Moving blissfully in tandem, their bodies sparking against each other like lightning, she leaned down to feast lovingly on his neck while he mapped the delicate curve of her undulating hips and spine. She licked him; he groaned. He moved a hand over her torso to capture a swaying breast and she rose up, his hand still holding her, and she arched like the front of a native bow as he squeezed the point possessively. Feeling himself throb as he stroked her, Eli knew that this was all he wished to do for the rest of his life. The heat of her skin drew him, the firmness of her hot little body bewitched him. The friction of their joining as they rose and fell coupled with the tightness of her flesh surrounding him made him stoke harder, faster, and then faster still. Spurred by his own orgasm rising, he clamped onto her hips to make her match his fierce pace, and when she screamed out her second release he orgasmed right behind her. Yelling his pleasure and filled with the insanity of a man making love to his wife, he kept thrusting until he thought he'd never stop.

He did finally, and when it was over, an exhausted Jewel collapsed on his chest and he dragged his arms around her to hold her close. For a moment the only sound in the kitchen was their ragged breathing, then she whispered, "Good, lord, Eli."

He smiled, tightened his hold, and kissed her hair. "You're welcome."

A few quiet seconds passed and he told her tiredly, "The floor is getting hard, Jewel. Can you let me up?"

"Sorry, but I can't move. It's what you get for choosing the kitchen floor."

Their bodies were still joined so he gave her a sultry stroke with his reawakening manhood and her eyes popped open with pleasant surprise.

The reaction charmed him. "You have two choices, Mrs. Grayson, either let me rise, or. . . ."

As their bodies began to move again, Jewel couldn't believe how greedy she'd become for his loving, so she leaned down, gently bit his ear, and husked out, "Mrs. Grayson will take the *or.*"

They eventually did get to eat the sandwiches, after washing up and changing into fresh clothes, then set out for the construction site to help with the house. As they drove within view, she was pleased with the progress her brothers and the other volunteers were making but at the same time she was impatient for them to be done. She was ready to move in, with Eli. It had come to her while she was lying spent on his kitchen floor that in spite of all her protestations at the beginning of their marriage, she was in love with him. How could she not be after all the tender care he'd shown her? He was funny, smart, kind, and true. She didn't want a divorce; she wanted to live with him in their house for the rest of her life. "I think I'm going to enjoy being here."

"I think we both will."

She wanted to tell him of her decision not to seek a divorce, but the moment didn't seem right so it remained unsaid. Looking over at him seated on the buggy bench beside her, she said, "We should probably get out before Pa starts to yell."

They could see Adam walking the construction site like a general commanding his troops. He was shouting directions to the roofers in a voice that could be heard clearly over the hammering.

"You're right." Eli's vision lingered on the woman slowly becoming his world. "Thanks for the stimulating repast."

His words instantaneously transported Jewel back to the kitchen. "Anytime."

The work on the house lasted until early evening and when her father finally dismissed everyone for the day, Jewel and Eli dragged themselves back to the buggy for the ride home.

As they lay in bed that night, Eli said, "Forgot to tell you I invited Maddie for dinner tomorrow."

"That's fine."

"I invited G.W, also. He's sweet on her."

Jewel flashed around and stared at his shadowy face. "What?"

"I was sort of amazed, too. Says he's more attracted than he's ever been in his life."

"To Maddie?"

"Interesting, don't you think?"

Jewel fell back onto her back and for a moment silently thought about the implications. "If she finds out we're matchmaking she'll kill us all. Including Hicks."

"Which is why I made a point of not saying anything to her about his feelings."

"Good idea. Hicks and Maddie," she said in a speculative voice. "Wouldn't that be something? She may eat him alive, but it could work."

Eli turned over on his stomach and contemplated her in the dark. "What happened to all the nightgowns you purchased in Niles, Mrs. Grayson."

Jewel had yet to wear any of the garments. She gave him a hastily mustered defense. "I'm saving them for a special occasion."

Eli responded by circling a finger around her breast. "Every time we're in bed together is a special occasion to me, Jewel."

*How could I not love this man,* she asked herself, and because she did, she felt she owed him the real reason for not wearing the sensual attire. "Truth is, I'm too prudish to try them."

His smile caressed her in the shadows. "This from a woman who let her husband make love to her in the middle of the kitchen floor?"

"That's different," she explained in a humor-filled voice. "You caught me with my guard down, and once we got started, I couldn't help myself."

"So it's all my fault?"

By then, he'd undone the three small ribbons holding together the front of her plain cotton nightgown and had slipped a hand in to tease a soft-skinned globe. Feeling herself succumbing, she whispered, "Yes, it was your fault. Besides, you never let me keep my clothing on for very long when we're in bed anyway, so it doesn't much matter what I'm wearing."

He leaned down and placed a humid kiss on her lips. "Sometimes a man just likes to take something off. "

She couldn't offer any riposte because her gown was now riding her waist and she was slowly being penetrated by the part of his anatomy that always filled her so splendidly.

By the time he'd brought her to her final orgasm of the day, she'd promised to wear to bed whatever he desired.

Maddie was late. Jewel, Eli, and G.W. were seated at the table in their small kitchen when she finally strode in. "Sorry I'm late. Had to deal with Widow Moss."

Jewel looked up from her plate. "What's happened?"

"Seems her precious Bibi just had pups and they look just like Blue Jr."

Eli grinned.

"She didn't think it was funny. Wants me to have Junior put down for assaulting Bibi."

Jewel shook her head.

G.W. asked, "Blue is your dog?"

Maddie took a seat and picked up a plate and began to fill it. "Yes. One of nine at the moment. Best pack of hunting dogs in the county. Do you hunt?"

"I'm afraid not."

She shrugged. "That's okay. What you and Eli do is important."

"You think so?"

Maddie buttered a biscuit. "Of course. These days, you all may be risking David Walker's fate after he published his *Appeal,* but no one seems to be backing down."

"You've read David Walker's *Appeal*?" The surprise and delight were all over his muttonchopped face.

She paused in the middle of raising her fork to her mouth and appeared to be thinking. "Start me off, Eli."

His voice took on serious tones. *"I am fully aware . . ."*

Maddie nodded and picked up the recitation, *"in making this appeal to my afflicted and suffering brethren, that I shall not only be assailed by those whose greatest earthly desires are to keep us in abject ignorance and wretchedness, and who are of the firm conviction that Heaven has designed us and our children to be slaves and beasts of burden for them and their children."*

Jewel took the next lines. *"I say, I do not only expect to be held up to the public as an ignorant, impudent and restless disturber of the public peace, by such avaricious creatures, as well as a mover of insubordination and perhaps put in prison or to death for giving a superficial exposition of our miseries, and exposing tyrants."*

G.W.'s head nodded approvingly. "He spoke for the race as no one ever had before."

In its time, *Walker's Appeal to the Coloured Citizens of the World* was hailed as the most inflammatory series of articles in the nation's history, surpassing in brimstone even the great Thomas Paine's revolutionary tract, *Common Sense,* which rallied the American colonists against the crown.

"And he was killed, just as he predicted he would be," Eli added.

In 1830, the forty-five year-old free-born Walker was found dead on the doorstep of his Boston clothing shop shortly after the *Appeal*'s third-edition publication. Many believed he was murdered for his impassioned call for slaves to defend themselves and for God to rain down vengeance on the Christian slaveholders of the United States.

G.W. had pride in his face. "I'm amazed that you all have the Preamble committed to memory."

Eli shrugged. "Only some of it, but it was and still is required reading at the Grove school."

Maddie explained further: "I wasn't allowed to attend, but Nate and Eli would come home and teach me everything they'd learned."

G.W. turned to Eli. "I thought you said school was mandatory here?"

"It is, but Maddie's father didn't believe in learning for girls."

G.W. studied Maddie closely and she responded with the truth. "He beat me anytime he caught me with a book in my hands."

His eyes widened.

"As much as I loved to read I took a lot of whippings," she relayed with a bittersweet smile. She then pointed at his plate. "You should eat before your food gets cold."

He sputtered. "Oh, yes. You're right."

But Jewel noted that he stole discreet glances at Maddie for the remainder of the meal.

After dinner, G.W. cited his need to take a walk so as to get a bit of exercise, per his doctor's advice. "The man's trying to make me lose weight," he declared, indicating his stomach's ample girth. "Says I might live longer." Turning to Maddie he asked, "May I be so bold as to ask for your company?"

She stood and smiled, "Sure."

So, off they went, leaving Eli and Jewel behind to clean up.

Jewel handed Eli a washed and rinsed plate to dry. "He's had his eyes glued to her all evening,"

"His intentions had better be honorable."

"This coming from the Colored Casanova of Cass County."

"The *former*, thank you very much, but Maddie's like the sister Nate and I never had and I don't want to see her hurt."

"Maddie can take care of herself, but it would be nice for her to have someone special in her life, besides Blue and the other dogs."

He agreed.

Later that evening, when dusk started to fall, Hicks and Maddie had not returned. A worried Eli stood out in front of his cabin scanning the countryside. "You don't suppose something has happened?" he asked Jewel, seated on a blanket spread out under a tree.

"They're probably talking, and have simply lost track of time," she offered reassuringly. She found his concern for Maddie touching and yet another indication of his good heart. "They'll return when they're done. Come sit with me." She patted the blanket.

He came over reluctantly, his features showing his mood. "Five more minutes and I'm going to go look for them."

"No, you are not. Maddie is not a babe in the woods." To distract him, she asked, "Have you worked on the editorial Hicks wanted?"

"Not yet," he answered distractedly, eyes still searching.

"Do I need to undo the buttons on my blouse in order to gain your full attention?"

He flashed around. "Would you?"

The heat and mischief in his gaze made her laugh. It also lit her senses like a flame to a wick. She was certain that with just the least bit of encouragement he could have her naked and screaming in the blink of an eye. Lucky for her, she spied their dinner guests returning. "Oh, look, here come Maddie and G.W. now."

"Damn," he pouted with mock disappointment. The two were walking slowly, arms intertwined. "Remember you said that."

"Said what?" she asked innocently.

Eyes filled with humor, he waggled a warning finger. "You are not getting off that easily, Jewel Grayson. I expect to see some buttons being opened later tonight."

Playing the role of the obedient wife, she grinned and dropped her gaze. "Yes, Eli."

"That's better."

He helped her to her feet and slipped an affectionate arm around her waist as they waited for Maddie and G.W. to rejoin them. They both looked so pleased that Jewel planned to interrogate Maddie first thing.

Maddie and G.W. stayed and enjoyed the Grayson's hospitality a short while longer, then, driving their separate vehicles, headed off in the same direction.

Eli noted. "I don't think G.W.'s going back to town, at least not right away."

"Me either. Hope he likes dogs."

"Hope they let him in the door."

For a moment they shared humor-filled looks after which Eli said, "Now. About those buttons."

Before Jewel could speak a wagon rolled into view. James Wilson sat behind the reins and beside him on the seat was Cecile. "What could they possibly want?" Eli asked crossly.

Jewel wanted to know the same. "Maybe he's driving her to the train station."

"We should be that lucky." Tight-lipped he watched the wagon's approach. When it got within hailing distance, James Wilson nodded. The smug superiority he sometimes exhibited was in full blaze. "Evening."

Eli viewed Cecile critically before responding. "Evening. What can I do for you, Wilson?"

"Came to get last week's wages. You told me to come by. Remember?"

What with all the comings and goings of the

last few days, Eli had forgotten the conversation. "Come on inside so you can sign the receipt."

Jewel's eyes hadn't left Cecile's the entire time. It was as if the women were sizing each other up.

Eli looked to Jewel and then Cecile. "We'll be right back."

Cecile replied, "We'll be here. Won't we Jewel?"

Jewel didn't reply.

After the men departed, Cecile fussed with her hat. The widow's weeds were gone and replaced with a fashionable green walking ensemble that Jewel remembered seeing in the front window of the new seamstress shop owned by the reclusive Adelaide Kane. The little green hat perched upon her glossy hair matched the dress. "I see you've shed the weeds."

"Yes. I'm sure my husband would prefer I plow ahead with my life. Black makes me feel so bleak. James sprung for this new gown. He's such a sweet man."

Jewel didn't know anyone who'd describe Wilson as sweet but she kept that unspoken. "That's nice."

"Unlike some, he refuses to hold my past against me."

"That's very Christian of him."

"Are you and Eli enjoying your marriage?"

"We are."

"I hear it was forced."

"You heard wrong."

She smiled falsely. "It took me a moment to

place you when we first met, but you're the youngest Crowley child, aren't you? The one who got lost playing Hide and Go Seek in the middle of the night."

"Yes."

"I remembered because Eli had to leave my bed to help with the search."

Jewel felt ice crawl over her heart.

"He was as disappointed as I. Tell me, does he still enjoy making love under the moon?"

The ice cracked and so did she. "Excuse me. I have chores. I'm sure they'll be right out." She hurried away.

A pleased Cecile called, "Hope to see you again, soon."

But Jewel couldn't hear over the sounds of her breaking heart.

Once she was in back of the cabin and out of view, she dashed away the angry hurt tears in her eyes and plopped down on one of the aged stumps left behind when the land was cleared decades ago. She told herself she had two choices, she could either ignore Cecile's painful digs or succumb and be miserable, but she was already miserable. *Does he still enjoy making love under the moon?* The smug question echoed again and again. The answer was yes, and Jewel had had no idea that the night she'd thought so special was just another one of the weapons in his Casanova repertoire. In light of all they'd shared, she felt like an absolute fool. Factoring in the admission that she was in love with him qualified her fool enough to be a clown in a traveling circus. Her heart hadn't ached this way since her mother's death.

"Jewel?"

She glanced up at him through the lowering darkness.

"Sweetheart, are you crying?"

She got to her feet and quickly dashed away the telling moisture. "No. Something in the air has been making my eyes itch."

Eli didn't believe that for a moment. "What's wrong?"

"Nothing. Not feeling well. I think I'll sleep on the sofa in case I'm contagious."

"The sofa?"

"Yep." After one more swipe at her eyes, she smiled falsely. "Wouldn't want you to be sick, too."

He placed a tender hand on her arm. Upon feeling her tense up sharply in response, his heart pounded with alarm. "Did Cecile say something to you?" It was the only explanation he could fathom that would make her distance herself this way.

"As a matter of fact, she did. She wanted to know if you still enjoyed making love under the moon."

His eyes closed in pain.

Jewel knew if she stood there for one more second, she'd start to bawl, so she whispered, "Good night, Eli. I'll see you in the morning."

He watched her go, then dropped down onto

the stump she'd vacated and put his head in his hands.

Cecile almost felt sorry for the little Crowley woman. Seeing the way her spirit had crumpled in response to the question about the moon had been touching, but it proved she was no match for Cecile or a threat to her plan of repositioning Eli into her life. Removing the green dress she'd sweet-talked Wilson into buying for her, she hung it up in the wardrobe in her rented room, then slipped into a robe. According to Wilson, Eli had come into a large sum of money. Word had it that his bank accounts were bulging.

Cecile sat down at the mirrored vanity table and took in her reflection as she creamed away her face paint. That Eli was now a wealthy man only increased her desire to reclaim him. She was in her mid-thirties, her beauty was beginning to fade like an aging rose. Soon it would be unable to get her what she wanted, so it was imperative that she find someone to ensure her future. Now. Someone who could take her to Mexico or maybe even Brazil until the heat cooled and the Pinkertons stopped looking. He wouldn't have to know the truth unless it became absolutely necessary, and if it did she planned to have him so enamored by that time he wouldn't care.

She'd wait to approach him for now, though, because she wanted her presence to grow on him, linger over him, force him to remember how it had been; how they'd felt in each other's arms; how nothing had been too carnal for them to try. He'd been a creative and inventive lover back then, displaying a level of expertise often lacking in men twice his age. She could only imagine how talented he must be now. With that in mind, she wanted him to relive the moments in her bed—the slide of their damp bodies; the orgasms they'd shared—and when she sensed he was haunted enough, only then would she cast her line. He had to be anxious, randy, in order to be susceptible to her charms. The lure in her had to be so strong that he'd turn his back on the Crowley woman, the same way he'd turned his back on Nathaniel.

Her smile was cold. Maybe coming back to this country turnip-truck town had been a sound idea, she told herself as she put away her toiletries. Maybe the fates intended for her to strike it up with Eli again. Pleased by the prospect and with her own cleverness, she blew out the lamp for bed.

Eli hadn't moved. It was dark and he was still seated on the stump pondering the disastrous effects of Cecile's visit. If someone had asked him earlier that morning how he and Jewel were getting along, he would have answered—on their way to happiness. Now? Now everything had crashed like a house made of straw. And truthfully, he had no defense; he had taken Cecile under the moon, just as he'd done Sally and most of the other women in his former Casanova life. He enjoyed outside lovemaking, the way the moonlight played over a woman's skin; the sound of her soft gasps against the quiet of the night had always been arousing to him, but that didn't make being in the moonlight with Jewel anything less than the very special occasion it had been. How to explain that to her and have her understand it was his problem. Or at least one of them.

The other was Cecile. Because of her foul deed, his anger knew no bounds. Were he the murdering type he'd search her out, strangle her with his bare hands, and leave her body for the scavengers. He knew her well enough to be certain that the question she'd posed to Jewel had been meant to maim, and it had achieved its goal. When he walked up and found Jewel sitting where he was seated now, he was glad night had been rolling in. The shadows had prevented him from seeing the depth of the hurt in her eyes because if he had seen it his inner pain would be all the more unbearable. He'd never wanted his past to wound her, yet it had.

Off in the distance he heard thunder. A few moments later lightning flashed in the western sky. The wind rose and he smelled rain but he didn't stand up and go inside. How did a man keep his heart from tearing apart at the sight of the sadness he'd put into the eyes of the woman he loved, he wondered—because he *was* in love with Jewel Crowley and had been possibly since the day they married. It was a life-altering admission for a man who'd planned on sampling willing women until he was old and gray. It didn't answer his question, though, and his heart was broken. Cecile had hurt Jewel through him and he didn't know how to fix it.

Raindrops began to splatter down. The flashes of lightning were brighter and the answering bass of the thunder rumbled loud and deep as the storm drew closer. He stood. Stretching with the weariness he felt both in and out, he headed to the darkened house.

Inside he moved about quietly, not wanting to wake her if she was sleeping. Her quiet snores let him know that was, so he walked over to watch her as she lay curled up on the sofa. She'd thrown a sheet over herself to ward against the night chill. As gently and as carefully as he could, he picked her up, sheet and all, and walked her into the bedroom. If anyone deserved to sleep on the sofa it was him. There was no need for her to make such a sacrifice.

He placed her down on the bed as if she were made of the most fragile crystal and stepped away. She moved around for a moment. He thought she might awaken, but she stilled and silently drifted back into the arms of Morpheus. "Good night, Jewel," he offered quietly. Exiting the room he closed the door soundlessly behind him.

# Chapter 13

Eli awakened to the smell of bacon frying. Wondering why his body felt so god-awful stiff it took him a moment to remember that he wasn't in bed, and why he was on the sofa instead. His long limbs were so cramped from curling up on the too-short space he wasn't sure he'd ever walk again. Bleary eyed, he rubbed at his hair, then rose unsteadily to his feet. Jewel stood watching him from the doorway and he instantly went still.

"Your breakfast is ready."

He saw no emotion or welcome in her eyes or stance. Wanting to offer her comfort but not sure how to do so, he simply said, "Thanks."

She turned and left.

He pulled in a deep sigh, and padded outside to wash up.

Jewel placed the plates and utensils on the table. She heard him come into kitchen behind her, bringing with him the clean familiar smell of his soap, but she kept her mind focused on what she was doing. She set the small platter of bacon on the table, followed it with the bowl of scrambled eggs, then took the biscuits out of the oven and turned them out onto a plate. "I'm going over to Calvin Center today to look at True Light's roses."

True Light was the community's Baptist church. Eli waited for her to take a seat before he took his own. Once he did, he looked across the table at the woman who wouldn't meet his eyes. "Jewel."

"Say the blessing, please." She bowed her head.

Eli offered a blessing and, when it was done, tried again, "Jewel,"

"Pass me the eggs, please."

Keeping his temper in check, he complied.

They ate in silence, and, when they were done, she began to clear the table. "I'll see you this evening."

He felt dismissed, and because he did and didn't want to push this into a full-blown argument, he stood, exited the kitchen and then the house without another word.

Left alone in the echoing silence, Jewel didn't know what to do with what she was feeling inside. She was aware that he'd wanted to talk about the wall she'd thrown up between them and probably attempt to make things better, but she was afraid she'd turn into a raging shrew given half a chance, and that nothing but more hurt would come out of it. She wanted to kick herself for being so naïve as to think she occupied a unique place in his life, or that their times together had been unique as well because according to the smug Cecile they were not.

Jealousy was part and parcel of her mood, too, she was honest enough to admit. It was a new experience seeing as how she'd never been in love before. The only saving grace was that she hadn't revealed the true depths of her feelings to him. If she had, she'd no doubt feel like an even bigger fool. Her battered heart wanted to turn back the clock to yesterday morning when everything between them had been fine, but since that was impossible, she finished up the dishes and went on with her day.

Eli burst through the doors of the Quilt Ladies' boardinghouse, scaring Caroline Ross to death. Viewing him with wide eyes, she asked, "What's the matter?"

"What room is she in!"

Caroline didn't hesitate. "Number five. Down the hall to the left."

Without a thanks, he climbed the stairs.

When he reached Number 5, he pounded on the door so hard the wood rattled on its hinges. "Open this damn door, Cecile!"

He pounded again.

She snatched it open, crossness on her face, but the sight of his fury put fear in her eyes. Alarmed, she stepped back into the curtains-drawn room and he followed, snarling. "Stay the hell away from my wife!"

"You can't come in here!"

He slammed the door behind him. "Be glad I'm not the woman-beating type or you'd be on the floor scrambling after your teeth."

"Hey!" shouted a male voice. "Don't talk to her that way!"

Eli's eyes seared the bed. Creighton Wilson was sitting up in the gloom, the wrinkled sheets held against his chest. The sight caused Eli to shake his head with disbelief. He viewed the triumph in Cecile's eye and said bitterly, "You are one of a kind."

"As you often told me," she purred, smiling slyly.

"This is not a game," he barked in a voice cold as winter.

Creighton was out of the bed, sheet wrapped around his waist. "Get out of here, Eli."

"Does your father know he's sharing?"

Creighton stepped forward to do battle, but Cecile placed a soft hand on his hairy chest. "No, darling. He isn't worth it."

The two men glared. Eli drawled, "Cray, you'd be better off taking arsenic."

"Get out!" Cecile snapped. "You're just jealous!"

"If you were lying in the road with your skirt above your head and your legs spread from here to Chicago, I'd walk right past you." His voice dropped to a low sinister tone. "This is your last warning. Stay away from my wife!"

Creighton made another move and Eli warned

him bitterly, "Right now, I could very happily beat someone to death, so if you want to be that lucky, come on."

But he didn't advance. Eli turned his menacing gaze on Cecile. Nothing further to say, he left them, slamming the door with such force it resonated like thunder.

G.W. was in the hallway, his face heavy with concern. A few of the other boarders viewed his angry exit with wary curiosity, but Eli ignored them all.

Downstairs, he stormed by Caroline Ross who was still wearing the stunned look she'd had on when he blew in earlier. His jaw tight with emotion, he gave her a terse nod then exited through the door and stepped back out into the chilly gray day.

Now, still fuming, he sat in his cousin's office. He hoped Cecile had enough sense to take him at his word, because if she did anything else to cause Jewel pain there would be hell to pay. When G.W. proposed contacting the local Pinkertons to see if they had any information that might shed light on what she'd been doing for the past few years, Eli hadn't really cared. Now he did. Very much so. He wanted to know chapter and verse on anything that could be found. Cecile was a snake and snakes only surfaced if they were threatened. Something had brought her back to the Grove and the time had come to turn over some rocks.

He forced himself to calm down, but the confrontation kept playing across his mind. And what in the world had Creighton Wilson been doing in her bed? The fact that she seemed to be enjoying the favors of both father and son spoke volumes about her claims to have turned over a new leaf. He wondered if James Wilson knew. He didn't impress Eli as being the type of man who'd be party to something so sordid, but who knew, maybe the elder Wilson didn't care. Were there others? Back when Eli had been her lover, he'd heard rumors of her entertaining other men. He remembered being disturbed by the prospect, but also, being young, he'd arrogantly convinced himself that he fucked her best; the rest were also-rans, so they didn't matter.

He rubbed his palms over his face—what a stupid ass he'd been. And he was still paying for it. He thought of Jewel and the tight, emotionless face she'd shown him this morning. Even though the wall between was less than a day old, he missed her. Terribly.

Wishing he had the luxury to sit and mope away the rest of the day, he pulled out his pocket watch and checked the time. He had to go. He had to take Nate's place at the monthly tenants meeting being held at the church.

The Graysons rented land to fifteen families, and the meetings had been set up to air grievances, deal with problems, and celebrate successes. Usually the meetings were nothing more than a chance to catch up on news or play checkers, but today Eli was presented with a problem holding serious implications. It seemed there was a tax being charged at the mill that Eli knew nothing about. "How long has this being going on?"

One of the berry farmers, Pete Dane, answered. "Few days after Nate and the doc went west."

"Really?" Eli replied, intrigued.

Another man, a farmer named Walt Bailey spoke up. "The charges are killing us, Eli. Do you think it can be rescinded at least long enough for us to get our crops in and harvested."

Eli freely admitted to not knowing as much about the Grove's business as he should, which was why Nate was the mayor, but he couldn't fathom his cousin imposing such an exorbitant fee on folks already struggling to make ends meet. "I don't know anything about this, but I'll speak with Mother and have an answer to this as soon as I can. I'll also be talking with Wilson."

That seemed to suit everyone, so the meeting adjourned.

He found his mother at the Lending Library having coffee with Maddie. Both looked at him with such concern when he walked in that he stopped in midstride. "What?"

"Did you threaten to kill Cecile this morning?" Abigail asked.

His lips thinned. "I may have, why?"

"It's all over town," she replied with curiosity in her voice.

"What happened?" Maddie asked.

He came farther into the room. "Just warned her to stay away from Jewel. That's all." Taking up a position in front of one of the bookcases he could feel the anger rising again.

The women shared a glance.

"And this started how?" his mother asked.

"With a simple question that shouldn't have been asked. By Cecile." In no mood to be further interrogated, not even by loved ones, he changed the subject. "Mother, what do you know about this new tax at the mill?"

The abrupt switching of topics made her pause and scrutinize him for a moment before replying, "What new tax?"

"The one Wilson is collecting at the mill."

She looked confused, so he told her what the farmers had told him.

Abigail's confusion deepened. "Nate hasn't implemented a new tax. What is Wilson up to?"

"Embezzlement sounds like. What do you want done?"

She shrugged, "If this can be proven, I say let him go. I admit to not liking him, never have, but he's been running that mill for fifteen years. I hate to think he's been stealing all that time."

"No, the farmers said the taxing started right after Nate and Viveca left for California."

"Well then, we have our answer. Give him his last wages and send him on his way. Do you agree?"

"Yes."

She studied him for a moment more. "Eli, can you tell me—"

"I don't wish to talk about it now, Mother. Jewel and I are at odds, and that's all I can handle at the moment. I'll take care of Wilson and see you both later."

He left, and as the door closed, a grim Gail and Maddie sadly shook their heads.

The skies opened up and a hard cold rain began to fall, which only soured Eli's already bad mood. Glad to have someone to take his lingering wrath out on, he contemplated the sacking of Wilson while he walked to his wagon parked in front of the mayor's office. Seeing G.W. waiting for him under an umbrella made him say coolly, "G.W. How are you?"

"I was going to ask you the same thing."

Eli reached into the bed of the wagon, found his slicker and dragged it on. "At the moment, that is the question of the day, so not to be rude, sir, but you'll have to get in line."

G.W. smiled. "That bad a day?"

Eli climbed aboard the wagon. "You just don't know."

"Well, go on home to that beautiful wife of yours. Just looking at her should make things brighter."

"That's the problem. Thanks to Cecile she may not wish to be my wife for much longer."

Standing in the rain, Hicks froze, stricken.

"My sincere apology for bringing her back into your lives. And to further my apology, I'll get the Pinkertons started on that issue we discussed earlier. I won't have snakes slithering around this Garden of Eden, especially now that I'm about to become a landowner and resident."

Eli smiled for what seemed like the first time that day and, for that instant, didn't feel the cold rain. "You're top drawer, G.W."

"I appreciate the compliment. Good luck with your wife."

Eli picked up the reins. "Thanks." Nodding his departure, he drove away. He was going to need it.

It took almost two hours for Eli to receive a reply to the telegraph message he sent to Nate out in California. In response to Eli's question as to whether Nate had imposed the new tax, Nate's answer came back with one word. *No!*

Armed with the truth, Eli proceeded to the mill. He found his quarry out back, covering some recently cut wood with oilskins to protect it against the now steady rain.

"What do you want?" Wilson snarled as Eli climbed down.

"Need to talk to you. Let's go into the office."

"Say whatever you come to say," he tossed out from beneath his sodden hat. "Unlike you, I have work to do."

Eli paused. The day was not getting any better. "You've been cheating the tenants. You have thirty minutes to clear out your gear."

"What?"

"You heard me. You're finished. The tenants told me about the tax you've been charging."

"A charge your cousin instituted before he left for San Francisco, if you knew anything at all about the business."

"I wired him. He didn't authorize it. Be glad I'm not hauling you off to jail."

"You? Hauling me?" he spat bitterly. "To hell with you. I'm not going anywhere, least not on your say-so. You're just mad because of me and Cecile."

Eli turned away and started toward the office. He called back over the rain. "Thirty minutes."

"I ain't going! I'm not turning this mill over to a man who used to be so drunk his own mother wouldn't even claim him! If Nathaniel wants to sack me, fine, but I'm waiting until he gets back."

Eli stopped and turned. The rain pouring down was as cold as his rage.

Wilson chuckled and taunted in ugly tones. "How mad is it making you knowing I'm the one bedding your mistress? Maybe I'll hop on that little Crowley whore next—make her scream my name the way Cecile does!"

The blow to Wilson's stomach packed enough rage to double him over, and the lightning-fast uppercut that followed stood him straight up again, but Wilson was a tough old rooster. He spit out a few teeth and grinned. "I've been waiting for this."

And the fight commenced. They fought in the

rain like two Titans grappling in the mud, ignoring the rain pouring down as fists connected and blood began to flow.

In the end, youth won out over age—that, and the fact that Eli was the Grove's undisputed boxing champion two years running.

Breathing harshly and standing over the moaning Wilson now lying in the mud, Eli reached down and snatched the ring of keys from the man's belt. He wiped at the blood filling his mouth and staggered into the office.

After securing the place, he came back outside and found Wilson and the wagon he always drove gone. Tired and beat up, he set out for home. He wanted his wife.

Jewel dragged back to the Grove that evening, cold, wet and covered with grime. It was bad enough that it had rained all day, thus making working outside on the roses next to impossible, but the roads were filled with wheel-swallowing mud and she'd had to stop twice to push and pull the horse and wagon free.

Now as night rolled in and she drove up to her brothers' house, all she wanted was a long hot shower and bed. She refused to use Eli's poor excuse for a washroom, and, besides, with things the way they were between them, she wouldn't know what to say to him anyway, so she was hoping to put off seeing him for as long as she could.

At the door, she removed her mud-caked boots and entered the foyer wearing her thick woolen socks. Not seeing any of her brothers and not really caring, she headed upstairs to her room. She opened the door and stopped abruptly as a middle-aged brown-skinned woman inside spun around with alarm. Jewel asked, "Who are you?"

"Ellie Chance."

"What are you doing in my room?"

"Your room?" Then her face relaxed and she smiled. "Oh, you must be Jewel."

"Correct, but we still haven't established who you are."

It was obvious the woman didn't care for the tone, but it was one more thing the weary and out-of-sorts Jewel didn't care about.

"I'm the new housekeeper."

"Ah." Jewel saw now that the room's walls and furniture had been changed. All of her personal effects were no longer about. "My apologies. I just came to wash up."

"I see," she said, critically eyeing Jewel's dirty denims, shirt, and canvas coat.

"They didn't waste any time moving me out, did they?"

Ellie opened her mouth in defense but Jewel waved it away with a smile. "It's okay. Where'd they move my things?"

"This way."

Her boxed-up possessions were in one of the spare bedrooms. After thanking the housekeeper, she took the long hot shower she'd craved. Once she donned clean, dry clothing she felt better than she had all day.

She entered the den where her brothers were gathered and saw Eli seated on the sofa next to Noah. She stopped, uncertain. He stood slowly in the now silent room. "Came looking for you after it got dark."

Noticing the bruises and contusions on his face, she stared. "What happened to your face?"

"Fight. James Wilson."

As she moved to get a better look, her first thought was to wonder if Cecile had somehow been involved but she pushed it away. "I hope he looks worse."

He grinned around his cut lip. "He does."

She reached up and gingerly turned his battered face this way and that. She scanned his swelling eye. "That's gonna be some shiner tomorrow."

"Yeah."

Their gazes held and a rush of feelings that had nothing to do with the strain between them filled her insides. "Let's get you home and see if we can't salvage the face beneath all this swelling."

"You sure?"

Noting that her brothers were watching with interest, she nodded, saying, "Positive."

After the Graysons departed, the Crowley brothers looked at each other and Paul said, "I say the first child will be a boy."

"I'll take that bet," Noah challenged. And the good natured-wagering began.

* * *

"What was the fight about?" Jewel asked, concerned. They were home now and she was placing moist warm cloths on the angry red whelps on his face. Lying propped up on the sofa, Eli basked in how wonderful it felt being taken care of after enduring such a hellacious day.

"He's been stealing from the tenants. Mother and I decided to sack him."

"I take it he refused to go quietly."

"Bull's-eye. Give the pretty lady a prize."

She smiled softly. She didn't like seeing him injured. "How long has he been stealing?"

"Started soon as Nate and Viveca left."

She was gently moving the cloth from bruise to bruise. "So he was using Nate's absence to line his pockets."

"Apparently."

"I'm glad you put a stop to it."

"So are the tenants."

She was seated on the edge of the sofa, ministering to him. As the cloth cooled, she stood to take it back into the kitchen and place it into the warm water heating on the stove, but he gently took her hand to prevent her from leaving just yet. For a few heartbeats they viewed each other silently, then he said to her softly. "I'm sorry my past reached out and hurt you, more sorry than you could ever know."

Standing there, she looked away for a long few moments and felt the pangs return.

"I have no defense, sweetheart. Yes, I made love to her, you already knew that but it doesn't diminish what we shared in any way."

"She made me feel common, foolish, used." The resentment and anger closed around her heart like a fist.

"I apologize for that as well. You are none of those things. Yes, I've made love to many women under the moon, but not a one ever had my heart. You do."

Emotion stung her eyes.

"None of them have ever heard me say this either: I love you, and I will forever."

Stunned, she stared through unshed tears. His declaration echoed again and again.

"Speechless?" he asked.

She wiped away the moisture. "I am. I never thought . . ." she was too overcome to find the words.

"I've also never made love to a woman in the middle of a kitchen floor."

She smiled.

He tugged at her hand and coaxed her back down beside him. He scooted over as far as he could and when she leaned into his chest, he wrapped her up and pulled her close. The sensation of holding her was so exquisite it was almost painful.

Jewel was moved as well and acknowledged how much moments like this had come to mean. "I've a confession to make."

"And it is?"

"I've loved you since I was fourteen and you waltzed with me at my birthday party."

He pulled back and stared down with surprise. "Truly?"

She nodded.

"Why didn't you say so?"

"And make that head of yours swell even larger? I think not."

She cuddled down again. He kissed her hair. "So, no divorce."

"Not unless I catch you making love to Cecile in the middle of my kitchen floor."

The threat was like music to his ears. "You won't have to worry. Rumor has it I threatened her life."

"Did you?"

He shrugged and told her of the call he'd paid that morning. "I was so angry I'm not sure what I said." He clearly recalled Creighton's presence in the room, but kept that to himself. For now. "I believe she got the message, regardless of what I said."

"Let's hope so."

Jewel looked up and silently studied the face of the man she loved, and who remarkably loved her in return. Cecile still loomed like a dark cloud, but Eli's love made the sun shine. "So, can we go back to having fun?"

"Yes. I'd like that." He traced her lips lazily. "I've missed you."

She whispered. "I missed you, too. And once you heal up and stop looking like a demon spirit from the underworld, I plan to show you how much. I'll even put on one of those gowns, just so you can take it off."

"And buttons?"

She smiled remembering the promise she'd made to him yesterday right before Cecile's visit sent everything sideways. "I'll open as many buttons as you like."

Loving his familiar countenance even if it was crooked and battered, a content Jewel Grayson placed a soft kiss on her husband's bruised cheek and went into the kitchen to rewarm the cloth.

The cold rainy weather held the Grove in a dreary grip for the next few days. Even though the calendar showed it to be late May, the temperatures were more reminiscent of April—early April. Being Michigan residents, though, the people were accustomed to the changeable weather, and so dressed accordingly and went about their business.

The mud hindered progress on the house, but the work was proceeding and Adam was convinced it would be ready to be occupied in another two weeks. Jewel couldn't wait. She spent those days helping at the house, seeing to pest-infested roses, and riding all over the Grove to deliver used clothing and other donated items to those in need of them on behalf of the Female Intelligence Society. Eli spent his days and some of his nights getting the office ready for the printing presses he and G.W. were looking forward to receiving, and polishing his editorial.

Jewel came home one evening and found him seated at the kitchen table scribbling away. After offering her a welcoming smile, he handed her the draft he'd been working on. "Read this if you would, and let me know what you think."

"Okay." Taking a seat on his lap, she read silently.

*How long must the Colored voter wait to enjoy the fruits of the Constitution promised to all? We compose no insignificant portion of the Republican Party, yet our needs are not only not brought forward, but are universally ignored. This is a government of the People, a commonwealth of equals, and no one party, race, or class can claim to have a God-given right to govern. The voter of color has been used, nay abused by those elected to speak on its behalf. The Lily White Republicans stand and do nothing while on the other side of the rivers of blood flowing through the south stand the Democrats, and among them men determined that we vote Democrat or not vote at all, preferably from the grave. What has happened to liberty, what has happened to the promises wrung by the thousands of black souls who gave their lives in order to aid this Perfect Union's need during the war. We protest the arrogance that would demand a return to the past, an arrogance that can be seen as the country turns away from the slaughter and disenfranchisement taking place under our very noses while offering up the nonsensical separate but equal. There are those in the national press who say we should be grateful. For what may I ask? I quote David Walker's* Appeal to the Coloured Citizens of the World *and ask again, are we to give thanks for our ancestors being chained and handcuffed? Or maybe for the brandings or having fire crammed down our throats? Surely we must be grateful for slavery and being kept in ignorance and misery. This editor is not, nor will he ever be until the freedoms guaranteed by the Constitution apply to one and All!*

Jewel handed the paper back to Eli. "This is very good."

"It's not the final version, but it is close."

"When will it be printed?"

"Soon as I think it says all that it should and hand it over to G.W."

"Do you think the country will ever do right by the race?"

He shrugged. "It's hard to be optimistic in the face of all that is happening."

She thought about the killing and violence in the South; the people burned out of their homes; the teachers tortured; the parents lynched and murdered in front of their children. It was hard to be optimistic. "Pa is convinced that in the future members of the race will be elected regularly to national offices and may even be nominated for president."

"To be alive to see that," he said wistfully. Eli couldn't imagine such a thing, but he could.

"It would be wonderful, wouldn't it?" She kissed his cheek. "Keep holding the country's feet to the flame and who knows, maybe one of us will run for president. A female perhaps."

The male in Eli shuddered. "You'll have to get the vote first."

"A minor detail," she told him leaving him to go back to work. "A minor detail."

* * *

The next morning, Jewel rode into town to see if the paint she'd ordered for the house had arrived at Miss Edna's store. The home she and Eli were to share was all but finished and now needed paint to give it character. On the way down the walk, she paused to stick her head into the Lending Library.

Maddie waved her in. "I want to talk to you."

"Let me go to the store first. Do you want me to bring back coffee for you?"

Maddie left the box of books she was readying to send to one of the fledgling Black colleges down south and came to the door. "No, I'll go with you."

On their way, they spotted Cecile up ahead. She'd just stepped out of the seamstress shop and was wearing a blue gown that was way too fancy for the Grove, and a matching hat.

When they drew even to her, she drawled cynically, "Well, if it isn't the little bride and the whore."

"Burn in hell, Cecile," Jewel tossed out, not breaking stride.

Once they were by the stunned woman, Maddie grinned. "I liked that."

Cecile must have recovered because she called out, "Send Eli my love. Tell him I'll be waiting in the moonlight."

Jewel wasn't impressed and hollered. "Poor comeback!"

Maddie eyes filled with humor. "That's what happens when you have your brains between your legs."

Jewel burst out laughing and continued all the way to the store.

They were back at the Lending Library drinking coffee and getting caught up with what had been going on with each other when Jewel asked over her cup, "So. How are you and G.W. getting along?"

"He is the nicest man. Wants me to marry him. I already said yes."

Jewel spit coffee across the table, and began to choke on the portion that had been going down her throat.

A chuckling Maddie slapped her friend on the back a few times, "Are you all right?"

Still choking, Jewel thought she'd die if she didn't stop soon. Shooting Maddie a smiling look, she finally regained control of her breathing and then wheezed out, "You said yes?"

"Soon as he asked. Of course when I told him the story of my life, he did what you just did. I thought he'd keel over then and there, but he didn't. I told him why I'd done what I'd done, and where and how I lived. In the end, he said, he didn't care."

Jewel thought that good news.

Maddie's voice softened. "I'd heard women talk of meeting a man they seemed to have been waiting for their entire lives, and that's how I feel about him."

"I'm glad you're happy."

"I truly am."

"Has he been married before?"

"Yes. Late wife died of pneumonia about ten years ago. They didn't have children and it was an arranged marriage. Not a love match."

"Do the dogs like him?"

"Not particularly, and he doesn't much care for them either, but I'm not giving them up and I'm not giving him up, so they're going to have to learn to coexist. What about you and Eli? I saw him yesterday after he confronted Cecile. He didn't look very happy."

"He wasn't." She told Maddie the story of why.

"And Cecile had the nerve to say that to you just now? 'Tell him I'll be waiting for him in the moonlight,'" she mimicked. "You should have knocked her into the mud."

"Maybe next time."

"I'm holding you to that."

Jewel was grateful to have such a supportive friend. "He and I are fine now." And they were. Jewel couldn't remember being so happy. "I've decided there'll be no divorce."

"No?"

She shook her head. "Can't divorce a man I'm in love with."

"Do tell?"

Jewel met the humor in Maddie's eyes. "He's in love with me, too."

"Funny how things work out, isn't it."

Jewel agreed. Everything had worked out. "I couldn't ask for a finer man."

Maddie raised her cup. "To love."

Jewel raised hers, too. "To love."

# Chapter 14

Two weeks later, on a beautiful early June afternoon, the cleared grounds around the Graysons' new house were filled with people come to celebrate the finished product. The newlyweds would be moving in that day and their guests had been invited to witness the long awaited event.

As with all Grove gatherings, there was food, fun, horseshoes, and gossip swirling around Cecile. Word was, now that G.W. was no longer footing the bill for her room at the Quilt Ladies' boardinghouse, she'd been forced to move out, and was now the houseguest of Reverend Anderson, of all people. His wife, Ida, a friend of Gail's and Edna's was not happy.

But Jewel was in too good a mood to let musings on Cecile intrude on one of the happiest days of her life, so when she heard some of the women whispering that the reason Cecile was at the reverend's place was because Lenore Wilson refused to have the father's paramour set foot in the Wilson home, she politely excused herself from the table holding the food and walked the short distance to the house.

Seeing it all spruced up with its green paint on the wood and creamy white gingerbread trim made her smile. On the big front sitting porch sat the gleaming rocker she'd built, seemingly waiting for her to come and sit and watch the sunset over the bluff.

Her father walked up beside her and for a moment the two filled their eyes with the spanking new home.

"It's beautiful, Pa. Thank you."

"Nothing but the best for my best girl."

She snaked an arm around his ample waist and hugged. "Eli and I are hoping to spend the rest of our years here."

"No divorce?"

"No, Pa. I love him and he loves me."

"Well, hot damn."

She grinned in response. "Are you ready for grandchildren? Not that I'm expecting yet, but maybe soon."

He turned and looked into her face. "Your mother would be so proud of you, Jewel. You filled her shoes and then stepped into your own. The boys and I will always be grateful for the way you took care of us."

His praise put the sting of tears in her eyes. "You provided the home, Pa. I just kept it picked up."

He leaned down and kissed her cheek. "Be happy, my Jewel."

"I am, Pa. I really and truly am. Thanks again for the house."

"You're welcome. We'll add more rooms next spring. If you're talking about grandchildren, you'll need them."

He headed off to return to the main celebration and left her standing there gazing contentedly at her new home.

The highlight of the gathering was the Opening of the Door. A large ribbon with a big bow was tacked across the front entrance. Jewel and Eli would cut the ribbon together and officially take possession, but first they had people to thank.

Eli stepped up first. Looking out at the smiling faces of families and friends, he felt his heart swell. "I'm not really sure what to say, " he said, hoping his voice was loud enough to be heard. "I know I want to say thank you to everybody who helped with the building, especially Adam and my brothers-in-law. This is very special to me. At one time in my life, I wasn't worthy of so many blessings"—he looked at Jewel with unabashed love in his eyes—"but God is good," he whispered over the lump in his throat.

Men nodded solemnly. Women dabbed at their eyes with handkerchiefs. Abigail had tears running down her cheeks, and Adam slipped his arm around her waist and squeezed her gently. Standing next to them were a gleaming Maddie and G.W. Hicks.

Jewel, as grateful as her husband for her own blessings, gave her thanks as well. "To my Pa, my brothers, and everybody who worked. To Abigail and Maddie." She turned to Eli, "And to the *former* Colored Casanova of Cass County. . . ."

Everybody laughed at the emphasis she'd placed on the word *former.*

"Thank you, Eli, for making me the wife of one of the finest men in the country. "

Affection glowing, he took her hand. He looked back out at the crowd and asked his mother, "Do you have the shears?"

Abigail, aided by her cane, stepped forward and handed them over. Eli passed them to Jewel. He placed his hand atop hers and together they cut the big blue ribbon in half. It fluttered down, freeing the door while cheers and applause greeted the official opening of the new home belonging to Mr. and Mrs. Eli Grayson.

Later, sitting on her husband's lap on a blanket spread out on the bluff so they could watch the fiery sunset, Jewel said, "This was a wonderful day."

"That it was."

"Liked your speech."

"Spoken from the heart."

"I think I'm going to go into our new house, wash up in my new washroom—with indoor shower."

He jostled her at the jab.

"And then find something very sultry to wear that my husband will enjoy removing."

He waggled his eyebrows. "Sounds like your husband's in for a good time."

"So is his wife."

Fresh from her shower, Jewel picked out the gown she wanted. Drawing it on and looking at herself in the mirror via the soft light of the turned-down lamp, she was instantly embarrassed, but that soon gave way to a smile The lace-edged white gown with its strategically placed ribbons was guaranteed to please, and she couldn't wait to see his reaction. Granted, Eli would probably make certain she didn't have the gown on for very long, but wasn't that the whole purpose?

That aforementioned purpose fueled her steps as she left the bedroom to seek him out. Tonight she planned to give as good as she got and more, because she wanted this first coming together in their new home to be as sensual as it was memorable.

Eli was outside on the porch looking up at the stars when she stepped out to join him. He turned. Upon seeing her in the thin white silk and the way it shone under the shadowy moon, all he could say was, "Oh, my."

His manhood instantaneously throbbed to life. The breezy night air played with the edges of the silk just enough to offer him teasing flashes of her skin, alerting him to the fact that his prim little jewel didn't have a stitch on underneath. The realization made him hard as the wooden banister he was holding on to. "Nope," he told her with a mesmerized shake of his head, his voice certain. "You're not going to have that on very long at all—but long enough . . ."

Pleased, Jewel eased closer and he leaned down and nuzzled her neck. "You smell sweet," he whispered.

She was already spiraling and they were just getting started. His hand was moving over her silk-covered breast, the nipple already hard. "I like the gown."

Jewel liked it, too especially the way his hands were sliding it up and down, and over and around.

"Like this little ribbon, too."

The thin silk ribbon positioned beneath her breasts was the gown's only closure. He undid it without a word, then eased his warm palms inside to cup her hips and bring her flush against the strength of his desire. "I hope you don't have anywhere to be tomorrow, sweetheart, because I'm planning on making love to you until dawn."

His mouth found her breasts and she drew in a shuddering breath. The hand playing a sweet night song between her thighs was expert and bold. Because he was so scandalous and made her so shameless, she widened her stance so he could make her senses sing. And they did; arias, cadenzas, soprano, and descant. By the time he knelt in front of her, his bold touch plying her, she was already in the beginning throes of the orgasm. "You're very wet, Jewel."

Braced against the banister, legs spread to receive his caresses, Jewel was in another world, one where she didn't care how she looked or what anyone thought of what she and this wantonly gifted man were doing. All she knew was that she was his, and because she was, he drew her forward and worshipped at the gates of her soul with a lingering, red-hot devotion until she was reduced to a strangled scream.

He picked her up and took her into the house. The little death had her arching and twisting and riding the waves as he carried her to their bed. She didn't remember being lain down, but when he entered her so magnificently she moaned with pleasure and greedily raised her hips to feast on all he had to give.

"Lord, woman!" he growled unable to do anything but stroke. Her sweet body fueled him faster and faster. There'd be time for dallying next round, the male in him reasoned. Right then, he couldn't have slowed if there'd been a gun to his head. She was too tight, too delicious, too tantalizing. If forced to stop he'd explode. He exploded anyway. The orgasm was staggering and he clutched her hips roughly while he stroked and roared, and stroked and roared.

In the silence that followed they could hear the call of insects through the open windows. The room was pitch-dark and they lay smiling next to each other on the bed.

"I guess you were pretty eager."

He turned his head her way. He could barely make out her face in the darkness, but he knew she was looking at him, too. "Didn't hurt you, did I?"

"Not in the least."

"Good. Wouldn't want that. I do want you again, though, soon as I catch my breath."

"Was hoping you'd say that."

He chuckled in the dark and slid a finger over a nipple that obediently tightened at his command. "Randy woman."

"Just doing a wife's duty."

He reached over and coaxed her on top. A second later he was slowly and sinuously filling her. She moaned.

He asked, whispered, "Better?"

Her reply was soft as the night. "Much."

They took things slow. While she rode him in the age-old dance of Eve, he kissed, touched, and suckled. Thrusting into her rhythm languidly, he met her blazing eyes and dragged his palms down over the hard points of her breasts. The last time they'd made love this way, they'd been in the middle of the kitchen floor, and she'd come away with floor burns on the edges of her knees. Not this time. With the mattress beneath them offering her soft support, and the springs beneath helping them mark time, Jewel Crowley Grayson was in heaven. The pictures in the *Kama Sutra* may have accurately portrayed the positions, but she didn't think any drawing could equate the bliss and joy.

And for the rest of the night, he gave her plenty of both. At one point, a shower was needed, and after the lusty interlude in the steam-filled stall Eli learned to sing the praises of indoor plumbing.

They initiated the house's beginnings well, and when the birds began to chirp and dawn pinkened the sky, the lovers shared a final kiss then slept in each other's arms.

It took Jewel a few days to get all their newly purchased furniture where she wanted, but when it was done she was pleased. Thanks to her father, brothers, and everyone else who'd helped raise the house, she had a good-sized front parlor, a large, well-set-up kitchen, a washroom with a shower that she couldn't pry Eli out of now, and two bedrooms: one large, one small. She and Eli used the larger room as their bedroom.

They turned the smaller bedroom room into Eli's office, giving him a space he could keep as cluttered as he liked. If Jewel didn't want to see the mess, she simply closed the door. It worked out perfectly for both of them.

Monday morning after breakfast, Eli headed off to town and Jewel began her chores. It was washday. As she stripped the sheets off the bed, she smiled remembering last night's lusty play. Eli gave her so much pleasure she couldn't believe she'd wanted to sleep alone when they first married. Now, she couldn't be pried out of bed with him with a crowbar. He'd professed to know all there was about making love and she had to admit, he did.

She was outside hanging sheets on the clotheslines erected behind the house when Abigail appeared. "Morning, Jewel."

Pleased by the visit, because she hadn't seen her mother-in-law in a few days, Jewel said with affection, "Morning, Abigail. How are you?"

"I'm fine, dear. How are things with you?"

"No complaints. I've coffee on the stove if you'd like some."

"No, thank you," she said taking a seat on the wooden bench that had been a wedding gift from Zeke and Noah. "I drink so much, that if I bleed, it's black, no cream."

Jewel loved Abigail's wit, but as she placed the last clothespin in the edge of the last sheet on the line she saw that Abigail's face was lined with worry. "Something the matter?"

"Yes. Cecile. She has turned this sleepy little place upside down. Now even Reverend Anderson seems caught up in her madness."

It was true. Two weeks had passed since Cecile had slithered her way into Reverend Anderson's household. Jewel asked, "Do you know if Miss Ida made it to her mother's in Indiana?"

"Edna received a letter a few days ago. She got there fine, but I still can't believe the reverend took Cecile in."

Everyone in town was talking about Ida Anderson going home to her mother. Gossips and non-gossips alike were pointing fingers at Cecile as the catalyst.

Jewel said. "At least Lenore Wilson had the good sense not to let her into her home."

"Amen to that, but at the store this morning I heard her father has shipped Lenore off to his sister's in St. Louis, so who knows where that terrible woman will build her web next?"

"I know it won't be here," Jewel responded emphatically.

"Amen to that, too," Abigail echoed, then paused for a moment before saying, "I'm really worried about Reverend Anderson. Is it my imagination or have his sermons been especially lurid the past few weeks."

"They have. All of this fire and brimstone about Eve tempting Adam, then Jezebel, and Bathsheba, and Salome dancing and the beheading of John the Baptist; there isn't a fallen woman in the Bible he hasn't condemned. And then he let Cecile get up and sing on Sunday? I was stunned."

"I know. Personally I was surprised that she even had the brass to attend the service. And wearing all white, too."

"And," Jewel added, "sat in Miss Ida's seat."

"I know. I was so dumbstruck I couldn't tell you whether she had a passable voice or not. My heart was pounding so loud, I don't believe I heard a note."

The congregation had been just as dumbstruck, at least most of them. Jewel spied a few of the men smiling and looking on as if Cecile were a lurid actress on the stage, but Jewel supposed that was who Cecile was in reality. "Did you notice the Widow Moss stand up and walk out?"

"I did. Edna said Temperance was muttering about Satan's handmaidens. Never thought there'd come a day when I'd agreed with Temperance Moss, but I do on this."

Jewel did, too. "Is there a legal way to make her leave town?"

"I'm sure there isn't, so I suppose we'll just have to wait for Nathaniel to return and hope he can figure something out. By then, though, the men here may be warring over her like she's the dusky version of Helen of Troy."

"Let's hope it won't come to that."

Abigail sighed and shook her head. "I'm going up Dowagiac later on today with Edna. The niece of the Patterson twins is due to have her baby. With Viveca away, Edna's midwife again."

"Okay. Does Pa know your plans?"

"Yes, I told him this morning before he left for Niles with your brothers."

"Have a safe trip."

"We will."

They shared a parting embrace and Jewel went back to her wash, wondering what would happen next.

Eli was happy as a man could be who had a beautiful passionate wife and a newspaper that would be up and running in another week. The newsprint he'd ordered from Grand Rapids had been delivered by wagon earlier that morning and he was stacking the boxes of it in a corner of the area where the new printing press would go when it arrived. Whistling with contentment, the tune trailed off as he saw the Reverend Anderson drive past the window. Next to him on the seat sat Cecile dressed in a crisp white outfit that looked new. He shook his head. Satan's handmaiden indeed. It was the first time he'd ever agreed with the Widow Moss in his thirty plus years of life. That Cecile had the reverend under her spell was obvious to anyone with the eyes to see. Eli had once been just as mesmerized but not anymore. Jewel was his world. He was just about to turn away when he saw James Wilson who'd been standing in front of the store step down off the plank walk and into the street. He approached the buggy. The reverend stopped. Eli could see their mouths moving but couldn't hear the conversation due to distance. Next he knew, Wilson's face was contorted with anger and the reverend stormed out of the buggy looking angry as well. The two looked ready to fight.

"Aw, hell," Eli groused aloud. As the stand-in mayor, he was also the stand-in constable, so he left the office and headed to the scene.

They were already rolling in the dirt by the time he approached. Fists were flying as fast as curses. Were it up to him, he'd have let them beat each other to pieces, but he was supposed to be the keeper of the peace, and one of the combatants was a man of the cloth—at least on Sunday mornings.

Eli yelled for them to stop. Vernon came running up, as did the five feet, two inch tall undertaker, Solomon Bates, and a few men from inside the store. They waded in. It took a few minutes to pry the combatants apart. Verbal insults filled the air as the two continued to strain against the men holding them at bay. The reverend appeared to have a broken nose. Miss Edna hurried out with wet cloths and her doctoring kit. Cecile sat on the bench looking pleased with herself.

Eli turned away from her in disgust and eyed the two grown men who'd been fighting in the street like lunatics. He paid no attention to all the folks standing on the walks watching. His voice stern, he announced to Wilson and Anderson, "I don't want to know why this started, but I do know how it will end. Both of you can either calm down and take yourselves home, or I can toss you in the lockup and fine you fifty dollars for disturbing the peace." He knew fifty dollars was a large sum and he'd intentionally set the fine high in order to keep this nonsense from being prolonged, or from happening again. "What's it to be, gentlemen?"

"This heathen attacked me!" the reverend said nasally while Edna packed his nose.

Wilson tried to have another go at it but the men holding him kept him away. The incensed reverend, riled again, twisted free from his holders and delivered a solid right hand to Wilson's jaw that dropped him cold.

Eli looked down at the knocked-out Wilson and drawled, "Guess it's the cell. Pick him up, fellas. Edna, when you're done, escort the reverend down to Nate's office, if you would, please."

"Will do, Eli."

Cecile came to life. "Who's going to take me to the hairdresser? I don't know how to drive."

Eli tossed back. "Guess you'll have to figure that out on your own." He told his helpers holding Wilson, "Bring him along, men."

Because Wilson was still out, the toes of his boots scraped the ground as he was dragged away.

Eli related the incident to Jewel as they sat on the porch after dinner.

"Are they still locked up?" she asked.

"No. Creighton came and paid his father's fine about an hour later."

"Where in the world did he get that kind of money?"

He shrugged. "I don't know, but I put it in the safe, and he took Wilson home."

"I wonder if it came from that phony tax he was charging."

"That did cross my mind."

"And what about Reverend Anderson?"

Eli thought back on the reverend and shook his head. "Ironically, the only person he could think to wire for the funds he needed to pay his fine was his wife. By the end of the day he hadn't received a reply, so I sent him on home."

"Poor man. I think Cecile has made him lose his mind."

"Apparently."

Eli dropped his head back against the porch

post. "I can't wait for Nate to return so he can take back this mayor's job. I swear, if I had to do this all day, every day like he does, I'd shoot myself."

"He'll be home eventually."

"But will it be before the rest of the men in town turn into lunatics is the question."

Jewel chuckled. "So, did Satan's handmaiden get someone to take her to the hairdresser."

"Yes. Sol Bates."

"The undertaker!"

"I'm afraid so."

"Lord have mercy."

"Exactly." He then asked her, "Would you do me a favor?"

"I'll certainly try. What is it?"

"Come here and let me open some buttons. I'm hoping it will make me feel better."

She laughed. "Speaking of lunatics."

But she granted him the boon, and lo and behold, they both felt better.

Cecile was lying in the dark in Sol Bates's lumpy bed while he snored loudly beside her. The short fat undertaker had not been a memorable lover, not because he was short in stature, but because he was short in the area where it mattered most. She'd given some of her best performances on her back but tonight, she should have been awarded a prize. She sighed. He'd offered her a place to stay, however, and that was what mattered most at the moment.

Now that she would be sharing Bates's bed, she could afford to discard the oh-so-righteous Reverend Anderson, and the judgmental James Wilson. Because of her return to town, their lives, especially the reverend's, were in tatters, and she was enjoying the turmoil tremendously.

Back during her marriage to Nathaniel Grayson, Anderson and Wilson had been two of the many lovers she'd commanded; however, when Nate divorced her and tossed her out of his life, neither lifted a finger to help. Penniless and in need of transportation to leave town, she sent messages to Miller, whose wife had still been alive at the time, but received a reply stating she was never to contact him again. Anderson, who'd told himself he was saving her soul by bedding her then and now, was suddenly too busy to do anything but walk past her as if they'd never met, let alone had had sex regularly in the choir stall at the church.

In her mind, both men deserved to be the subjects of public scorn. She knew the moment she saw them again that they wanted her, and what better way to get her revenge than to ruin them. The only one who seemed immune was Eli. Him, she'd wanted back simply for the sheer pleasure. It never occurred to her that he'd not want her for the same reason. The day he'd shown up at her door, he'd been so angry, he'd frightened her. She'd managed to hide it, but knew from that moment that he was lost to her and would not betray the little Crowley whelp the way he'd betrayed his cousin.

Oh, well, she told herself. At least Anderson and Wilson's life were in shambles, or at least Wilson's would be once he learned she'd been sleeping with his son, and she couldn't wait to alert him to that titillating fact. She guessed the good reverend would be looking for a new wife and possibly a new church if only to escape the damning gossip.

All in all, it had been a good stopover in turnip town, she decided, and as soon as she got her hands on a little bit more money, she'd be on her way somewhere else.

On the last Friday night in June, everyone turned out for the annual Sweetheart Ball sponsored by the Grayson Grove Female Intelligence Society. It was always the group's most successful fund-raiser, and this year, from the looks of the numbers of people in the well-dressed crowd, the profit would be a record breaker.

The dance was held at the town hall. The decorating committee had tacked red doily hearts to the walls and strung white streamers across the ceiling. Vernon and his band were playing, and the cakes, pies, and homemade candies that were always for sale at the dance filled a white-clothed table.

Jewel was dancing slowly with her husband to the ballad being played by the band. "Everybody looks so nice."

Eli agreed. Even Maddie, dancing with G.W., was wearing a lovely green gown instead of her usual buckskins. "Maddie must really be in love if she's wearing a gown."

Jewel looked toward them and nodded. "She looks very beautiful, don't you think?"

"I think G.W. should get some lifts for his shoes."

Jewel swatted him playfully on the arm. "Be nice." Maddie was a good five inches taller than her beau. "You know, this is the first year she and I have ever come to the dance and not been behind the punch table serving. So thank you for being my escort this evening."

"You're welcome. Did I tell you how fetching you look?"

"Yes, you did." Jewel had made a special trip to Niles to purchase the indigo gown she was wearing from Sally Payne's shop, and she felt like a queen twirling around the floor with her handsome husband dressed in his formal wear. "You look very fine, yourself, Mr. Grayson."

"Thanks. How about we take a long time undressing each other when we get home?"

She laughed and whispered, "Behave yourself."

"Only while we're here at the dance. Once we leave, I won't be responsible for my actions. Ever made love in a buggy?"

Wondering what she was going to do with this outrageous man whom she loved as much as she did breathing, she told him, "Dance."

"Yes, ma'am."

When the band finished the selection, Eli led her off the floor and over to the punch table. As one of the hostesses ladled out portions for them into short glass cups, they sipped and fed on each other with their eyes.

Jewel told him quietly, "You really should stop looking at me that way."

He sidled close enough to smell her rose-scented perfume. "What way?"

"As if you want to remove my clothing."

"Didn't I already say that?"

She shot him a humorous look.

He grinned over his cup. Eli couldn't wait to get his wife home. He was just about to tell her that when he noticed James Wilson enter the hall alone. Eli hadn't seen him since the day of the fight but heard he was working in Chicago on the docks during the week and returning to the Grove on weekends. Eli had no idea if Wilson had chosen to work so far away so as not to see Cecile being squired around by her newest pet, Sol Bates, but Eli didn't really care. He just wanted Wilson not to cause any trouble.

Jewel looked across the hall to see what was causing her husband's cool glare. Spying James Wilson, she said, "The reverend has already blessed the gathering and gone home, so we're spared them coming to blows and ruining the dance."

The band struck up a lively tune, but Eli, still watching Wilson, saw him stagger into a chair. "He's drunk," he said stonily.

Sure enough, Jewel could see Lenore and Creighton's father moving about on wobbly legs and bumping into some of the dancers. Eli handed Jewel his cup. "I hate being mayor."

She watched him thread his way through the crowd. As wary couples moved away from the stumbling Wilson, the floor cleared. The band stopped playing and all eyes were directed Wilson's way.

Suddenly, he yelled drunkenly, "Kill the whores! Kill them all!" Then he began to cry, tears running down his face.

Jewel saw Eli reach out and gently take hold of Wilson's arm, intending to steer him outside, but Wilson snatched free and shouted emotionally, "She slept with my son! That whore slept with my boy."

A collective gasp shot through the hall and Jewel shook her head sadly.

"Kill her!" he yelled again angrily, doing his best to fight off Eli and the men who'd come to aid him. "Kill the whore!"

But in the end, Wilson crumpled to the floor and the sounds of his pain-wracked sobs filled the silent hall.

Eli and the others finally managed to escort the broken man away and once they disappeared, the place buzzed with reaction.

Maddie and G.W. walked over to where Jewel was standing and Maddie said, "Satan's handmaiden, indeed."

"I know. I never thought I'd feel sorry for Mr. Wilson, but I do now."

G.W. voiced tersely, "And to think I brought this woman here."

Maddie sought to reassure him. "Don't blame yourself. If it hadn't been you it would have been somebody else."

Jewel saw Abigail imploring the band to commence playing, and once they began, couples moved back out to the dance floor, but the whispers went on for the rest of the evening.

Jewel drove home alone and waited up for Eli. She was in bed reading when he returned a short while after midnight, and his face was grim. "We left Wilson at his house. Didn't see Creighton."

"Do you think he was telling the truth about Cecile and Creighton."

Eli nodded. "He was in her room the morning I warned her to stay away from you. I wondered at the time if Wilson knew he was sharing Cecile with his son, but I guess we have the answer now. What a mess."

Jewel agreed. "There should be a law to make her leave town."

"No law against a woman bedding a husband and his son. Just like there was nothing against a husband and his cousin when I was the one in her bed."

"Well, you're not anymore, so come, let's go to sleep."

He nodded and removed his black coat and then the shirt beneath. After the disastrous evening, Eli's desire to make love to his wife had been diminished. "I'm not much in the mood for lovemaking after what we witnessed tonight."

"Neither am I."

So when Eli finished undressing and the lights were extinguished, he eased his arms around Jewel. A short while later, she drifted off to sleep, but it took Eli much longer.

It was late. Bates had been called away to attend to the sudden death of someone somewhere in the Grove. Cecile hadn't been interested enough to remember the name, so when she heard footsteps enter she assumed it was him returning, and plastered on a phony smile. "Sol, darling, is that you?"

"No," came a familiar voice.

Surprised she got out of bed and met him at the bedroom door. "What are you doing here? Leave. I'll meet you in the morning. Bates may be back any minute."

"Just came to pay my last respects."

Confused, she asked, "Are you leaving?"

"No. You are."

As he advanced and grabbed her, her eyes widened, but it was too late. His hands were already around her throat. She fought for air, but he was strong. Her clawing and twisting were to no avail.

He increased the pressure of his hold, crushing her windpipe and she finally went limp. Her death made him smile. He picked up her lifeless body and left the house with it as silently as he'd come.

# Chapter 15

Eli and G.W. were in the *Gazette* office the following morning admiring the new printing press that had been delivered. In the past, due to his lack of funds, Eli had always been forced to buy someone else's discarded or rebuilt equipment and the idea that this one was brand spanking new put a smile on his face.

"Like it?" the beaming G.W. asked.

"There are no words to describe."

He was just about to say more when Solomon Bates hurried in. Seeing him made Eli remember last night's scene at the dance, and Cecile. "Morning, Sol."

"Have you seen Cecile?" he asked in a rush.

"No. Why?"

"I think something has happened to her."

"Why?"

"She's gone."

Eli studied the undertaker's agitated face. "What makes you think she hasn't just run off?"

"All of her clothes and things are still at my place."

"That doesn't necessarily mean she's gone, Sol. She could be out visiting somewhere or decided to leave the Grove altogether."

"She's gone, Eli, I tell you. Something's happened. She wouldn't just take off without a word to me, and she wouldn't leave all her possessions behind."

Before Eli could respond, Sol's face clouded with anger. "Never mind. I'll look for her myself."

As he stormed out and drove away in his wagon, which also doubled as the town's hearse, Eli said to no one in particular, "Would somebody please wire my cousin and tell him to get his ass back here so he can take this job off my hands."

G.W. smiled at that, but then asked, "Could she really be missing?"

He shrugged. "Who knows, but if she doesn't turn up by this evening, I'll pull a search party together and we'll go looking."

"Sounds reasonable."

"More reasonable than she deserves."

By noon, they had the new press up and running. When word got around as to what they were doing various people stopped by to take a gander at Eli's fancy new printing press, including Abigail, Jewel, and Maddie. The office had become so crowded by midafternoon that Eli was having difficulty maneuvering so he could run the test sheets that needed to be printed in order to get the proper ink saturation. He was just about to throw everybody out when Maddie glanced out of the window and said sadly, "Sol Bates is coming up the street in his hearse. Looks like a body in the back."

They all went to the window. "Who do you think has died?" Jewel asked, turning to Eli.

As he and G.W. shared a look, Eli fought off an eerie chill. Neither man had said anything to anyone about Sol's visit that morning and how worried he'd been about Cecile.

"He's stopping out front," Abigail said.

Eli made his way to the door and walked outside to where Sol sat atop the wagon. "Sol?"

The undertaker's eyes were red and swollen. "I found her," he said, choking back tears. " Somebody strangled her, Eli. She's dead."

Eli sighed. Cecile had finally met her fate. "Where did you find her body?"

By then a crowd made up of those from inside the office and from the walks and storefronts close by had gathered around.

"On the field behind the school."

Eli said to him, "Go ahead and make whatever preparations you need to get her buried and I'll wire the authorities at the county seat. They'll probably send someone down to investigate."

Sol drove away and Eli turned to the people looking on in shock. "If you know anything about what happened to her, or who did this, it's your duty to come forward."

No one did. "Okay. Go on back to whatever you were doing, everyone. Show's over."

And once again, the Grove was abuzz.

Needless to say, Eli didn't get much more newspaper work done that day. He drove over to Calvin Center and spent the balance of the afternoon sending wires back and forth to various county officials and law-enforcement agencies about the murder. When he returned to the Grove, he had to keep reassuring those who stopped by the mayor's office that the Grove continued to be a safe place for them and their families. However, he was disturbed knowing there was a murderer lurking amongst them and hoped the culprit would be exposed soon.

He was finally preparing to leave Nate's office for the day, anxious to head home with Jewel, when a man he didn't know walked in. He was White, middle-aged, and tall and thin as a scarecrow. His brown suit with its frayed cuffs showed its age. "Are you Eli Grayson?"

"Yes. And you are?"

"The name's Swan. I'm with the Boston Police office."

Eli went still. He looked out through the windowpane at Jewel seated on the wagon waiting for him so they could drive home. He didn't think it would be anytime soon now. "What brings you to Grayson Grove, Mr. Swan?"

"A Mr. G.W. Hicks wired the Pinkertons a few weeks back about a Cecile Green?"

Eli gestured to a chair. "Have a seat. Excuse me for a minute. Let me send my wife home so that you and I can talk."

Swan nodded.

Outside, Jewel asked, "Ready?"

"No, you should probably go on without me. The man inside's a policeman from Boston."

Her face showed her surprise. "Really. Why is he here?"

"G.W. wanted to find out if Cecile had been involved in anything seamy before her return here."

"Do you think he found something?"

"No idea."

"Have you told him she's dead?"

He shook his head. "Not yet."

"I'll head on home, then."

"That might be best. I'd like to keep Swan being here just between the two of us, for the time being. No sense in adding to the commotion. We've had enough for one day."

"Of course. I won't tell anyone."

Her answer pleased him. "Have I told you lately what a wonderful wife you are?"

She smiled. "I'll see you at home. Be careful."

"I will." He looked up at her beautiful face. "I love you, Mrs. Grayson."

"I love you, too."

He watched her drive away, then went back into the office. "So," he said to Swan after settling into the chair behind the desk. "What have you found, if anything?"

"We've learned that the woman you know here as Cecile Green is more than likely Cecile Briles. The Pinkertons turned the information over to us when they found out she was wanted for murder in Boston."

Eli sat up.

"She's also tied to a string of questionable marriages that stretch from California to Massachusetts."

He proceeded to tell Eli about the woman the Pinkertons had dubbed the Black Widow. "She marries these men, stays in their lives just long enough to get access to their funds, and once that is accomplished, she cleans them out and disappears."

Eli didn't know why he found the report surprising, but he did. "And she's wanted for murder as well?"

"Yes. A woman named Bethany Briles, the daughter of Lucius Briles, Cecile's last husband. Miss Briles, whose married name is Carter, was found clubbed to death in Cecile's bedroom."

Eli sighed and shook his head.

"I'm here to take her back to Boston to stand trial. Do you know where I might find her?"

"Yes. Bates Undertaking down the street. Somebody killed her."

Swan stared. "She's dead?"

"I'm afraid so."

"When?"

"Close as we can figure, sometime last night."

"Any suspects?"

"Probably half the town. She had more lovers than Old Glory has stars; even I was one years back."

It was obvious from the way Swan was staring that he was as much taken aback by Eli's revelations as Eli had been by his. "How was she killed? Has that been determined?"

"Undertaker says she was strangled."

"Then we have a murderer to find now."

Eli nodded. "Yes, we do."

"Is there time for me to visit the location where the body was found before nightfall?"

"Yes. Let's go talk to the undertaker. He discovered the corpse."

Eli and Swan gathered up Bates and rode to the school. When they arrived, he pointed out the place where'd he found Cecile. Eli watched Swan look around at the surrounding landscape, then bend low to look at the dirt field they were all standing in.

The curious Bates asked, "What are you searching for?"

"Nothing in particular, just seeing what there might be to see." He continued to study the soil. "Footprints." He looked up. "Mr. Bates can you come here and identify the ones that belong to you."

Because Bates feet were so small, his were easy to distinguish from the larger ones pressed into the dust.

Eli studied the prints. "That's your standard Grove boot. We all wear the same kind. Miss Edna sells them at the store."

The scarecrow nodded. "Certainly doesn't narrow it down. Does it?"

"No," Eli answered solemnly.

Swan stood and wiped his hands on his trousers. "Let's go back to town. I need to find a room for the night and write my report. I'd like to start interviewing some of your residents in the morning, if I could Mr. Grayson."

"I'll assist however you think best."

His blue eyes pierced Eli. "Good, because I'd like to start with you."

Eli knew he had nothing to hide. "We can talk first thing tomorrow."

Swan nodded and they walked back to the wagons.

That evening as Eli and Jewel lay in bed, she said, "Once Mr. Swan is finished interrogating you, he can start looking for the real killer."

Eli smiled in the dark. She hadn't been happy to learn that her husband would be questioned first. "I don't mind answering his questions because I've nothing to hide. And yes, then we can look for the person really responsible for Cecile's death."

"James Wilson should be on the top of the list."

"I agree. Swan will probably want to talk to Reverend Anderson, Creighton, and lord knows who else, too."

"I hope he finds the culprit quickly. It's very unsettling knowing we may have a killer loose in the Grove."

"I know." He reached over and pulled her close until she was spooned against him. "I want you to be careful when you're out driving. I don't want anything happening to you."

"Neither do I." She turned so she could look into his shadowy face. "You do the same. I don't want anything happening to you, either."

He kissed her softly. "You're my life, Jewel. I'm not sure I could cope if you came to harm."

"I'm pretty handy with a gun, remember?"

"I do," he said thinking back on her and her bird gun. "Anybody wanting to tangle with you should think twice."

"True, but I will be careful."

He placed his lips against her forehead. "That's all I ask. One more question?"

"Yes."

"How many buttons are on this nightgown?"

She chuckled. "I'm not real sure. Would you like to check?"

"I think I might."

There were five and after he spent an inordinate amount of time opening them, the only sounds in the bedroom were the squeaks of the bed and the cries of the little death.

When Swan walked through the open door of the mayor's office the next morning, Eli greeted him with a nod and gestured him to a seat.

Swan sat, and then asked, "Are you ready?"

"As ready as you are."

He studied Eli for a long moment and then said, "So, tell me about your relationship with Mrs. Briles."

"She was my cousin-in-law when I first met her."

Swan looked surprised, and as Eli's story continued, the surprise was replaced by grim shakes of his head. "You were sixteen at that time?"

Eli answered.

"And your cousin divorced her as a result of the adultery?

"Yes."

He then asked Eli where he'd been on the night Cecile was killed. Eli related the story of James Wilson's drunken display at the dance. "We took him home and afterward I went home to my wife."

Swan was making notes. When he finished, he seemed pleased. "Thank you, Mr. Grayson. I needed to hear your story. Want to make sure the person I'm working with is not on the top of the suspect list."

Eli smiled. "I understand."

Swan stood and stuck out a hand. "So let's you and I start over. I'm Bryson Swan. Most people call me Bryce."

Eli stood and met his hand. "Call me Eli."

The scarecrow's blue eyes twinkled, "Glad to meet ya. Now, let's go see Mr. James Wilson."

But the elder Wilson wasn't in the mood for callers, and the shotgun he raised toward them when they reached his gate emphasized that. "Get off my land!"

Eli sighed loudly. "Wilson, this is a policeman from back east; he wants to talk to you about Cecile's death."

"Hope she's burning in hell and the man who killed her gets a medal. That's all I got to say. Now, get off my land before I shoot you for trespassing."

Eli called back angrily, "This is a sworn officer of the law, Wilson. You can't refuse to talk to him!"

"The hell I can't!"

Swan touched Eli's arm. "We'll come back. If he was as drunk as you said he was the night she died, I doubt he's our man. Let's save him for later."

Eli gave him a tight nod and they got back on the wagon.

For the next two days, he and Swan crisscrossed the Grove talking to people near and far, and the only thing they learned for sure was that the list of her paramours was much longer than Eli had imagined. Men he would never have suspected confessed to having trysted with her. Her conquests were both young and old, and she stole from each of them.

A talk with the Reverend Anderson that afternoon in the mayor's office revealed his previously unknown, long-term relationship with the murdered Cecile.

When he finished his sordid tale, Eli was stunned. "So she was sleeping with you, too, while Nate was away fighting the war?"

Anderson looked ashamed, but he nodded. "James Wilson as well."

Eli didn't believe this. It was difficult not to be bitter knowing he'd been the only one ostracized after Cecile left town.

"James and I pretended we weren't involved with her when your cousin found out about you and her. We didn't want to risk his wrath, and I didn't want to lose the church I'd just become the pastor of."

Eli had trouble hiding his disgust.

Anderson walked to the office windows and looked out. "I've begged my wife's forgiveness, and I've begged God's forgiveness, too, but neither seem to be in a charitable mood right now, so I continue to pray."

Swan asked, "Did you kill Cecile Briles?"

The reverend turned. "No. I wanted to when she confessed that she'd intentionally set out to ruin my life because of the way I'd turned my back on her those many years ago. And she has." He looked at Eli. "I suppose your mother's going to want me to find a new church?"

"That would probably be best."

He turned back to the window, was silent for a long while, and then said, "I was weak. She tempted me like Eve with the apple. Like Adam, I was but of flesh."

Eli who'd been around progressive women all of his life, wasn't buying the excuse. "And like Adam, you made the choice to take that fruit, Reverend. Cecile didn't hold a gun to your head."

Anderson apparently didn't appreciate Eli's insight. "Do you need me for anything else?" he asked tersely.

Swan replied, "No, but don't leave town. I may have other questions for you at a later date."

"I understand." He met Eli's hostile eyes then looked away. "Good day, gentlemen." He exited without further word.

Eli glanced at Bryce. "Well?"

Bryce shrugged "He could be the one. Loses his wife and his church. He wasn't happy with you sticking a pin in that excuse balloon he was attempting to send up. We'll keep him on the list."

Eli agreed.

Next up was Solomon Bates. They found him at home in his apartment above the funeral home. He ushered them in politely then stood, waiting.

Swan said, "Thanks for agreeing to see us, Mr. Bates."

Bates nodded.

Eli knew that Sol had buried Cecile yesterday and had been the only one at the graveside. Not even the now-disgraced Reverend Anderson had come to see her put into the ground.

"Are her personal items still here?" Eli asked.

"Other than the gown she was buried in, yes."

"I'd like to see them," Swan stated.

Eli thought the short man would refuse at first. The look on his face showed he was not happy with the request, but he seemed to think better of defying the policeman and so led them into his small bedroom. On the short dresser were two handbags. The doors to an armoire were open and her gowns could be seen hanging inside.

Swan asked, "Have you gone through any of her things?"

"Of course not. Why would I?"

Eli and Swan shared a look.

Swan said to Eli, "You take the handbags. I'll take the drawers and the armoire." Eli dumped the contents of the first bag on the bed and as he began to look through the train ticket stubs and other detritus, he asked, Bates, "Have you checked your safe since she became your houseguest?"

"What?"

"Your safe, Sol. Is everything that is supposed be in there still there?"

"Are you asking if she stole from me? That's a terrible question to ask."

"Just go look in the safe, please."

"Cecile wouldn't—"

"Man, get your head out of the sand. If everything's as it should be, I'll apologize."

Solomon stomped over to the wall safe hidden behind a picture and opened it. He moved the contents inside around for a few moments, and then his searching became frantic and his eyes were wide.

Eli shook his head as he dumped out another handbag and hit the jackpot. "This what you're looking for?" he asked and tossed the undertaker a small but heavy coin bag.

Sol made the catch and dragged open the drawstring. Inside was almost three hundred dollars. "Oh my!"

Swan said to Eli, "Guess you won't have to apologize."

"Guess not."

While Swan and Eli continued their search, Bates dropped silently into a chair and placed his head in his hands.

# Chapter 16

Jewel was missing Eli something fierce. For the last few days he'd been coming home late and leaving before she got up as he and the Boston policeman continued to search for clues that might lead to Cecile's killer. Everywhere she went people stopped her and asked if Eli had found anything new, and each time she told them no, but that he was still looking. Thanks to her monthly and the ongoing investigation, she felt as if they hadn't made love in months. She didn't complain because of the importance of what he was doing, but she did miss having him near.

That morning, he was once again gone by the time she got up, so she padded out to the kitchen to see if he'd made any coffee. She froze at the sight of Creighton Wilson sitting at the table. "What are you doing here!"

"Didn't mean to scare you, Jewel, but you're the only person I know to talk to."

She noticed how dirty and unkempt he and his clothing were. He looked like he'd been sleeping on the ground in the forest. "Eli's been looking for you, Creighton. He's been talking to everybody about Cecile's death and he has some questions he wants to ask?"

"Figured he would. I want you to go with me so I can turn myself in."

He then looked up at Jewel and she saw the sadness in his eyes. "I killed her," he whispered.

Her first thought was to wonder if she could be in danger as well, so she casually glanced around the kitchen in search of something she could use to defend herself should it become necessary. "You want something to eat," she asked, trying not to show the nervousness making her heart pound.

"Yeah. I'm pretty hungry. I've been too scared to go home or into town."

She fried up some eggs and bacon, reheated some of the biscuits left over from last night's dinner with Eli, and put everything on a plate. "Here you go."

He dove in like a man starved, and while he was preoccupied with eating, she slipped a very sharp boning knife into the pocket of the apron she'd put on when she began cooking breakfast. Too wary to eat herself, she poured herself a cup of coffee and stood by the stove, well out of his reach as she sipped slowly. She prayed that somebody, anybody, would stop by for a visit so she'd have help with this. And she preferred someone large in stature like her husband, father, or one of her brothers because Creighton was a big man as well.

He looked up at her and she froze. A cold smile spread across his face and lingered in the formerly sad eyes. "You think I'm going to hurt you, don't you?"

"It has crossed my mind, yes."

"I am, Jewel. I've always wanted you for myself, but I'm going to wait to do it after I tell you why I killed that whore."

Jewel fought down the terror that was threatening to buckle her knees.

"You're scared, aren't you?"

"Yes."

"Cecile was scared. I liked that."

Jewel tried to determine if she could make it to the door behind her quickly enough to escape.

"If you run away, Jewel, I'll have to hurt you more, so don't try, okay?"

"I won't run, Cray. I promise."

"Good. Thanks for feeding me. Do you want me to put the plate in the sink?"

"No. I'll take care of it later. You were going to tell me about Cecile."

He seemed to go away in his mind for a few moments, then said, "She told my father I was seeing her. No, she told him I was fucking her. Such a crude word, *fucking*. I thought she was the most beautiful woman I'd ever met, besides you, but she was only beautiful on the outside. Inside she was a crude whore."

Jewel's insides shook.

"You'd never use that word, would you?"

"Never."

That seemed to please him. "My father was angry at her, and at me. He told me I wasn't his son anymore. Started drinking and told me to get out." The pain he carried was easy to see. "So I left."

"I'm sorry, Cray."

He snapped coldly. "You weren't sorry when your brothers laughed at me. You weren't sorry when Pa and I came across you that night sitting on Eli's lap."

Jewel's heart was pumping so hard from fear she found it difficult to breathe.

"But you'll pay, Jewel Crowley. Just like Cecile."

She knew then that she had to get out. The unbalanced anger in his eyes was terrifying. "I thought you wanted to turn yourself in?"

"I did, but I changed my mind. I'm going to have you first, then show you how I killed the whore. Where's the bed you and Eli use?"

Horror screamed in Jewel's mind. She'd kill herself first before she'd let him rape her in the bed she and Eli shared. She turned to run, but he was quick for a man his size. He grabbed her with a hand around her throat, and from that point on time seemed to slow. She saw his other hand reach out, but by then, she'd already drawn the knife. Feeling the pressure closing down her windpipe cutting off her breathing, she jammed the razor sharp blade into his groin and jerked it up as far and as hard as she could, slicing through bone, tissue, and sinew. His hands fell away, his screams filled the air, his blood spurted everywhere, and she gasped for life-giving air on legs too jellied to run, but she forced herself to stumble toward the door. He was screaming like an enraged bear and came after her, but by that time, Jewel was down the back steps and into the yard before he could catch her. Running, she looked back, her eyes wide, her throat on fire, and saw him clutching his blood-stained belly and cursing her as if he wanted the vile words to kill her because he could not. He fell from the steps, hit the ground and didn't move again.

After Eli and Swan completed another fruitless day, they returned to the mayor's office. Eli asked, "You want to come home with me and have dinner? I'm sure Jewel has food waiting and I doubt she'll mind."

Swan studied him. "I'd hate to barge in on her without a proper invitation."

"It will be okay."

"You sure?"

"Positive."

"Then the answer is yes."

As Eli drove, Swan looked out over the land and said, "Looks a lot like home."

"Does it?"

"Yes, it does. Makes me miss it and my wife."

"I didn't know you were married."

They spent the rest of the drive talking about Swan's life back in Boston, his wife, Beatrice, and his two sons, Ethan and Cyrus.

"How long have you been a policeman?"

"Too long, I think sometimes, but fifteen years come December."

"That long?"

By then, they'd reached the bluff and as Eli drove up the incline he could see his wife sitting on the porch in the rocking chair she'd made and his heart smiled at the sight. But as they grew closer, he paused, sensing something not quite right. The rocker was moving way too fast and she was holding the chair so tightly he could see the bulges in her arms from where he sat on the wagon bench. Only then did he realize that the woman he loved more than life was covered with blood! He tossed the reins aside, jumped down and ran to the porch. Swan ran, too.

"Jewel?" Eli called softly as he kneeled beside her. Speckles of dried blood were all over her face in her hair and on the front of the old blue shirt she was wearing. Seeing it put his heart in his throat. "Sweetheart, what's happened? Are you hurt?"

She continued to rock. The eyes that had been staring straight ahead suddenly filled with tears and then met his. She whispered. "I knew you'd come if I sat here long enough. I knew."

He reached down and grabbed her up, blood and all. She held on to him as if for dear life. "It was so awful," she cried. "I had to kill him, Eli. I had to."

Swan left them and disappeared inside the house.

"Who, darling? Who?'

"Cray. He killed Cecile. He wanted to kill me, too."

Eli clutched her tighter. "God!"

"I knew you'd come. I knew you would."

Heart aching, he carried her inside and sat her down on the sofa. When she began to rock again his worry heightened.

Swan walked into the parlor. "How is she?"

"Not sure. I think she may be in shock."

"She's a pretty brave lady. Whoever he is, she gutted him like a trout. Found the knife she must have used on him lying on the floor in the kitchen."

"He's Creighton Wilson. James's son. She said he killed Cecile."

Eli looked at his staring and rocking wife with rising concern. "I don't want to leave her, so could you drive back to town, go to the store and tell Miss Edna what's happened and that I need her as fast as she can get here."

"Will do."

"And ask her to get word to my mother and to send someone to tell Jewel's father, Adam."

"I'll send help back fast as I can. Can I use the wagon outside to take the body back to town?"

Eli nodded.

"Oh, and the kitchen floor and walls are splattered with blood, you might want to keep her out of there until everything's cleaned up."

"Thanks."

After Swan's departure, Eli went to Jewel, put her in his lap and held her against his pounding heart. That she had almost been Creighton's second victim tore him up inside, but the knowledge that she was alive and in his arms made him feel blessed. "Is there anything you want me to do for you, Jewel?"

"Just hold me," she whispered.

Eli had no problem honoring her request. He'd hold her until the sun became the moon if it would help her shake off the terror she must have experienced. He and Swan had been looking for Creighton for days now, but had they known he was the person responsible for murdering Cecile, they would have moved heaven and earth to find him. Instead, Creighton found Jewel. Eli tightened his hold, so sorry he hadn't been there to help her, but she'd evidently done all right without him.

Jewel had never felt so safe. With Eli's arms around her, she knew no harm would touch her, ever, and all the anxiety and fear roiling inside seemed to be fading. "I need to wash up," she told him softly. She hoped that ridding herself of the blood and being clean again would aid in righting herself.

"Do you want me to help you?"

She shook her head. "I think I'll be okay on my own, but will you wait outside the door?"

"I'll wait in hell if you need me to."

She looked up. "I love you, Eli."

"You are my heart, Jewel."

* * *

When Adam, Abigail, and Miss Edna arrived, Jewel was clean and sitting up in bed. Dressed in a plain cotton nightgown, Eli thought she still looked very pale, but all the blood was gone and he hoped to never see her that way again. It hurt him too much.

To give Jewel some privacy while Miss Edna examined her, Eli, Adam, and Abigail stepped outside the room.

"So what happened?" Adam demanded.

Eli told them as much of the story as he knew.

At the end of the tale, Adam was furious. "Be glad he's dead," he fumed. "Otherwise the boys and I would be hunting him down like a rabid wolf."

Abigail patted him on the arm reassuringly. "She's fine, Adam. Thank God she kept her wits about her, though."

Eli was thankful for that as well, and he attributed her survival to the fearless way she'd been raised. "Be proud of the way you raised her, Adam. I'm not sure she would be still with us if you hadn't."

Adam nodded, but he was impatient to speak with his daughter. "How long is Edna going to be? I want to see Jewel."

"She'll be done in a few moments," Abigail said to him. "Just be patient."

As Abigail predicted, Miss Edna came out of the room a short while later. "Physically, she's fine. She's had a horrible experience, so it may take some time for her to go back to being the Jewel we know and love."

Eli asked, "But she's not hurt in any way?"

"Just her spirit."

Eli was glad to hear that.

Edna looked to Adam Crowley. "She's asking for you, Adam."

He nodded and walked to the door.

Jewel looked up when her father came in. "Hello, Pa," she said quietly.

"How's my Jewel doing?" Studying her, he sat down on the edge of the bed.

"I've been better."

He looked off into the distance for a moment as if thinking back on what she'd had to endure, then said, "I'm real proud of you."

"Why?"

"Because you did what you had to do to survive. Not many women can do that."

"They didn't have you as a father," she reminded him. Suddenly, the memory of the awful encounter returned and she did her best not to let it reclaim her soul. "I killed a man, Pa."

"It was either kill or be killed."

"I know, but . . ."

"But what?" he asked gently.

"I wish I hadn't had to, I guess."

"Truthfully, better him than you."

Adam looked into the face that so resembled his late wife. "When you were born, you were so small you could fit into the palm of my hand."

Their eyes met and she smiled softly. "I must have been quite a shock after all the boys."

He nodded. "You were, but your mother was so

very happy. I was, too." He quieted for a moment. "No offense to Abigail, but I miss her."

"I do, too."

"I know. I think you took her passing harder than anyone, including me."

"It was the first time death ever took someone I loved from my life."

"I'm glad it didn't take you from mine today."

"So am I."

Father and daughter shared a look of love, then he hugged her tight. "Are you sure you're okay?"

Tears stung Jewel's eyes as she hugged him back with a love that welled up from her heart. "I am."

He kissed her cheek and rose to his feet. "Then I'm going to leave you alone now. Your brothers are probably here by now and I know whoever else is outside is chomping at the bit to get in here, but don't let them tire you out. You hear?"

"I hear. And Pa?"

He turned from the door and looked back.

"Thanks for being my father."

He nodded. "Thank you for being my jewel. Rest up."

And he was gone.

For the next little while, the people Jewel loved the most stuck their heads in the door to see with their own eyes that she was okay. Her brothers, Abigail, Maddie, G.W., Anna Red Bird. Half the town would have paraded into the room had they been allowed to do so, but Eli gave them verbal reports instead and eventually everyone went home.

* * *

Later, he came into the bedroom carrying a tray holding dinner. "Hungry?"

"A bit, yes."

"You look better."

"I feel better."

He took a seat in a chair he pulled up next to the bed. As he'd been doing for most of the day, he silently gave thanks that she hadn't been harmed. Although she looked a hundred times better than she had when he'd found her on the porch earlier, the haunted look remained in her eyes.

Jewel ate as much as she could, then set the tray on the bed. "I need to tell you what happened so that maybe the memories will leave me alone. Is that okay with you?"

He nodded.

Jewel began the story with finding Creighton in the kitchen, then told him what came next, and she ended it with Creighton's death in the yard. "Miss Edna said it might be a week or two before the bruises on my neck heal."

Eli could see the ugly red splotches on her throat above the collar of her nightgown. They'd turn black and blue before they faded. The anger he felt toward Creighton filled him with a quiet rage, but he kept that out of his voice as he told her, "Thank you for telling me the whole of it, Jewel. I needed to know what happened."

"Even though I didn't want to talk about it, I knew you wanted to know." What he didn't know, however, was that the retelling only served to make the memories more vivid. "Has everyone gone home?"

"Yes. You and I are the only ones here."

"Then will you come to bed with me. I need you to hold me."

He nodded.

After taking the dinner back to the kitchen that Maddie, Edna, Abigail, and the Crowley brothers had scrubbed clean of all the blood, he returned to the bedroom, removed his clothes, and got into bed beside her. Holding her close, he kissed her hair. "I'll be right here when you wake up."

"I love you, Eli."

"I love you more. Sleep now, sweetheart."

But as they lay together in the darkness, it was a long time before either of them closed their eyes.

# Chapter 17

Jewel awakened the next morning and sure enough, she was in Eli's arms and her love for him knew no bounds. He was still asleep, so she remained still so as not to awaken him. Blessedly she hadn't dreamed last night, yet she felt so tired she was certain she hadn't slept well, but never having have been one to sleep late, she carefully got out of bed, slipped her arms into a robe and left the room.

Creighton remained in the back of her mind. She hoped busying herself with her morning routine would keep him at bay, so she washed up and walked into the kitchen intent upon starting breakfast. However, the moment she entered, the memories hit her like a bucket of ice cold water and she began to tremble. She was thankful to whoever had cleaned the blood from the walls and the floor, but she didn't know how to clean it from her mind. Looking at the kitchen table, she saw Creighton, so she turned away. Her eyes settled on the back door and the sight brought back the panic and fear. No matter what she tried to do to set the terrible incident aside, it wouldn't leave, so she left the kitchen and went out and sat on the porch.

And that was where Eli found her when he stepped outside a short while later. She looked over at him with her haunted eyes and said quietly, "I can't go into the kitchen."

Eli's lips tightened and his heart went out to her. "That's understandable, sweetheart, so I'll cook breakfast. How's that?"

She gave him a small smile, "You're going to cook?"

"Yep. I may not know how to light the stove but I'll manage."

Her first instinct was to force herself to handle the chore herself but the memory of the knife being in her hand and how she'd had to use it, overrode all. "Okay."

"I'll try not to burn the house down."

True to his pledge, he didn't burn the house, but he did burn the bacon and eggs. He also managed to burn some leftover biscuits he found in the breadbox, but Jewel ate around the blackened parts of the meal, and with their love for each other filling their hearts, the Graysons began their day.

Eli didn't go into the town but stayed by her side. A number of family members stopped by to check on her, and Maddie brought over some food and books. Although Jewel was buoyed by their concern and their presence, she wished Creighton had never entered her life.

The Boston policeman Swan stayed in the area for another few days in order to help the Michigan authorities wrap up the investigation and the paperwork surrounding the deaths of Cecile and Creighton. The morning he was to leave, he had Vernon drive him over to the Grayson's place before heading off to the train station, so he could say his goodbyes.

Standing by the wagon, Eli looked up into Swan's blue eyes and said, "Thanks for everything, Bryce."

"Thanks for your help, too, Eli. How's your wife?"

She was standing on the porch watching their exchange but did not venture over. "Doing okay, considering."

Swan nodded his understanding, then said, "Give her my regards. If you ever come to Boston be sure to look me up."

"Will do. Godspeed."

Swan acknowledged the blessing and Vernon drove away.

Eli walked back to the porch where Jewel stood and asked her. "What do you want to do today, Jewel?"

She shrugged. Three days had passed since her encounter with Creighton, and no matter how hard she tried, the incident wouldn't leave her be. "You should go on into town. Aren't you and G.W. supposed to be printing the first issue today?"

"Yes, we are."

"Then go. I'll be fine here."

Eli was eager to get the presses rolling but not at

her expense. He'd stay by her side until the snow started falling if it would help. "I don't want you here alone, Jewel."

"I appreciate the concern, Eli, but you have things to do and I told Maddie I'd stop by and see her today, so I'm going to drive over."

Eli was torn. He didn't want to leave her, because he knew she was still suffering.

She sensed that. "If I told you I'd feel better if you left me, would you go then?"

"Trying to get rid of me, are you?"

"Of course," she teased.

He eased her into his arms and held her against his heart. For the hundredth time he wished he had been the one to take on Creighton, but since he hadn't, all he could offer her was his love and care. "Okay, I'll go to town and you go to Maddie's. I'll see you later."

He placed a solemn kiss on her brow, then went to get his buggy.

Once he was gone, Jewel forced herself to enter the empty house. It echoed with silence. She still had a hard time being in the kitchen and was purposefully avoiding it. Her lovely new kitchen and home that had been erected with so much love was now fouled by horror and death, and she had no idea how to remedy that either.

Jewel drove up to Maddie's front gate and the dogs barked happy greetings. She smiled and reminded herself to ask Maddie if the dogs and G.W. had come to a truce.

"They are still negotiating," Maddie replied when Jewel posed the question as the two friends sat on the porch drinking coffee. "The dogs have yielded enough to let him enter the gate, and he has stopped asking that they be penned up when he visits."

"Sounds like progress."

"I'm taking it a day at a time."

"Eli and G.W. are putting out the first edition of the new *Gazette* today."

"That's pretty exciting, isn't it?"

Jewel could see Maddie watching her with concerned eyes and she looked off.

"How are you getting on, Jewel?"

"Scared to be in my own kitchen," she stated flatly. "Silly isn't it."

"Not really. Bad memories in there."

"Never had anything scare me the way he did."

"But you handled yourself, and you're here. That has to count for something."

"I killed a man in my own home, Maddie. I see him every time I walk in there."

"I imagine you will for a while, but what were your choices? You could have been weak and we would have already buried you, or you could have been strong like you were and be here to stand up with me at my wedding next month."

"Next month?"

Maddie nodded.

"Really?"

"No sense in waiting. It's not as if we're dewy-eyed virgins." She brought the subject back around. "Jewel, I want you to do something for me. Each and every time you walk into your kitchen, think of how strong you were that day. Think of how brave you were. Creighton may have taken Cecile's life but you didn't let him take yours."

Jewel mused over the advice, but wasn't sure if she could follow through on the suggestion.

"Will you at least think about it?"

"I will."

"Promise?"

Jewel didn't know what she'd do without the people she loved. "Cross my heart," she replied, making the sign with her finger.

"I'm holding you to that. Now let's talk about the wedding."

Jewel had her first nightmare that night. Creighton was chasing her. His skull face was covered with blood and he had his hands around her neck. Jewel was fighting him in and out of the dream. She didn't have the knife this time and Cecile was in the kitchen, too, screaming for Jewel's death.

Jewel's screams awakened Eli instantly. She was screaming and fighting and rolling all over the bed. He grabbed her hands and called her name.

"Nooo! Let me go!"

"Jewel! Jewel! Baby, wake up. It's a dream. Jewel!"

Jewel's eyes popped open, and seeing Eli above

her, she grabbed him and held on tight. "Oh, god."

He rocked her, shushed her, and kept her close.

"Bad dream," she whispered, glad it hadn't been real. So glad.

"It's okay."

"Creighton was there. Cecile, too."

"The only ones here now are you and me, and I love you." Eli was shaken but fought for calm so he could comfort her. "Do you want some water?"

"No. Just hold me."

After a few more moments, she took a deep breath.

"Better?" he asked

"I think so."

He peered down into her shadow-filled face hoping he'd be able to see that she was, but it was so dark he was unable to take her true measure.

"I've never had nightmares before."

"You've been through a lot."

"First I'm scared to be in the kitchen, now I'm going to be afraid to sleep." She paused and said, "Remember the three wishes you asked me about when we first got married?"

"I do."

"One is that I wish this had never happened."

He kissed her brow. "Me too, but we'll get through it, and we'll do it together."

She nodded then placed her cheek against his heart once more. She found his solid presence an anchor, a port in the storm that had taken over her life. "I'm sorry I woke you up this way. Did I hit you?"

"A couple of times," he chuckled softly, "but I'll be fine. Do you think you can go back to sleep?"

"No."

"Then how about we get the checkerboard out?" He was hoping to find a way to distract her from the dream and it was the first idea to pop into his head.

She looked up. "Checkers?"

He shrugged. "Why not? Might take your mind off things, especially when I win."

"Excuse me?" she begged to differ. "Do you know that I am the Crowley champion?"

He chucked her chin. "But I cheat."

She couldn't help herself, she laughed and hugged him tight. "You are so wonderful and so good for me, Eli Grayson."

"Can I get that in writing?"

She felt her love for him banish the remnants of the awful dream. "I'll shout it from the rooftops if you'd like."

For Eli, holding her soft body brought home the fact that they hadn't made love in a dog's age, but since he didn't feel as if now was the time to broach the subject, he got up to light the lamps and find the checkerboard.

Jewel found out after they began the first game that he hadn't lied. He did cheat. Repeatedly. "I don't believe you," she said laughing at his attempts to jump his checker to a spot where he knew he couldn't.

"What?" he asked innocently. "There's nothing in the rules saying I can't jump here."

"You know good and darn well you can't jump that way. Move that piece."

Eli was grinning and so was she.

He moved his piece, albeit reluctantly, and she won the game two moves later.

"Told you I was the champion."

"Told you I cheated."

They were seated on the floor with the board between them. "I've never played checkers at four in the morning before," the happy Jewel confessed.

"Just trying to put more fun in your life."

"And you're doing a great job."

She ran her eyes over the handsome planes of his face and acknowledged once again how good it was to be married to him. She also acknowledged that it had been quite a while since they'd made love, and she wanted to rectify that because she missed the intimacy of their marriage. "Since you can't beat me in checkers, even cheating, how about we play something a bit more challenging."

"Such as?"

"I believe it's called, The Dance of the Little Death."

Eli smiled. "I've heard of that game. I'm very good at it in fact."

"Are you really? Can you teach it to me?"

"Thought you'd never ask. . . ."

He pushed the board away and coaxed her onto his lap. "First," he husked out against her ear, "I have to take off your gown."

Jewel was melting just from the low, thick timbre of his voice. "Why?"

He opened the two buttons on her gown and when it fell open he brushed his mouth over the hollow of her bruised throat, "Because that's a rule . . . and so that I can kiss you here." He took a nipple into his mouth and felt her shimmer in response. Only after the bud was tight and damp did he transfer his attention to the other side, "And then here." He spent such a long lazy time on the second bud, she couldn't help but moan with pleasure.

"I think I'm going to like this game," Jewel whispered.

"I think so, too."

And they were both right because he made love to her with all the tenderness and passion he could muster. He wanted his kisses to replace the terror of her dreams. Wanted her to think only of the two of them making love when she climbed into bed at night. He pleasured her slowly, fiercely, and so completely that she danced the little death until the sun came up and then slept.

But in spite of that passionate interlude, the nightmares continued to plague her, and she often awakened Eli with her tossing and screams. Each time it occurred he pulled her close, held her until she calmed, and waited for her to drift back into sleep.

They plagued her so totally that she took to sitting out on the porch at night to escape them. She moved through her days like a wraith—silent, alone. Eli could feel her slipping away from him but he didn't know how to bring her back, and it was killing him. They hadn't made love again, but he didn't miss that as much as he missed her smile, her laugh, and her sass. He forced himself to be patient and to give her as much time as she needed to get herself sorted out, because he didn't know what else to do.

And then one morning, he awakened to the smells of bacon frying. Thinking he might be the one dreaming now, he sat up and sniffed the air. It was bacon. Tossing aside the thin blanket, he left the bedroom and padded into the kitchen. He half expected to see his mother or maybe Maddie standing by the stove, but it was Jewel. "Good morning," he said, unable to keep the surprise out of his voice.

"Morning." She knew he was wondering what she was doing in the kitchen she'd been so pointedly avoiding for the past few weeks. "Surprised?"

"A bit, yes."

She cracked some eggs in a bowl. "I decided, I had to get over this and the only way to do it was to do it. I was getting so sick and tired of running scared that last night while I was out on the porch, I finally decided to take Maddie's advice." She told him what Maddie had asked of her. "I didn't let Creighton take my life but I was letting him take my soul."

Eli studied her. "So does that mean I have my wife back?"

"Most of her. I can still see him sitting there at the table." And she could, but she was doing her best not to let the sight rattle her to the point that it forced her to crawl back into her shell. "I am a Crowley after all."

"And a Grayson, I might add," he said with a smile. He was glad to see her finally taking the bull by the horns. He'd been so worried about her. Happy that she was beginning to fight back, he came up behind her while she was scrambling the eggs in the skillet and placed his arms around her waist, nuzzled the soft skin on her neck. "We Graysons may not be as well known for our courage and bravery as the Crowleys, but we are known for our loving, and I know the perfect way to help banish Creighton from our table once and for all."

She turned, her face serious. "How?"

He grinned.

She chuckled. "Eli Grayson. We're supposed to be having breakfast."

"I prefer to have you first, so I'm going to wash up and when I come back I want you sitting on that table, buttons open and your denims off."

Her eyes widened.

He pressed his lips to hers. "Say, 'Yes, Eli.'"

Grinning at her very scandalous husband, she answered, "Yes, Eli."

He left, and when he returned his wife was seated on the kitchen table without a stitch on. His manhood hardened instantaneously. "You are such an obedient wife, Jewel Grayson."

"It's because I know my husband will give me a reward."

And he did, until she filled the kitchen with husky cries of pleasure.

A tired but ecstatic Eli entered the mayor's office and whistled as he took his seat behind the desk. His next stop would be the *Gazette* office, but first he wanted to scan the mail he'd picked up from Miss Edna. While he did, Jewel came to mind; and he was savoring the memory of his hot little wife twisting with passion on the tabletop when he heard what sounded like cheering. "Now what?" he asked the silence.

Going to the door, he stepped out onto the walk, and the sight of his cousin Nate, Viveca, and their children coming up the street in a wagon Nate was driving filled him with joy. The cheers were coming from the folks on the walks. Nate and his family were waving like participants in an August First parade, and the townspeople were waving back, and no one was happier to see them returning than Eli.

He stepped down into the street. His nieces, Magic and Satin, spotted him first and suddenly Magic jumped from the back of the wagon and ran in his direction. "Cousin Eli!" she screamed.

Nate was barking at her, of course, but the fifteen-year-old Magic didn't slow. She ran into Eli's outstretched arms with such force she almost knocked him over, and he hugged her with all the love he felt. "How are you?" he asked laughing.

"I'm fine. Oh, it is so good to be home! And we had such a wonderful time!"

By then, the wagon had reached the office and as Nate, Viveca, and the remaining three children stepped down, they were swallowed by the crowd of well-wishers.

Once the return celebration ended, it was Eli's turn. He greeted them all with strong hugs. "Come on inside and tell me about the trip. It's good to have you all back."

Nate, who favored Eli enough to be his brother, nodded. "Good to be home."

They all looked weary but happy, and the children spent the next little while telling him about California, a place he'd yet to visit.

Joseph, who was older than his twin brother, Jacob, by two minutes said, "Cousin Eli, we saw a lion and a tiger and a elephant."

"Really? Your *abuela* took you to Mother Africa?"

Jacob laughed. "No, we went to a circus."

"My," Eli responded, sounding impressed.

Satin, younger than her sister by a year, had always been a very elegant child growing up. Her family looked disheveled and hot from the heat, but she didn't have a wrinkle anywhere. "We missed you, Cousin Eli."

"I missed you all, too. Very much."

Magic, knowing the adults wanted to talk, asked, "Can we go see Miss Edna? We won't stay long."

Viveca, smiling at her children, nodded her approval, and the brood trooped out. Nate said, "I see my town is still standing."

"Barely."

Nate peered at him through his spectacles. "What's that mean."

"It means, I have a whole new respect for you and what you do to keep this town running, cousin."

"What went wrong?" Nate asked suspiciously.

Viveca cracked, "Did somebody finally tie the Widow Moss to the train tracks?"

"No, I wish," Eli chuckled. "Have a seat. Do I have a story to tell."

So he began with Cecile, but he didn't get to tell it all because Nate interrupted, shouting, "Cecile was here!"

"Just long enough to turn the town upside down, then she was murdered."

"What?" Nate and Viveca yelled in unison.

"If you don't stop interrupting I'm never going to finish."

Nate shared a wide-eyed look with his wife, then said to Eli, "Go ahead."

Eli continued the tale by relating the circumstances of Cecile's death, and then Jewel's encounter with Creighton Wilson, and both Nate and Viveca looked stunned.

Viveca said, "Poor Jewel. How is she?"

"Doing much better." Eli dropped the next bombshell. "She and I married while you all were away."

"What?" they shouted again.

So he told them about that and how it came to be.

Viveca said with a small smile, "I'm surprised she didn't shoot you and Adam."

"We were as well. Oh, and hold on to your seats for this one—our Maddie is getting married."

Of all the shocking news Eli had related, this last tidbit left them speechless and with their heads spinning.

"How about I finish the rest of this later, after you all get settled in at home?"

Nate asked, "There can't possibly be more, can there?"

Eli playfully touched his chin, "Let's see, Jewel and I had a house built. The Reverend Anderson had to give up his job at the church. Jim Wilson has moved away. Yep, there's more."

Viveca shook her head. "We may have to leave town more often."

Eli replied, "Oh, no. I'm not sitting in for Nate ever again. My hair's turning gray from all this excitement."

Nate chuckled. "It's good to be appreciated. Stop by the house later so I can hear all of it. Not sure my heart can stand any more, but I want to know."

"Will do, and I'll bring Jewel, too."

"Congratulations on the marriage, Eli," said Viveca.

Nate cracked, "Not sure this family can handle another Crowley, but my congratulations as well."

* * *

Maddie and G.W. married a week later. Half of the people in the county turned out to view the outdoor ceremony, mostly because they didn't believe the rumors of her marrying were true. Viveca and Jewel stood up with Maddie, while Eli, Vernon, and Blue did the same for G.W.

After the wedding festivities, Eli and Jewel drove home just as dusk began to roll in. "It was a nice wedding," Jewel said.

"It was. G.W. didn't seem to mind taking the ring box from Blue."

She smiled at the memory. "I guess he and the dogs have finally come to an agreement."

"Looks that way." He turned to her. "Speaking of looks. I like the looks of all those buttons on your dress, Mrs. Grayson."

"I purchased it especially for that reason."

"Did you now?"

"Yep. And do you know what else? I figured out my last two wishes."

"And they are?"

"That the babe I'm carrying not be a lunatic and cheater like her father."

Eli pulled back on the reins so hard, the horse almost tripped. "What?"

"And my last wish is that her father keep loving me as much as I love him."

Eli's wide eyes were eclipsed only by his stunned, dropped jaw.

Jewel laughed. "Never seen you speechless before, Eli Grayson. You might want to drive, though, you have a lot of buttons to open before the sun comes up in the morning."

He looked into her eyes, saw the love for him shining there, and said, "Yes, ma'am!"

Later, the sun was coming up when the sated and very satisfied Jewel said to her husband. "I love you, Eli."

He kissed her softly. "And you are the jewel of my heart."

"I'm glad we got married."

"So am I."

As Eli and Jewel cuddled close and drifted off to sleep, they were at peace with themselves and their future life together in Grayson Grove.

# Author's Note

Eli Grayson and Jewel Crowley first appeared in my second Avon historical romance *Vivid*. It has taken me thirteen years to return to Grayson Grove so I hope their story was worth the wait. The Black press has always played an integral part in the African-American community, second only to the churches in importance and influence. Although their numbers have decreased in the past fifty years, they continue to beat the drum for justice. If you do not own a copy of *David Walker's Appeal to the Colored Citizens of the World*, I suggest you get one. No Black history collection can be complete without it. It is truly a remarkable work, not only for its fiery intellectual rhetoric but because it serves to dispel the Hollywood myth that members of the race spoke only in dialect. According to historians, Walker's *Appeal* was widely read and discussed by the free Black population in the North. It was also well known in the South and secretly read in the slave quarters by those who could read, to those who could not. As a result, slave owners were so alarmed by the *Appeal's* calls for armed rebellion that bounties as high as ten thousand dollars were put on Walker's head. The legislatures of Georgia and Louisiana passed laws against its circulation, promising imprisonment or death, and in North Carolina, teaching a slave to read became a crime. The race would not see the likes of Walker again until Malcolm Little changed his name to Malcolm X.

For readers interested in the historical sources I used for Jewel, here is a partial list.

Dann, Martin. Ed. *The Black Press: 1827-1890.* New York: Putnam, 1971.

Fields, Harold B. "Free Negroes in Cass County Before the Civil War." *Michigan History*, 44 (December 1960) 375–383.

Giddings, Paula. *When and Where I Enter.* New York: William Morrow, 1984.

Sterling, Dorothy A. *We Are Your Sisters: Black Women of the Nineteenth Century.* New York: Norton, 1997.

Walker, David A. *David Walker's Appeal to the Colored Citizens of the World*. Baltimore: Black Classics Press, 1993.

Vennum, Thomas, Jr. *American Indian Lacrosse: Little Brother of War.* Washington, DC. Smithsonian Institution, 1994.

I'm finishing this book in 2007, and it has been a good year. Avon graciously published a tenth-anniversary edition of *Topaz*, and the cover was so beautiful I cried. I traveled to places like Baltimore, Austin, Dallas, St. Louis, and Houston. I met with many book clubs, and in August toured Indianapolis and Chicago, along with eighteen other African-American authors, courtesy of book distributor Levy and the good folks at Wal-Mart. Thanks, Pam! In October, Ava and Gloria headed up another outstanding BJ PJ Party, and almost a hundred fans attended. Later that month, I was invited to speak and sign books at Detroit's Charles H. Wright Museum of African-American History, the largest museum in the world devoted to African-American history, and I was truly honored. As I said, it was a good year, but the best part of all was seeing you, my readers. From Valeria and her book club ladies at Nicola's Books in Ann Arbor, to Donna and her girls in Houston, to the women in Baltimore who came to see me at Sepia, Sand and Sable—one of the few African-American bookstores still operating—to the Ft. Lauderdale chapter of the National Coalition of Black Women. Bless you. You fuel me with your love and support. For those of you I didn't meet on the road in '07, here's hoping I see you in '08. Thanks, everybody. Until next time. B